C000142725

WOLF SISTERS

Paul Goetzee

Grosvenor House
Publishing Limited

This book is published by
Grosvenor House Publishing Ltd
Link House
140 The Broadway, Tolworth, Surrey, KT6 7HT.
www.grosvenorhousepublishing.co.uk

This book is a work of fiction. Any references to historical events,
real people, or real places are used fictitiously. Other names,
characters, places and events are products of the author's imagination,
and any resemblance to actual events, places or persons, living or
dead, is entirely coincidental.

A CIP record for this book
is available from the British Library

ISBN 978-1-83975-448-7

For Gillian, Jack, Katharine and George

Preface

WOLF SISTERS was inspired by the research of Russian genetic scientists Dmitri Balyaev and Ludmila Trut into Siberian Silver Foxes. Balyaev fell foul of the Russian authorities because his research implied that genetics not ideology determined what kind of human being you would turn out to be. This was not a wise thing to assert in post-war Stalinist Russia.

Fortunately, Balyaev survived and did not suffer the fate of his fictional counterpart in this book, nor of the real-life genetic scientists who were imprisoned or executed.

The relationship of politics and science is, as the world has seen in 2020, urgent and contemporary, but I hope that setting events in another time and another place will give the reader some perspective on what is happening now.

Josef Stalin never visited a scientific outpost in Siberia to my knowledge. Nor did Lysenko, though he did claim it was possible to grow lemons in the Arctic. Stalin did not have an aide called Volkov and he never travelled the length and breadth of the USSR by train, at least not in 1948.

Otherwise, every effort has been made to be historically accurate.

My apologies to the Evenki people if I have misrepresented them in any way. Too many homelands and habitats are being destroyed globally and one can only hope the nomads -and the wolves- of Siberia continue to resist the onslaught.

Paul Goetzee
December 2020

PART ONE

1

The Siberian Grey howled then bared his front tusk-like canines and yawned. His mate lay curled around her two remaining cubs. The other pack-members shambled and padded about aimlessly. The Central Siberian early autumn air was already cool. The sky was grey with some promising gleams of silver and the clouds swept to the Yenisey and the mountains in the east. The male was uneasy. There was a scent in the air he didn't much care for but couldn't quite place. His mate whined and growled and licked her cubs. Two females, born late in the season to a small malnourished pack. They had to be protected at all costs.

Irina fired into the air. The pack scattered. The female remained where she was but stood up. The cubs squirmed in their pine-needle bed, mewing and whimpering. Another shot. The male fell dead. The female fled, torn between maternal instinct and survival. Irina ran forward and scooped up the cubs and thrust them into the open canvas satchel across her body. There was a shout from Semyon. Irina turned. The female was bounding towards her, fangs bared, running at full speed. Another shot rang out and she dropped, a bullet through her skull. Her dead weight fell at Irina's feet and she looked up.

Semyon grinned.

'She nearly had you!' He laughed.

'Not funny, Semyon.'

He said nothing but continued laughing. A big bearded Georgian pushing sixty.

'How are the pups?

'Whining like babies. We need to get back and feed them.'

She looked down at their mother and was suddenly very sad. A wave of grief passed through her and her eyes pricked. The mother was a beautiful Grey with a collar of white fur. She might have been asleep but for the blood pulsing from the hole beneath her ear. Semyon would take her and her mate, skin them and sell the fur. Despite being brought up to hunt since she was a child, she felt somehow small and shabby.

She clambered back into the old wartime ZIS army truck with the rear caterpillar tracks. Semyon threw the carcass of the mother and father into the back. The rest of the pack paced at a safe distance, leaderless and lost. Semyon fired into the air and the wolves immediately dispersed. Irina knew that if she hadn't been there, he would have tried to claim a few more pelts with his rifle. He went round to the front of the truck to fire it with the starting handle, a task which required his bulk and strength.

After a few turns, the engine clattered and spluttered into life. Semyon got into the cab and they began their drive home across the marshy plain. Irina filled a small pipette with reindeer milk she had brought with her. The cubs sucked at it eagerly, indifferent to the fact that it was cold and not from their mother's teat. She looked down at the cubs. The darker one continually pushed the lighter one out of the way of the proffered pipette. The lighter one whined in protest but had to yield to her more assertive sister.

'I'll call them Grusha and Masha.'

'Which is which?'

'Grusha's the greedy one, a character from Dostoevsky. Fiery, wild. Masha is Chekhov, more gentle, troubled.'

Semyon grunted dismissively at this display of anthropomorphism on Irina's part. Besides which, he didn't know what she was talking about. He could barely read.

Irina stroked Masha's head and was rewarded with a warm tongue. She did the same to Grusha and felt needle-like teeth in her finger.

'Ow!'

Semyon roared with laughter.

The truck shuddered to a halt an hour later at the Pustinya Field Centre for Animal Behavioural Studies. Irina was nauseous from the diesel fumes and had a headache - partly from the fumes but mainly from the responsibility of looking after the two cubs in the bouncing, rattling cab. They were vulnerable and only days old. They had to be this young, as her father kept reminding her, or the experiments would be inconclusive.

The Field Centre was set on a slight mound and surrounded by the endless pine, fir, larch and birch of the taiga. There was a central wooden building which served as living quarters for the scientists and several smaller outbuildings. Beyond this was a semicircle of spacious cages which housed several wolves, some on their own, others in groups of two or three.

Scenting the dead animals on the truck, the wolves set up a series of discordant howls, blended with whines and yelps and the occasional deep-throated growl. A large uncaged white wolf bounded toward Irina as she staggered from the truck.

'Kolya! Here boy!' Irina shouted, forgetting for a moment her two tiny charges in the canvas satchel.

The white wolf leapt up at Irina as a dog would and went to greet her with his rotten-meat breath and sticky, dripping tongue, but immediately caught scent of the cubs and his expression changed. He pulled back on his haunches and gave a threatening growl, his fangs bared, ears flat against his skull.

'Semyon, take the cubs in to the house. Kolya isn't happy.'

A man in his forties appeared on the porch of the main building. He was tall and slim with thinning brown hair combed back and flecked with grey. He wore steel rimmed spectacles and he had a pipe clenched between his uneven teeth. Irina waved to him as she made friends with Kolya, who was now completely won over and scampering round her like a puppy. She dived on him on an impulse and wrestled him to the ground. The animal growled and leapt free and then pushed her to the ground in turn. Irina just reached up and hugged him and laughed, completely confident that the animal would do her no harm.

Semyon opened the bag and showed the man their booty with some pride. The man took out the darker cub, who struggled and tried to bite him. Then he reached in and brought out the lighter one who was much more passive.

'Only two?'

'They are all she had. Last winter was bad.'

'It's against all odds, but I think we might have a good pair.'

'The mother nearly killed Irushka by the way. She's in the back of the truck with her mate.' He grinned and ran a finger across his throat.

The man raised his eyebrows briefly, then sucked on his pipe, which had gone out.

'But you looked after her – as always. Thank you, Semyon.'

'I'll skin them now.'

'Will you be eating with us tonight, Semyon?'

'No. I've got traps to inspect. I'll eat in the forest.'

The man knew not to argue. He shrugged, took out the oilskin pouch in which he kept his tobacco and refilled his pipe.

The red hot ashes collapsed with a sigh in the stove. Irina opened the door of the stove and put in another birch log. She closed the door carefully so as not to disturb the two cubs now curled up together in the basket lined with a scrap of wolf fur salvaged from their mother. She knelt a moment and looked at them with affection. She felt her father looking at her in the same way and turned.

'What?'

'It's almost like you are their mother.'

Irina stroked one of the cubs. The cub snuffled and mewed then squirmed back around her sister.

'Well someone has to be. You are going to tag them and observe and monitor them and write them up and then cage them when they get too big. Not much of a life.'

'Irushka, are you getting sentimental?'

Irina looked up and smiled. No, she wasn't sentimental, but she had feelings for the wolves that were brought to the field centre, that *she* brought here. She knew all of them by name. Some snarled at her, others licked her face. But they were all members of her family.

What for Irina was a matter of intuition, for her father was a matter of scientific investigation. Dr Grigori Grigorivich Medvedev had spent his working life trying to discover the link between the wild wolf *Canis lupus* and the domestic dog *Canis lupus familiaris*.

She watched him relight his pipe in the warm buttery glow of the cabin lights as the evening grew darker. Grigori stood and went over to the gramophone. He selected one of the bakelite discs stacked up on the shelf above it in their stiff grey-green paper sleeves. He looked it over for scratches, gave it a wipe from his own sleeve and placed it on the turntable. He wound the handle and lowered the needle. There was a brief scratch and hiss followed by the unmistakeable strains of Billie Holliday singing 'Love Me or Leave Me'. The high-pitched, nasal voice backed up by a five-piece jazz band filled the room.

Jazz was not an approved musical form. '*Lumpenproletariat* syncopation from the descendants of African slaves', as her father put it with more than a hint of irony.

'Your mother would have loved this,' he said as he sat down again.

Irina had never really known her mother. She was only three when she'd died of diphtheria. She was buried in the field centre grounds, her grave marked with a simple Orthodox cross. This was removed when any officials from the Institute visited. Religion, like jazz, was taboo.

Irina sang *sotto voce* the alien lyrics. 'Love me or leave me or let me be lonely. You won't believe me I love you only.' It was impossible not to respond to the beating heart of the music and the emotional life of the song. Grigori had visited a Finnish University before the War and had been introduced to jazz by fellow post-graduate students who had smuggled in discs from Sweden. He had built up his own collection in the same, illegal way.

He was all the family Irina had, unless you counted Semyon and the wolves. She had turned down a place at Moscow University studying behavioural science, so that

8

her father would have someone who could help him with his work. It didn't feel like a sacrifice. She couldn't bear to think of him without someone to take on the domestic chores and organise his papers.

Grigori looked at her for several seconds. He shook his head.

'What's the matter?' Irina asked.

'One day... when my research is published, then you must go. Take wing. Leave the nest. I won't want to see you until you have a degree and a husband, a job in the university and three kids.'

She laughed and she could feel herself blushing. It was as if he knew what she was thinking. She took the opportunity to turn back to the cubs. Her father's words filled her with warmth and sadness at the same time. He had taught her to read and write, introduced her to the great figures in Russian literature, kept her away from the horrors of the war, taught her to shoot and drive and hunt. Taught her all about the behaviour of wolves. She owed him everything. He had tried to be a mother to her too, which was excruciating in her early teenage years.

The song came to an end and the record hissed and crackled until Grigori lifted the arm of the gramophone.

He stretched. 'I'm going to bed. See you in the morning.'

'I'm going soon. I'll give Grusha and Masha one last feed then set my alarm for the next one in two hours time.'

Her father looked at her, then smiled and left the room. Irina got up and warmed a small pan of reindeer milk on the stove, poured it into a bowl, then brought it to the cubs who were mewing fiercely. With the pipette she fed them again and then watched as they fell asleep. She picked up her book but soon dozed off.

She was woken by a prolonged howl. Her heart pounded in her chest and a cold sweat broke out all over her body. Another howl rang out, desolate and savage.

There was no pack nearby. A group of Evenki herders were camped in the area and that would always be an attraction for the wolves, even though the herders mounted vigilant guard and had rifles and dogs. Irina decided to investigate.

She pulled on her woollen coat and rabbit skin hat and her thick hob-nailed army boots, several sizes too big for her. The cubs would be asleep for a little while yet. She took her rifle and went out into the cold night.

Irina called Kolya's name knowing he wouldn't respond immediately. He was a wolf not a dog, but he and she had a bond that rational scientists like her father would never understand. There is wild in all of us, she mused, as she walked under a canopy full of ice-cold stars towards where the sound had come from.

Kolya emerged from nowhere and joined her on her walk. The air would be full of irresistible reindeer scents. Urine, faeces, skin, fur.

Irina had to be careful not to let Kolya stray too near the Evenki camp or they would shoot him without hesitation. They didn't see a dog. They saw a wolf. Wolf was sacred in their ceremonies, but a menace near their reindeer. Besides, Kolya would be no match for three or four of their camp dogs.

The moon was full. The chill was bone-piercing. Winter was never far away. She could see the Evenki fires in the forest, hear their drumming and singing. Suddenly a scream rent the still night air and a frisson ran through Irina's body. Kolya stood stock still, his ears trying to trace the origin of the sound.

Irina ran toward where she thought it had come from. Another scream. And another. She ran harder. Kolya followed outstripping her. She had no control over him, but he slowed of his own volition so she could keep up. They ran together into the trees. The drumming had stopped and there was shouting from the herders' camp, as they ran towards the sound of the scream.

There was a fire burning amongst the trees some distance from the Evenki camp fires. The scream seemed to come from there. Irina ran as fast as she could, the frosty air scorching her lungs. Why was this fire so far apart from the others?

When she reached a clearing, she saw why.

It wasn't a camp fire. It was a burning torch made from a pine log standing horizontally. It's yellow and orange flames lit up a makeshift reindeer skinning frame of birch saplings used by the herders. On the frame was the body of a creature which had been freshly skinned and gutted. In front of it, a woman was kneeling, her head forward retching and vomiting and screaming by turns. The creature on the frame wasn't a reindeer, nor an animal of any kind. It was a man.

He was naked and spread-eagled across the frame, bound by ropes at wrist and ankle. His abdomen had been opened and his intestines spooled greasily in the snow. Dark patches on the snow showed where the blood had run and started to freeze. The skin had been scoured from the flesh in the same way a reindeer was relieved of its hide. It fell in folds from raw and bleeding muscle. The skin of the face had been cut away with a very sharp knife, exposing a hideously grinning skull which seemed to laugh as the light from the flames flickered across it.

Irina felt her own gorge rise at the sight and at the same time experienced a strange distancing feeling as if what she saw in front of her was secondary, a picture in a book maybe, a painting by Goya, but in no way real.

The men cut down his body. Irina wanted to call out to stop them. When the police investigated they would want everything left as it was, so that no clues would be disturbed surely? The next thought that followed was that they would take no notice of her, and a third swiftly-following thought: who was she fooling? The police investigate a killing among native tribespeople? The idea was laughable. The Evenki were no friends of the authorities. Soviet policy was to collectivise their herds and keep them penned up in specific areas. The tradition of following the reindeer in the old nomadic way didn't fit with modern Soviet Russia. There had been arrests and in some cases violence. The authorities regarded the Evenki as ignorant savages who worshipped bears and wolves and stank of reindeer fat. This would be put down to a tribal squabble, someone would be arrested at random and tried and convicted - and probably executed - and everything would return to normal. That is to say, seething with tension and resentment.

As a young Soviet Russian, Irina didn't like the cynical path her thoughts were taking but she knew it was true. As she watched them take down the body and gather up its entrails and folds of skin, she knew this was not a tribal dispute. The Evenki didn't do things this way. Sure, they had their own ways of meting out justice amongst themselves, but it wasn't barbaric. This was the work of a maniac.

She shivered and held Kolya to her, as much for reassurance as to make sure he didn't get too close to the corpse. She could feel him tensing and thick slaver was foaming at the blackened corners of his mouth. Where she saw a brutal murder, he smelt food. He whined softly.

One of the men looked up and saw her. He shouted at her in Evenki and pointed to Kolya. The words she didn't understand but the gesture was clear: *Get him away from here!*

She thought, I'm a witness. I saw the body. Surely the police will listen to me if not to the Evenki? She would contact the police as soon as she got back to the house.

She trudged back in the moonlight, her mind racing. The sight of the butchered man flashed through her mind again and again. She could hardly believe that she had seen it. The war had never really reached this part of Central Siberia, but she had heard stories of what the Nazis did to her people. They were butchers beyond butchery. But this was the first time she had ever witnessed something so violent, so mindlessly cruel done to another human being. Whoever did this had to be hunted down and stopped. But the Evenki wouldn't call in the authorities. She would have to call the police herself and explain what she'd seen.

She couldn't call them until morning. The nearest phone was in a fur-trading post ten miles away. Who precisely would she call? The local militia? She stopped. Kolya paused and looked up at her briefly then stared straight ahead. The local militia would only arrest the first drunken Evenk they could find and throw him in jail. No, she would write a letter. To Moscow.

2

Lieutenant Ludmila Sirotovska of the People's Militia East Moscow District took aim with the old Mosin-Nagant rifle and fired five shots at the straw-filled dummy. The straw head disintegrated as each round followed the other in an almost straight line. She reloaded and emptied the magazine into the dummy's heart.

'We won't have any targets left if you carry on like that, lieutenant Sirotovska!' shouted the instructor, a small round bald man in glasses.

'Isn't that the point, comrade instructor?'

The instructor was impressed but not amused by the fact that he would have to procure a new dummy. Comrade Sirotovska was famous. As a girl she'd been a sniper in Leningrad and had nineteen Nazi scalps to her credit. Everyone knew that. Still, he had to find another dummy – or end up making one himself from straw bales and old clothes.

'OK, enough!' the little man shouted through cupped hands.

Ludmila handed in her rifle without any expression then made her way to the station front desk. Last night she had brought in a violent drunk who was cooling off in a cell. He had tried to hit her with his empty vodka bottle, but she had disarmed him and broken his wrist in the process. She still hadn't completed the paperwork. She turned back to look at the firing range and the hapless instructor trying to piece together the target dummy. Anyone else might have found it funny, but not lieutenant Sirotovska. She rarely smiled, never told a joke or funny story. She would sit alone and drink her tea oblivious to the gossip from her fellow officers.

That she was the centre of gossip was partly because of her aloofness, her reputation as a child-sniper and the fact that she was striking to look at. Not particularly tall, she had a feline assurance in her movements and her light-green eyes were penetrative and cool, even cold.

As she went to find an available typewriter, she was aware of an uneasy feeling that rendered everything lifeless and dull. Her blood felt as if it was congealing inside her veins and she couldn't shake off a constant low-level fatigue. The fifteen-year old orphan who had pinned down German infantrymen in Leningrad was now a lieutenant in the People's Militia, a staunch member of the Party, ruthlessly efficient as a law enforcer on the streets of Moscow and bored to distraction.

She sat at the typewriter and inserted the appropriate form with carbon copy skin into the roller. She looked round the office. An NKVD officer was arguing with the station commander about taking in someone who had been arrested some days before. The officer, who was young and impatient, was claiming that the arrested man was his to interrogate as an enemy of the state. The station commander, overweight and sluggishly impassive but with a gleam in his eye that suggested he was enjoying himself, told him until he brought him the correct documents, the man stayed in his cells.

The young officer eventually marched out of the station with a threat that he would be coming back. The station commander shrugged and looked over at Ludmila and winked. She didn't respond. A pale, tall woman with teeth too big for her mouth walked past with a stack of paperwork in her arms. Ludmila asked her if she had anything interesting.

'A murder in Siberia. Not our concern.' She nodded towards a letter on top of her pile. 'Central Siberia. Middle of nowhere,' she continued. 'It's a letter from a scientist working out there. Looks tribal. Reindeer herders or some such.'

Ludmila took the letter and read:

Pustinya Field Station 57N91E
13ᵗʰ September 1948

Dear Comrade Militia Chief
My name is Irina Grigorievna Medvedenka. I work with my father in the Pustinya Field Study Centre for Animal Behavioural Studies. As the name suggests it is a wilderness with only a latitude and longitude to identify it.

Recently I was disturbed to come upon a reindeer herder of the Evenk people who had been brutally murdered. There was something horrifically savage about the killing —he was bound to a wooden frame and skinned and disembowelled- that I think only experienced police officers would be qualified to deal with it. Hence my letter to you.

I would be very grateful if you could send a team of detectives and a squad of militia officers familiar with tracking in wild terrain right away.

I await your reply forthwith.
Many thanks

Irina Grigorievna Medvedenka

Ludmila's brow furrowed and something approaching a smile crossed her features. A 'team' of detectives? A 'squad' of militia? To the back of beyond? To what was in all likelihood a tribal killing? She looked across at the map of the Union of Soviet Socialist Republics and traced latitude and longitude given in the letter. She snorted. Almost three thousand miles away! Was the woman out of her mind? The station chief would laugh and file it in the nearest waste paper basket. And yet there had been a murder and it sounded a little out of the ordinary to say the least. Maybe that's how they settled scores out in Siberia. Nevertheless a crime had been committed and the role of a police force was to solve crime and bring the perpetrator to justice. She asked if she could take it to the station commander. The other officer shrugged and said he'd already seen it. Ludmila took it anyway and approached her senior officer.

'Comrade commander.'

'Yes, comrade lieutenant. What is it?' He looked at her over his reading glasses. The folds of neck flesh rolled over his tightly buttoned collar as he hunched over his desk reading a newspaper.

'This letter has just arrived.'

'I know. I've read it.'

'Has anyone been assigned to the case?'

'What case would that be?'

'A man has been murdered.'

'The letter will be forwarded in due course to whatever local militia they have in … wherever the hell it is. It's not Moscow's concern.'

'It seems a pretty brutal murder.'

'Do you know any murders that aren't, comrade lieutenant?'

The sarcasm was lost on Ludmila.

'I would like to be assigned to the case.'

The station commander brushed the remains of his breakfast blini from his uniform shirt front, lit a Bulgarian cigarette and blew two columns of smoke from his nostrils. He coughed violently and leaned across the desk.

'Comrade lieutenant,' he began. 'Comrade lieutenant, decorated heroine of the Soviet Union you may be, but what you are not is a detective…yet.'

'No, that's true, comrade commander, but if I don't work on a case I never will be.'

He cut across her, flicking the letter.

'And I can't send a 'team' of detectives to Siberia. Only comrade Stalin can do that!' He erupted into a phlegm-rich gravelly laugh at his own joke and almost couldn't get his breath. Ludmila was a little shocked. His irreverence could get him into trouble.

She looked at him coldly. 'Be careful, sir.'

The station commander immediately stopped laughing and narrowed his small hooded eyes.

'You weren't thinking of reporting me, were you, lieutenant Sirotovska?'

'It is my duty as a loyal party member to report any breach of protocol by an official of the Soviet State.'

The station commander looked at her. Was she threatening him? Or was she just stating a fact? Despite all his years as a police officer, he couldn't tell. If this was anyone else he would have said the former but this girl was a strange one. He decided on discretion. More to the point, he decided on survival.

'Would you like me to assign you to this … case?'

'Yes, comrade commander.'

'You understand that we can't supply you with any other officers. You would be completely on your own.'

'Yes, comrade commander.'

'You should have things cleared up within the week. It will do no harm to let those savages in the arse-end of nowhere know that the hand of Soviet law enforcement has a very long reach.'

'Of course, comrade commander.'

'Then the case is yours. I will see to your travel papers.'

He handed her the letter.

'I am grateful for your trust in me.' She felt the excitement rise through her like a transfusion.

The commander looked up over his spectacle frames.

'Siberia is a wild and dangerous place. Take care, comrade lieutenant.'

3

Ludmila tried to sleep as the train swayed out of the Moscow suburbs and rattled past endless birch forest. She hunched herself into her woollen uniform greatcoat and jammed her fur hat on to her head. An old woman and a little girl sat opposite her. The girl sat wide-eyed as Ludmila opened the parcel she had brought with her containing dark rye bread and sausage. She had divided it in two and offered half to the girl who had accepted eagerly. She offered the old woman half of what remained but the woman shook her head and thanked Ludmila effusively for giving the girl her food. She then went into a long story about where they were going but Ludmila eventually told her she was tired and needed to sleep. The old woman shrugged and was silent. Ludmila lent her head back and drifted into sleep. She was seven and walking into the cramped dark kitchen in their flat in Moscow. She had come home from school. Dmitri Kanovich had punched her and she had been invited to Olga Betsuva's name-day party. She called her mother again. There was no answer. She looked up and saw her mother hanging by the neck from a rope she had fixed to a hook in the ceiling. A hook that must have been bored into a timber beam for it to have held her weight, she noted. Her mother's face was purple, almost black, her tongue protruded and there was a puddle of urine on the kitchen tiles. She screamed and woke up. The old woman and the child were staring at her.

She must have cried out in her sleep. The girl's mouth was wide open.

'I was just having a bad dream,' she said to the girl.

The old woman said nothing but turned and looked out of the window at the big red sun and the honey-tinted woods. The girl continued to stare.

'What did you dream about?' asked the girl.

'I found my mother dead when I was seven. She committed suicide. I dream a lot about that,' Ludmila answered.

The old woman pulled the girl to her and crossed herself, then glared at Ludmila briefly before turning away in disgust. The girl's eyes remained wide and fixed on Ludmila, her mouth still open. Ludmila closed her eyes and pretended to sleep. Her mind was fixed on the Siberian murder and the almost gravitational pull it seemed to exert on her.

Two and a half days later, the Trans-Siberian Express pulled into Krasnoyarsk, 2400 miles from Moscow.

Ludmila pulled her bag from the string luggage rack and climbed down the steep steps on to the platform. She looked around and sniffed the air. Cold, clean, pure, with hints of sulphur and burning coal from the aluminium smelting plants. Caucasian and Asian milled about, rushed along platforms, hauling trunks, suitcases, chicken coops, children. Vendors sold cooked food which she didn't recognise but smelt of hot spice, onions and boiled flesh from stalls and handcarts and improvised tables. Krasnoyarsk had been a vast railway junction since Tsarist times. A gateway to the East. She watched as a cattle truck emptied its cargo of prisoners destined for Kansk, a gulag 120 miles away. Chained, shaven-headed, wrapped in whatever they could find to keep warm, men and women and teenage children, shuffled towards waiting military trucks.

'You look lost, officer.'

The voice came from a tall slim middle-aged man in steel-rimmed spectacles with a pipe clenched between his teeth and a dark fur hat on his head.

'No. I know where I am. I just don't know how to get to where I want to go.' Ludmila looked at the man evenly. He grinned at her robotic logic.

'And where's that?'

'I need to get to a Scientific Field Centre.'

'Called Pustinya by any chance?'

'Yes. How did you know?'

'I work there. Is it about the murder?'

'Yes. I am here to investigate. I have a letter from....' She pulled a folded sheet of paper from her greatcoat pocket. '... From Irina Medvedenka.'

'That's my daughter. She got your reply. We didn't think anyone would come. So, welcome! Follow me.'

Grigori escorted her to the ZIS and Ludmila climbed into the cab. He made several back-wrenching attempts on the starting handle and finally the engine roared into life.

'How long is the journey?' she asked as Grigori hauled himself into the driver's seat. 'And tell me all you know about the murder.'

The answer to her question was over four hours. Grigori took the vehicle off the main highway east and drove north, the road soon becoming a rutted and muddy track.

The landscape grew wide and open. They followed the Yenisey river for a large part of the journey, then turned north west into vast expanses of conifer and birch. Ludmila sniffed the air again. It was purer here, like drinking in the clearest spring water, leaving her lungs feeling light and clean. She listened to what the scientist told her about the murder, logging every detail in her notebook.

'And that's it really,' Grigori concluded. 'That's all we know. Some poor bastard brutally murdered as if he were an animal. By someone who knew what he was doing.'

'In what sense?'

'In the sense that he killed the man like his victim would kill and skin a reindeer.'

'And your daughter saw the body?'

'Yes.'

'And she didn't prevent them from cutting it down?'

Grigori looked at her and then resumed his concentration on driving the lurching, roaring monster of a truck. 'They wouldn't have taken any notice.'

'Primitives.'

'Well, yes, but they have certain formalities when it comes to a funeral. The body is left in the open for the animals. The ground is usually too hard for burial.'

'So there will be little evidence for me to work with.'

'I'm afraid not, no. Oh, and the other thing is, they believe the murder was committed by a spirit.'

Ludmila looked at Grigori slowly. A frown crossed her face.

'A spirit?'

Watching from the kitchen window of the cabin and kneading dough for dumplings as the ZIS rumbled to a stop, Irina was surprised and pleased to see a uniformed officer dismounting from the tailboard. She watched as the militia-woman seemed to sniff the air like an animal then stand perfectly still moving only her head as she took in the field station buildings. She took her suitcase from her father then marched to the house. Irina ran to greet her, wiping her hands on her apron.

'Hello, are you coming to investigate the murder?'

The militiawoman stopped in her tracks and looked at the slim, fair-haired young woman of about her own age wearing an apron over men's military trousers and oversized boots. This was presumably the woman who had written the letter. The daughter.

'Who are you?' was all she replied.

'Oh sorry, my name is Irina. You've already met my father. So, there's just you?'

'You seem disappointed,' Ludmila remarked flatly.

'No, well, in a way. I thought murders were investigated by ...'

'A man? A 'team' of men?'

'Several officers put it that way. But I'm glad you're here. Come in. Let me take your suitcase.'

'I can carry it. Just show me where I can sleep.'

'There's a spare room, at the back. It's kept ready for visitors. Come, I'll show you.'

The women went into the house. Grigori walked out past them.

'Semyon! Semyon!' he shouted.

Semyon emerged from one of the cages in the wolf compound where he had been feeding the tamer wolves. A huge black wolf, called Ivan the Terrible, eyed him from his solitary confinement with a lip-curling snarl. He was fed through an opening in the cage. No one went into the cage with him. Semyon looked at him impassively and Ivan stared back, yellow-eyed, ears flat against his skull, the growl deep and threatening. All of a sudden, he threw himself at the wire cage, his powerful teeth and jaws tearing at the steel mesh. Semyon didn't flinch, but just burst out laughing

'You wouldn't be laughing if Ivan got out of that cage, Semya. You'd be his first meal.'

'He should be let out, not locked away here.'

'Perhaps. I need to make more observations anyway.'

They watched the wolf together as he withdrew from the mesh and paced at the rear of the cage.

Semyon asked, 'Who's the woman in the uniform? What does she want?'

'She's come to investigate the murder of the Evenk.'

'Just her?'

'Yes, she'll have her work cut out.'

Semyon said nothing but moved on to the next cage.

Over a supper of sorrel soup, reindeer dumplings and sweet pancakes washed down with the honey-sweet *medovuka*, Ludmila asked them everything they knew about the killing of the Evenki tribesman and the people generally. Semyon was persuaded to eat with them, but wolfed down his food and left the table, muttering about inspecting his traps. Ludmila watched him go. She spooned her soup and ate slowly and methodically and listened as Grigori expounded on the Evenki and his own work at Pustinya. Ludmila noticed that occasionally Irina would look in her father's direction and widen her eyes, as if warning him against saying something he might regret. Her father did not seem to notice.

'So, what exactly do you hope to prove with your experiments on these animals?' Ludmila asked, looking at Grigori directly.

'To prove?' Grigori took another large sip of Georgian wine having moved on from the *medovuka*. Irina could tell he was already a little drunk – or at least drunk enough to let his guard down. 'The hypothesis –and scientists always have a hypothesis- the hypothesis is that some wolves have dog in them, but the problem is proving it. I mean, it seems obvious doesn't it? Dogs look like wolves, well a lot of them do. Christ knows how we got Pekinese and Dachsunds and St Bernards, but you know what I mean.' He laughed at his own joke and Irina could see that he was stimulated not just by the wine but by the presence of an attractive young woman who was apparently very interested in his work. The militia woman didn't smile in response but her attention was fixed, intense.

'Dad, don't bore our guest with work...' Irina began.

'She asked a question and I want to try and answer it, Irushka. You're not bored, are you, lieutenant?'

'I am only bored when something doesn't interest me,' Ludmila said without a hint of having said anything amusing. Or obvious.

Grigori laughed anyway. 'Very good, very good. Where was I? Yes...dogs. Dogs as we all know are loyal and affectionate creatures. They could even be said to display empathy in certain situations – such as at the death of their owners or protecting small children and so on. Wolves, however, have none of those qualities, at least not to human beings. And to each other they function as pack members with a certain behaviour according to rank. But I have discovered through working with wolves most of my adult life, that there are some born into a pack who show the behaviour we associate with domesticated dogs. As a behavioural scientist, this has always fascinated me.'

'In what way?'

'In how it links with the way human beings behave.'

Irina's eye-play clearly not having any effect, she blurted out, 'Dad, do you think we should attend to Grusha and Masha? They need to be fed.'

'Who?' Ludmila asked.

'Our new arrivals. Irina always names them.' Grigori pointed to the basket next to the stove where the cubs lay fast asleep. 'Yes, Irushka, see to them, but as I was saying, lieutenant, one can –though one perhaps shouldn't without sufficient evidence- but one can extrapolate from the behaviour of wild animals to the behaviour of so-called civilised humans…Imagine we are all dogs but in our midst live wolves who look just like us and who we think are dogs just like us….' He tailed off, allowing the conclusion to speak for itself.

'Do you mean like psychopaths?' Ludmila asked bluntly.

'Yes, like psychopaths. Human beings with little sense of danger or the consequences of their actions, completely ruthless, lacking in empathy.' Grigori took a large sip from his glass and looked at Ludmila over his spectacles, a smile hovering around his mouth.

'A psychopath is someone who has no sense of collective responsibility and therefore no place in Soviet society. He must be constrained and if possible re-educated.'

'Do you think such a self-seeking wolf can be turned back into a compliant dog, lieutenant?'

Irina was becoming more and more agitated, something that didn't go unnoticed by Ludmila.

'Dad, where are the pipettes? I need to feed the cubs.'

Grigori looked at her with raised eyebrows. 'You know where the pipettes are, Irina.'

'I ... I broke one and can't find where you put them. You keep moving things.' She stared hard at her father. Grigori rose to his feet. 'They are in the cupboard on the right in the lab. For goodness sake…'

'Dad, the cubs are hungry.'

Masha and Grusha squirmed and started to protest, almost on cue.

Grigori threw down his napkin. 'I'm sorry, lieutenant. Just some necessary house-keeping.'

Father and daughter left the room together, Grigori grumbling unintelligibly and shaking his head.

When they entered the lab across the narrow corridor, Irina closed the door and whispered fiercely, 'Dad, you're talking too much. She's a police officer and a Party member. If she starts talking back in Moscow, we could be in big trouble.'

'Nonsense, Irushka. She's very intelligent and just wants to know about our work.'

'She's here to find a murderer, not discuss science.'

'Irushka …'

'Dad, you've had too much wine and she is a pretty face. Just watch what you're saying, ok?'

'She's not as pretty as you, Irushka.'

Grigori kissed her on the cheek and laughed and went back into the stove-warmed living room.

They found Ludmila examining the rifle that Grigori kept over the stove. She cocked it expertly and looked down the barrel.

'It's old but well-oiled. A bit like me,' said Grigori.

Irina stared at the back of his head furiously. How had he survived so long and been so trusting, so carefree?

'It's old but functional,' Ludmila said matter of factly, pulling the trigger with a snug click. She put the gun back in its place.

'Irina is the crack shot.'

Ludmila looked at Irina.

'I suppose you have to be - in a house surrounded by wolves.'

The rest of the evening was spent quietly enough. Irina fed the cubs with warm reindeer milk, Ludmila asked some questions about the Evenki and their customs. Irina bit her lip at the police officer's complete lack of understanding of how the nomads lived. She talked about them as if they were not herders but herded creatures themselves, fit only to be organised and collectivised by dictates from the Central Committee on Agricultural Production and Indigenous Peoples – or whatever committee it was that 'dealt' with Siberian people. Semyon appeared briefly saying all the wolves were fed and he was going to sleep. Ludmila asked questions about how long Semyon had been working for them, where he slept, how a Georgian was so far from home? There was one moment when her father in a bid to break the endless interrogation offered to put on a record. Irina jumped to her feet and grabbed the Moscow State Choir singing Ukrainian folk songs before her father had a chance to expose the zealous Party member to the bittersweet -but illegal- tones of Billie Holiday. Again, the daughter's jitteriness was noted by Ludmila. Irina could sense being under a police microscope and began to wish she hadn't written that letter to Moscow.

4

Ludmila stared out of the kitchen window nursing a glass of hot sweet tea. Behind her, Irina was rolling out the dough for blini. Earlier she had baked rye bread and the kitchen smelled warm. *The professor has no wife so the daughter does all the cooking and cleaning. And she helps with her father's work.* Ludmila made mental notes. The sound of typewriter keys being hammered and the occasional curse and ding and whirr demonstrated that the professor had been up early too with his work.

'I usually type up his notes. But sometimes he likes to do it himself – even though he hates using the machine,' said Irina as she laid a circle of dough into a thick heavy pan.

Ludmila said nothing but watched as Semyon backed into the yard. He was pulling the carcass of a female reindeer. He stripped the flesh from the back legs and inserted a branch through the exposed main tendons and attached this to a rope and hauled the body up a frame made of young birch stems. He took out a short fleshing knife and began work. First, he tackled the throat and worked his way across the face, peeling the fur from the purple-white fascia as if it were a garment. He worked with skill and assurance. Ludmila guessed the knife must be razor sharp as the skin came away so easily. There was little blood. His attention was focussed on the fur, which was useful and valuable. The rest was wolf-meat. Next, he cut along the belly and up around the hind parts, pulling it all back and away as he went. Finally, he freed the fur from the bluish embryonic form the deer had now taken on.

'He's good,' Irina said when she saw what Ludmila was looking at.

'A butcher and a hunter,' murmured Ludmila. Out loud, she said 'I will need to question the Georgian properly.'

'Why? You don't think he has anything to do with the killing, do you?' Irina looked up from the pan where the pancake had now browned appetisingly.

'Can you take me to the native encampment as soon as possible?' was all the reply she received.

The ZIS lumbered over the marshy terrain toward the Evenki encampment. Irina drove and Kolya padded alongside, big shaggy head down, tongue lolling from his jaws. She tried to paint a picture for Ludmila about the Evenki, attempting to dispel the prejudice Ludmila had demonstrated the previous evening.

'The Evenki are normally in small groups. There are tribes but they identify not so much as families as brigades. The one we are going to – where the murder happened – they are two or three brigades who have come together for a festival. They race reindeer and drink and dance. There is a shaman who co-ordinates everything. They are so shocked by what has happened.'

'Could it be that someone in another group has a grudge?'

'Possibly. But when there are disputes, they don't slaughter each other. They come together and argue and even fight and they have their own laws.'

'Which I do not recognise as an officer of the Soviet Union.'

'No. Obviously. But it is good to know their ethical beliefs and how they conduct their disputes isn't it?'

'All information is useful - until it isn't,' said the militiawoman staring straight ahead of her. 'Do you have any contacts in the camp?'

'There's a little boy I'm friends with. Innaksa. He is so cute …'

'Does he speak Russian?' Ludmila interrupted.

'… Yes. Yes he does.' Irina stepped on the accelerator and was pleased to see Ludmila lurch forward.

Before they went into the camp, Ludmila wanted to visit the scene of the murder. The frame was still there, the ligatures hanging where they had been cut by the Evenk. The pine torch had burned to a black stump. Ludmila asked Irina detailed questions about the murder victim, the position the body was in, exactly what had been done to him. She looked methodically over the ground under the frame, moving out on the right in a tight spiral and asking Irina to do the same on the other side.

'What am I supposed to be looking for?' asked Irina.

'Anything that shouldn't be there.'

'That's helpful,' muttered Irina, resentment growing at the way she was ordered about.

Suddenly, the militia woman stooped and picked up something. Something metallic, shiny.

'What have you found?' asked Irina, curious now.

'Some sort of religious medallion. Look.'

She had picked it up with a gloved hand. She held it out for Irina's inspection.

It was a Russian Orthodox cross, but quite large, not something an ordinary person would wear. For one thing, it would be hard to conceal. This would take up the palm of a man's hand.

'My first piece of evidence,' said the militiawoman and put it into her greatcoat pocket. Then she took out her notebook and wrote in it, glove between her teeth. She writes with her left hand, like me, Irina observed.

Ludmila had insisted they take the truck even though the camp was barely two miles away. Irina suspected it gave her more authority rather than turning up on foot. She stopped two hundred yards from the camp and called Kolya over. Reluctantly he came and she tethered him to the truck with a length of chain. Rope or leather would have been useless as he would simply have chewed through them. Ludmila looked at her questioningly as she dismounted from the tailboard.

'The Evenk won't have him near their camp and I don't want him shot,' Irina explained.

'Do you think it could follow a scent if I needed it to?' asked Ludmila.

'Kolya is a he, not an it. And you're asking if a wolf can follow a scent ...?' Irina laughed.

'What's funny?'

'A wolf can follow a scent ten times better than a dog. Getting him to do what you want is another matter.'

She exchanged licks, much to Ludmila's disgust, with the big white wolf and ruffled the fur round his neck. He strained, whining, at the chain as the two women walked towards the camp.

They went into the birch trees at the edge of the taiga and a little further to where larch, fir and spruce dominated. They passed reindeer pens made of birch logs tied loosely together and standing at intervals on lashed tripods. The animals moved away as the two women approached. The smell of dung, urine and musk was strong and Ludmila held a handkerchief over her mouth. The camp dogs growled and barked but didn't attack. In a clearing of traditional conical tents a man in ceremonial clothing was dancing and chanting. On a platform of saplings a human form was sewn into reindeer hide. Later the remains would be taken further into the forest for the birds and animals to devour. The members of the brigades sat around, watching the shaman perform the funeral rites. Some of the men were drinking the vodka they distilled themselves. A huddle of women were crying and wailing. An old woman on her own was singing in counterpoint to the shaman's chanting. Children, restless and unsettled, moved about the clearing in small groups. A baby cried. Innaksa, a six-year old with a round beaming face and bright brown eyes, rushed over to Irina when he saw her and held her hand. He shouted to his parents that Irushka was here with a 'soldier woman'. His parents looked up. The mother, breast-feeding, smiled shyly, the father nodded curtly, then went back to drinking with the other men.

'Who is the commissar here?' Ludmila asked Irina.

'Innaksa's father, that man there.'

'He looks drunk,' Ludmila said with steely disapproval.

'He will be drunk. All the men will be drunk. It's traditional at funerals. Like it is with us.'

Ludmila looked at the boy who had grabbed Irina's hand. 'You, do you speak Russian?'

Innaksa nodded.

Ludmila pulled the cross from her pocket. 'Does this belong to anyone here?' she asked. She held it up. The mourners looked up briefly then looked away. Some shook their heads.

'Some of the herders became Christian in tsarist times but they prefer their own religion. I doubt it belongs to them,' said Irina.

34

Ludmila put the cross back in her pocket. 'I need you to tell your father and everyone here that I have come to find the murderer and arrest him and that I want to look at the body.'

Innaksa looked at Irina, then went over to his father. His father took in the information. The other men in his drinking circle looked as one at Ludmila. The father went over to the shaman and spoke to him. The shaman stopped chanting and dancing, turned to Ludmila and delivered a speech to her angrily. He came close to her but she stood her ground and looked at him unflinching. The shaman stood, waiting for a response.

'What did he say?' asked Ludmila.

Innaksa looked again at Irina who gave him an encouraging smile.

'The shaman said…he said, you won't catch the murderer because he is a wolf-spirit, not human, and that you can't see the dead man because that is wrong.'

Ludmila looked around the camp and then back to the shaman. Irina watched her. She had to admire her courage. Or is she just stupid? she wondered.

'This is what has to be stamped out. This superstition. That is why we got rid of priests in the first place. They disseminate lies to control the peasants. Tell your priest that the murderer is not a spirit. He is a man and I will find him and take him back to Moscow to be tried and executed.'

Innaksa hesitated.

'Tell them,' Ludmila insisted.

The boy spoke to his father who spoke to the shaman. The shaman went into a frenetic dance and chanting, banging the deerskin drum with his stick. He stopped suddenly and looked at Ludmila ranting and gesturing to the forest and the world beyond the forest, stabbing his stick into the ground for emphasis. Briefly, he roared something at Irina with another broad sweeping gesture. Just as suddenly he stopped, more for breath than anything else.

Ludmila said calmly to Innaksa, 'Tell me what he said.'

The boy looked at Irina and his father again for reassurance. The father interrupted, speaking in halting Russian.

'The shaman is angry...he said you take all the land from us...where can we move our herds? He say not to interfere. He will banish wolf spirit. Also...' The man, sturdy, sun-burned with a broad, creased Mongolian face and a mouthful of crooked teeth, paused. He looked at Irina.

'Go on,' Irina said quietly.

'He say you keep wolves in prison. That is bad.' He shrugged, then took Innaksa by the hand and moved to one side. The whole camp was silent now, watching the two women intently. Finally, Ludmila spoke. 'So, I will have to work without their co-operation.' She directed her next comment to Innaksa's father. 'All this will be in my report. Tell your priest.'

Innaksa's father muttered something to the shaman, who laughed and recommenced chanting and drumming around the platform on which the dead man lay.

Ludmila turned on her heel, as Irina gestured apologetically to Innaksa's father. He stared at her without expression, but Irina knew what he would be thinking. *Leave this to us. This is our business.*

Irina waved goodbye to Innaksa, who waved back with the hand-carved figure of a squirrel he always had in his hand.

Irina caught up with Ludmila as she marched toward the truck. Kolya got to his feet as he saw them approach. He pulled at his chain and whined, but wagged his tail like an over-excited puppy. Ludmila turned to Irina, angrily.

'Savages!'

'They're not…' Irina began.

'Primitives! How am I supposed to find the murderer if they won't co-operate?'

'I don't know. Perhaps, if you try a different approach…'

'In what way?'

'Be a bit more diplomatic maybe. Win their trust?'

'Impossible. You heard what their priest said. And they all seem to listen to him. Diplomatic? I should arrest him.'

'That wouldn't be wise. You're a lone militia officer, far from home. In country you don't know.'

'If they harmed a Soviet officer, they would be severely punished.'

'Listen, they're not a violent people. They need the space and it's being taken from them, to build dams and factories and mines. But they're not violent. You can't expect them to be keen to help.'

Ludmila looked at her blankly, then turned to the truck.

'We need to get back. I will have to make a report. Is there a telephone at the field station?'

'No. You'd have to go ten miles east of here. There's a fur-trader's state collective at Sobol Cherny. They have a radio that sometimes works.'

'So, how am I to make my daily report?'

'I don't know. This is Pustinya. Not Moscow.'

Irina, deeply irritated by the other woman's abruptness and intolerance, turned to the starting handle. She cursed herself for having turned off the engine. She knew she wouldn't be strong enough but she gave the handle the turn it needed to fire the pistons. Nothing. Again. Nothing. She winced in pain as she pulled a muscle in her shoulder.

'Here, let me.' Ludmila pushed her to one side, but she had the same lack of success.

'We'll walk back. It's not far. Semyon can come and get it later,' said Irina, as she unchained Kolya. He immediately ran into the forest.

Ludmila looked at the truck with disgust, shook her head and followed the tracks it had made in the marshy ground back towards the field centre.

They walked together in silence. Irina tried to engage Ludmila in conversation, asking her about how she became a police officer, where she had gone to school, her family. Ludmila replied with one-word answers. Then Ludmila asked her questions but expected full, detailed answers. Why did she work out here in the middle of nowhere? Did she have any friends? Where had she gone to school? What had her father done in the war? Irina was happy to answer but felt a creeping resentment at revealing anything to this automaton who revealed nothing about herself.

The air was cold and the clouds suggested snow even though it was only late September. Suddenly, Irina put her hand on Ludmila's arm and motioned her to be quiet and still. The two women stood immobile, listening. At first nothing, just the cawing of squabbling crows and the desolate mewing of a buzzard high in the sky. Then there was a grunting, snuffling sound and the light crash of branches being pushed aside. A brown bear emerged from trees two hundred yards away. It didn't appear to notice the two women and continued its unimpeded crashing through the undergrowth. Irina swung her rifle from her shoulder. Irina grabbed her arm and looked at her with a mask of furious warning, eyes widening, teeth clenched. However, the movement was picked up by the bear and it stopped and looked short-sightedly toward the two, long neck stretched out, nose picking up their scent. Ludmila shouldered the rifle and fired. The bear dropped. Ludmila fired again. The bear's bulk absorbed the shot with a brief shudder, then it was still.

'What the fuck have you done!' Irina cried incredulously.

Kolya appeared from the forest and ran toward the lifeless animal.

'Kolya, get away! No!'

Kolya looked at his mistress, who stared him down and growled at him. He backed away. In the distance there were shouts from the men in the camp and their voices were getting nearer.

'Do you know what you've done?'

'Saved our lives. It was going to attack us.'

'Only because you were going to shoot.'

A group of Evenki men and boys ran up to where they were standing. They shouted to one another and went over to the dead bear and seemed to be arguing with one other. Then they pointed to Ludmila and shook their heads.

Irina saw Innaksa's father. 'I'm so sorry. He saw us and we think he was going to attack.'

He looked at her with suspicion. He could see the trail the bear had made.

'Bear going *away* from you.'

'I know but he stopped and turned... we were scared.'

Innaksa's father turned from her abruptly and went and joined the group standing round the bear. He gave orders for them to chop small trees down. A couple of men went back towards the camp.

'What are they doing?' Ludmila asked.

'They're going to make a sling to carry it back to the camp.'

'Then what?'

'Then they'll eat it. It's like a festival. They have to appease the spirit of the bear. Whether the shaman will let them eat it I don't know. They're angry with us.'

'If I hadn't shot it, we would be dead. It's simple. Let's go.'

Irina made another half-hearted gesture of apology and followed Ludmila. What more damage was she capable of?

5

Frustrated by the absence of any convenient telephone contact with police headquarters and by her encounter with the Evenk, Ludmila scribbled angrily in her notebook. *Refused sight of murder victim by hostile herders. Religious cross found at murder scene. Not herders'? Query property of murderer? Native herders' hostility suspicious. Indication of complicity? Need to question them further. The Georgian Semyon also uncooperative. The scientist. His daughter. Suspect everyone.* The last sentence was written so fiercely she tore a hole in the page.

She was sitting at the kitchen table. Irina place a glass of tea in front of her which she took and drank without acknowledgement. Irina looked down at the young police officer. So pretty. Beautiful really. Am I as good looking? She looked in the little cracked mirror on the wall. She saw what she always saw. A young woman whose features were only ever noticed by her father, a gruff Georgian, a six-year old Evenki boy and a pet wolf. Striking eyes even without make-up. Dark blonde hair in need of a wash. Good cheekbones. Full mouth. She didn't like her chin though. It was cleft, like a man's. As was the militiawoman's she noticed. Didn't that mean stubbornness or something? Well then, they must be both as stubborn as each other.

'You're welcome,' she said to the ungracious Ludmila.

'What?' Ludmila looked up from her notes, irritated.

'Nothing', said Irina, moving over to prepare the evening meal. Potatoes and tinned beef and stuffed cabbage leaves. Gingerbread and condensed milk for dessert. As she picked out the dark grey patches of decay in the potatoes with a knife, she spoke to Ludmila, feigning casualness.

'We could always try again with the Evenki. Maybe, if we took them something as a peace offering and just asked if we could talk to, say, the woman who found the body…just a thought.'

Ludmila put aside the irritation she felt at being told how to do her job, turned over the logic of what Irina was saying in her own mind, then nodded curtly.

'Good. I'll bake two gingerbread cakes and take one to them. I want this killer caught as much as you do. I don't think the Evenki will have had anything to do with it, but I realise you need to question everyone to be sure.'

'That is the first sensible thing you have said since I came here,' said Ludmila and turned back to her notebook.

Irina looked at the vulnerable downy neck bent over her notebook and imagined plunging her sharp little knife into it.

Semyon had retrieved the truck and later that afternoon, Irina drove Ludmila back to the camp, leaving Kolya behind. Three men were busy skinning and butchering the bear, watched by excited children. The cake placated Innaksa's father a little and the shaman made surly noises but didn't interfere. Ludmila questioned the woman who had found the body, using Innaksa as an interpreter. The woman was in her forties and spoke little Russian. She had gone out into the wood to relieve herself when she had seen the torch glowing through the trees. Then she had seen a dark shadow move through the trees. At first she thought it was a bear and very quickly forgot the main reason she was crouching exposed and vulnerable in the forest. She had jammed a fist into her mouth so that the bear –or whatever it was- wouldn't hear her. What was it, the shape? Ludmila insisted. A bear? Or a man? The woman said it was too small to be a bear, but big for a man. Did you see his face? No. He had a fur hat pulled well down, she thought. He was moving very quickly. Then he did something really strange. What? What did he do? The shaman had come over at this point and was listening intently. The woman looked at him for support. He willed her on with a look. 'He put his hands to his mouth and howled like a wolf,' she said. He was a wolf-spirit, she was sure. Then she came upon the body. At this point she started weeping uncontrollably and was comforted by a younger woman, who seemed to be her daughter. Irina could sense the growing impatience in Ludmila at the mention of wolfmen and spirits and laid a warning arm on hers gently. Surprisingly, Ludmila took the hint and continued to ask questions with professional thoroughness.

After Ludmila had noted the woman's details for 'when this comes to trial', they took their leave of the Evenki. Irina wondered how Ludmila would ever find the woman and even if she did whether she would give evidence - the Evenki's suspicion of Soviet authority being so strong - but she said nothing.

On their arrival back at the field station, the two women were regaled with a deep baritone voice singing slightly off-key what sounded like a hymn. Some of the wolves were howling - either in chorus or in protest it was hard to tell. In the flickering yellow hurricane lamps by the cages, Semyon was busy feeding the wolves with the deer and wolf meat collected in the last couple of days. He wore a greasy blood- and offal-stained leather apron as he threw chunks of meat into the cages from a bucket. His huge barrel chest and thick-muscled neck seemed to resonate as he sang. The convexity of the cage arrangement and the still Siberian night added to the effect of a vast open-air cathedral. In the lamplight, he was silhouetted like a bear.

'He likes to sing while he feeds the wolves. They like it,' said Irina.

'What is the song?' asked Ludmila.

'I don't know. I think it's from church. Semyon was brought up as Orthodox before the Revolution.'

'So he is still religious?'

Irina saw where Ludmila was going and tried to head her off.

'No. He just likes to sing. Listen to his voice. It gets you, right here, in the belly. Don't you think?'

Ludmila looked at Irina coolly.

'No', she said.

Ludmila went straight to her room as soon as she had finished her meal. A candle burned dimly on the rickety wooden chair by the narrow bed. It was a tiny room with a small window whose frame had been stuffed with old newspaper but still rattled in the wind. Kicking off her boots, she lay on the bed fully clothed and stared at the low timbered ceiling. The only sound was the throb and hum of the diesel generator at the back of the cabin. Her hand went to her forehead and the tiny chicken foot-shaped scar she had always had there. Barely noticeable by eye, it felt like a considerable lump to her fingertip. She unbuttoned her woollen trousers and her hand strayed between her legs where she rubbed vigorously and mechanically until with a barely audible gasp and a convulsion she came. Now her head was clear. She was relaxed. Normally she would have drifted off to sleep, but her mind was racing.

The murmured voices of Irina and Grigori were audible in the next room. Semyon had excused himself and gone. Where did he go? Irina had told her he had his own cabin in the woods, not too far from the field centre. He preferred his own company apparently. And this religious singing. She had never heard anything like it. Her mother had told her about the shawled old ladies who stubbornly crossed themselves and muttered prayers when she had seen them in the Moscow streets. But the priests had gone, the churches closed. The one thing that had kept them mentally enslaved under tsarist rule had been expunged from society. And what about the professor? Always laughing. Everything so amusing. And the daughter. Covering for her father and the surly Georgian. Were they hiding something? If so, what? She had asked him about his work with the wolves and the daughter constantly interrupted and tried to change the subject. He let her type up some notes but sometimes used the typewriter himself, even though he hated typing. The herders. A closed, backward people. They resisted everything the State tried to do for them. *The killing was done in exactly the same way as they slaughtered and skinned their animals ...* Her mind turned and turned, until eventually she fell asleep.

She awoke cold and shivering. Sleepily, she pulled back the old blankets and the threadbare sheet and was about to pull off her tunic and trousers and get in to bed, when a wolf howled somewhere in the compound. There were answering howls and loud growls and the cages rattled and thudded as some of the wolves threw themselves at the wire mesh.

Ludmila listened as Irina and then Grigori came out of their rooms and were talking. She pulled on her boots and went into the living space. The stove was still warm and the two cubs were mewing and squirming in their basket. They were due to be fed by Irina but the commotion outside had disturbed and excited them. Grusha was even attempting an infantile howl herself.

Grigori was pulling on his thick woollen coat and Irina was jamming her rabbit skin hat on her head. She took a rifle from its place on the wall and loaded it.

'What's happening?' Ludmila asked, searching for her great coat.

'We don't know,' Irina said.

Grigori was lighting a hurricane lamp, then he opened the cabin door and they went outside. The sky was clear and the stars and Milky Way spectacularly beautiful. A full moon sailed high in the heavens. The wolves continued to howl.

'Check all the cages. Where's Semyon? Semyon!'

The Georgian appeared at the corner of the cages rubbing his face and beard. He was fully dressed, Ludmila noticed. Gregori repeated his order and they went to every cage, checking that they were still secure. Suddenly, Irina called out, 'Ivan's gone! His cage door is open! Who the hell's done that?'

They all rushed to Ivan the Terrible's cage. The door was open and the wolf gone. Irina looked out into the dark strip of taiga. Grigori was examining the catch. 'It doesn't look as if he forced it,' he muttered.

'Somebody has let him out. Who?' said Ludmila.

'That howl…' began Irina.

'What howl?' Ludmila looked at her in the flickering lamplight.

'The first howl. It was what I heard the other night. It wasn't a wolf. It was someone imitating a wolf. I'm sure of it.'

'The catch is weak. Ivan has pushed and pushed and finally it's given way,' said Semyon.

'I don't think so, Semyon. Do you think the herders might have done it? They don't like the way we cage the wolves.'

The Georgian shrugged. 'Maybe. But this bastard was always trying to escape. Now he has.' He turned and walked into the darkness, back to his cabin.

'What about the howl?' asked Irina of his retreating figure.

Semyon turned. 'Ivan,' he said simply.

He disappeared into the darkness. Irina shook her head.

'There's nothing else we can do now. At least we have all his documentation and we have him on film.' Grigori was trying to be positive, but it was clear this was a blow. Not only that it was disturbing. If Irina was right, then they had a prowler.

'Give me the rifle. I'm going to investigate,' said Ludmila abruptly.

Irina was open-mouthed. 'What? Where are you going?'

'If someone opened the cage, they can't be very far. Give me the rifle.'

Grigori said, 'I wouldn't advise it. It's starting to get very cold and you don't know the area. It's pitch-black.'

'The rifle. Please.' She held out her hand. Irina looked at her father, who shrugged, and she handed over the rifle.

Ludmila slung it across her shoulders by its worn leather strap and began walking with short, fast strides. Irina and Grigori watched her go.

'I've got to feed the cubs,' said Irina. 'If she's not back in half an hour, I'll take Kolya and go after her.' Grigori nodded then they turned and went inside.

Ludmila broke into a trot. The cold air with an edge of frost pricked her lungs and a strong pine scent filled her nostrils as she neared the taiga conifers. The ground was still marshy underfoot but slowly crisping as the temperature dropped. The sky was cloudless, blotched with stars and lit by the sharply-focused disk of the moon. Late September in Central Siberia heralded winter after a short, hot summer. Ludmila buttoned up her coat as her breath steamed in the cold night air. She felt light and full of limitless energy, despite having little idea of where she was going or who or what she was looking for. She was hunting.

She moved deeper and deeper into the taiga. Occasionally she would pause and hold still, a hand against the rough flaking bark of a larch, listening intently and sniffing the air. Her eyes were next to useless in the gloom and growing darkness of the forest, as the trees blotted out the blue-white illumination of the moon. But her ears and nose were more than adequate, she felt. She was an animal, a part of the forest. The city streets of Moscow were her usual territory. You needed your instincts to survive. This was no different.

She stood perfectly still. This was as near absolute silence she had ever experienced. No wind, no bird or animal calls, no rustling. Her boots sank into the decades of pine needles on the forest floor. The only thing she could hear was her own breathing and …*something else*.

The first thing she noticed was the smell. It was heavy, musky with a slightly acidic edge. It wasn't an animal, like a reindeer, because there was no hint of breathing or snorting and no movement. As her nostrils flared and remained open and she breathed in as deeply as she could, she thought she detected alcohol, tobacco and stale sweat. It was human and male and close by. Whoever it was, he was stalking her and keeping still whenever she was still, quiet when she was quiet. But he couldn't disguise his scent. She slowly lifted the rifle from her its place in front of her body, but as she did so she heard a loud grunt and someone grabbed the rifle from behind her and pulled it against her throat. He was big and powerful and she could feel his breath close to her cheek. It smelt like rotten meat, like dog's breath. She pushed hard with her hands on the rifle barrel and stock but she was no match for his brutish strength. Vainly, she hit back with her head, hoping to smash him in the mouth and cause him to momentarily lose his grip. The man pulled the rifle to her throat and her hands were the only thing preventing it crushing her windpipe. Then she felt the rifle loosen and the man grabbed her hair and pulled her head backwards and she saw a blade glint in the moonlight. He was going to cut her throat. She jabbed her elbow into the man's abdomen. There was a gasp and the knife disappeared and the grip on her hair loosened. Using the metal-edged heel of her boot, she back-kicked the man's shin and scraped it down his leg. The man howled in pain. Ludmila spun out of his grasp and faced him. He was holding the knife at face height tilted down aiming at her throat. She was aware of a head in a military balaclava and a thick dark beard. She raised her arm and the knife caught the back of her hand. Then she heard Irina shouting her name. She called back. Irina responded and shouted 'Kolya!' The next thing Ludmila saw was a blur of white as the wolf sprang out of nowhere and on to the man. The man automatically put up his forearm and fell to one knee. He retrieved his knife as the wolf's jaws bore down on his arm causing him intense bone-crushing pain. He brought the knife up at the wolf's stomach and there was a yelp and Kolya leapt backwards giving the man enough time to escape.

Irina ran panting to Ludmila. Kolya had got to his feet and was about to pursue the man, but Irina called him back, clutching him around the neck. Ludmila found the rifle half buried in pine needles in the dark and picked it up. She loosed off a couple of shots in the direction the man had run, then swore.

'Give me the wolf and I can go after him!' she shouted at Irina.

'No! No!' Irina screamed. 'Kolya's hurt and you'll get yourself killed! You see what he tried to do!'

Kolya was whining under Irina's weight as she held on to his thick leather collar. He was clearly eager to go after his attacker.

'Anyway, you're bleeding too,' Irina said looking at the other woman's hand.

Ludmila followed Irina's eyes. The knife had sliced the back of her hand. She flexed her fingers. Nothing serious but the pain was just starting to kick in.

'That will probably need stitching,' said Irina. The blood, black in the moonlight, was oozing freely from the wound and showing no sign of stopping. Irina took out a handkerchief and bound it tight around the cut. A deep lapping sound announced that Kolya had gratefully given up any idea of pursuit and was starting to take care of the wound on his own leg.

'How badly is the wolf hurt?' asked Ludmila

'I think it's only superficial, thank heaven. He was aiming at his stomach.' Irina was sobbing and trying to stop the violent shaking running through her body as she stroked the big animal's head and scratched behind his ears. Kolya continued his instinctive medical procedure, whining a little in pain but no doubt savouring the taste of his own blood. Ludmila looked down at them feeling a searing, throbbing pain in her hand and wondering at Irina's tears. She held out her hand. Irina looked up and then at the proffered hand. Irina wiped the tears from her eyes and the clear thick phlegm from her nose and felt suddenly warm towards Ludmila. She reached out and felt the militiawoman's strong warm fingers. Ludmila pulled her to her feet… and promptly let go of her hand and marched back towards the field centre. Bitch, thought Irina.

An anxious Grigori ushered them back into the warm cabin then bolted the door. He hugged Irina and then tended to Ludmila's hand. Kolya remained outside, as guard and because he was allowed nowhere near the cubs.

'Don't worry, I did a year's medical training before I went into behavioural studies and I have morphine,' Grigori said, unwrapping a coarse green cloth which contained scissors, syringe, glass phial and a needle and sutures. He produced a bottle of surgical spirit and cotton wool and began to clean the wound.

'I don't need morphine,' said Ludmila.

'Oh yes you do. It's a nice clean incision but it will need to be stitched. Roll up your sleeve.'

Ludmila refused and told Grigori to get on with it. Irina was incredulous. She obviously could not bear to lose control. Grigori shrugged and threaded the black suture into the curved needle and put in the first stitch. Ludmila yelped and pulled back her hand. Irina grinned inwardly.

'Now will you have the morphine?'

Ludmila nodded. Irina tightened an old belt on the militiawoman's upper arm. Grigori snapped off the top of the glass phial, filled the syringe, tapped for a vein and expertly injected the drug. Irina could see her visibly relax. She even smiled. Grigori got to work, knotting each stitch as he went and snipping the surplus with the surgical scissors.

'I can feel the pain but it is somewhere out there,' she said, her pupils beginning to dilate into black discs. She grinned widely.

'That's the first time I've seen you smile,' said Irina.

'It's the morphine,' said Ludmila sharply.

Father and daughter exchanged amused glances and Grigori went on with his work. Irina fetched bandages and bound up the wound.

Later, Grigori found a bottle of vodka and three glasses. Ludmila, as with the morphine, was reluctant to drink but the opiate had the effect of lowering her resistance and she drank the vodka offered to her. She asked where Semyon was and received the reply that he had gone to his cabin and was presumably asleep. No point waking him now. Ludmila considered this for a moment but said nothing.

Grigori chatted lightly about how they had brought Ivan to the compound as a pup, how he had bitten anyone who came near him and no amount of human affection would soothe or tame him. Ludmila said nothing. Irina looked at her. She knew what Ludmila was thinking. She wished her father wasn't so open and at the same time so closed, secretive. The attack by the unknown man in the woods had upset Irina emotionally and thrown Ludmila into a cerebral turmoil. Grigori was doing his best to take their minds off it. Suddenly Irina sprang up.

'Dad, just … stop! We need to do something about this madman who's stalking the place and killing people! He tried to kill her and he'll try again with us or with one of the Evenk! Don't you understand how vulnerable we are?'

She stood, shaking.

'It's all right, Irina, I'm sorry. I know. I just wanted to take our mind off things. I'll tell Semyon in the morning. Tonight we bolt all the doors and windows. Kolya will make sure we're safe.'

He took hold of his daughter, tall and slender like him and hugged her. She broke into sobs and then brushed the tears angrily from her face.

'I don't want to cry. *She* doesn't cry.' She turned to Ludmila. 'Why don't you cry? Why? We were attacked and nearly killed and you're like…like a stone! You're not human!'

With that, she stormed out of the room.

Ludmila woke up in the dark. A coarse prickly woollen blanket had been placed over her. She could hear the soft mewling of the cubs by the stove and the low hum of the generator. Her head felt light and airy as a balloon, but her limbs were sluggish. She didn't remember falling asleep. Her hand throbbed painfully. The bandage felt damp and sticky. She forced herself to pull back the blanket. Irina and her father must have gone to bed. Her eyes grew accustomed to the almost complete lack of light. There was a strip of illumination on the floor in the direction of Grigori's study. He must be in there working. She had no idea of the time. Moonlight filtered through the window of the living room, enough to allow her to find her way to the study door. She tried the handle gently and felt resistance. It was locked of course. She remembered there was an outside window to the study. Still feeling intensely light-headed and, wading through molasses, she opened the front door and went out into the chilly night. Kolya looked up at her from his place on the porch but laid his head back down across his front paws with a faint growl and sighed.

The temperature had dropped to zero at least and she shivered involuntarily. Someone had taken off her boots but she didn't want to make any sound looking for her footwear and crept to the study window in her socks. The cold damp earth penetrated the soles of her feet. A low light flickered in the window. Carefully, she raised her head over the ledge and peered into the room.

Grigori was at his desk, head bowed. He lifted his head and drew his hand across his face, pulling at his nose briefly and sat staring into space. Ludmilla watched as he absently filled his pipe with tobacco from his pouch, but then failed to light it. His face looked sad, haunted. Guilty.

She ducked out of sight and made her way back into the cabin. She took off her socks and warmed her cold, sodden feet against the stove. She hauled herself to her feet, stumbled into her room, crawled under the blankets and fell fast asleep.

Her dreams were more than usually vivid. As usual, she saw her mother hanging from a hook in the ceiling, but this time her mother looked like someone else, someone she had seen before, a younger woman, fresher-faced, not lined and worn down prematurely like her own mother had been. She was walking through the snow in bare feet. Wolves were running beside her, in front of her, cutting off her means of escape. She tried to run but her legs were heavy and refused to move. She was high up in a tree. She launched herself into space and for a brief moment felt that she was flying, then she fell and hit the ground.

6

Ludmila woke to the sound of the heavy diesel engine of the truck as it drove into the compound. She pulled back her threadbare woollen curtain and watched Semyon haul another deer carcass from the back of the truck. She supposed he bought them from the herders to feed the wolves. Her head was pounding from the vodka and morphine and she felt sick. Her hand still throbbed and the wound had been bleeding. She pulled out her notebook and scribbled down everything that had happened and interrogated herself on what it meant.

She looked out of the window again and noticed that Semyon was limping as he made his way back from the birchwood frame where he had hung the fresh reindeer. She dressed hurriedly, aware from her own smell that she would need a bath or thorough wash at some point, and went into the kitchen. As usual, Irina was at the stove. She looked up briefly as Ludmila entered. Ludmila caught her lowering her eyelids and deduced that she was not in favour. Her father was sitting at the table eating his breakfast. He looked tired and drawn but managed a nod to the militiawoman. Semyon was helping himself to tea from the samovar. Placing the glass on the table, he reached for the sharpening steel which hung from a rack together with pots and pans and kitchen implements. He glanced briefly at Ludmila and began to sharpen his skinning knife in quick, practised movements.

'Have you injured yourself?' Ludmila asked him.

'No,' replied the Georgian.

'I thought I saw you limping just now.' Ludmila looked directly at him. Irina turned to him and Grigori looked up. Semyon turned back to his sharpening with increased vigour. Without looking at any of them, he replied, 'I caught my leg with the axe setting sable traps.'

'Not like you, Semyon,' said Grigori.

'No,' said Semyon. He returned the steel to its place on the rack and left the cabin without another word. Kolya growled as he passed him.

'Does the wolf always growl at Semyon?' she asked.

'He's a wolf. What do you expect? He should sing?' Irina replied.

'How's the hand?' asked Grigori, as Ludmila helped herself to tea and sat down. Irina placed a blini on a plate in front of her.

'Sore.'

'I'll change the bandage later. We don't want to risk it getting infected.' He turned to Irina. 'I have to take the truck to Bakta to pick up fuel later Irushka. I'll take Semyon.' He got up from the table, left the room and closed his study door.

'I'll need a bath. How does one go about that?' She had already experienced the outside privy and knew not to expect too much in the way of luxury.

'There's a zinc bath which you can take to your room and you just boil up a big pan of water on the stove,' said Irina without a hint of apology.

After her breakfast, Ludmila decided to question Semyon. She walked into the compound and could feel that the temperature was already starting to fall, far earlier even than in Moscow. She pulled in lungfuls of the clean air. The scent of conifer resin was still present under the overpowering scent of wolf. They were going frantic as they watched –and smelt- Semyon dismembering the reindeer. He affected not to notice her and continued with his work. Ludmila watched closely as he performed his butchery. It had more the appearance of surgery as Semyon cut and sliced through the thick flesh, peeling it back from the fascia almost without drawing blood.

'Is it hard to work with one arm?' Ludmila asked.

'I'm not working with one arm.' Semyon glared up at her, red-faced, the veins snaking at his temple.

'Your left arm looks a bit weaker. You're using your elbow and forearm a lot.'

'I hurt my arm as well setting the traps.'

'Careless.'

Semyon said nothing.

'Where were you last night?'

'Why?'

'You left after we discovered the wolf had gone. Why did you go?'

'I was tired. I wasn't going to chase after an escaped wolf in the middle of the night.'

'You heard what happened?'

'To you and Irina. Yes. It was stupid to go into the forest after dark.'

'Don't you go into the forest after dark?'

'I know what I'm doing.'

Ludmila tried to get closer to him to see if the big Georgian smelt the same as last night's attacker, but each time she moved closer, he moved away. It was futile in any event, as the powerful stench of freshly killed reindeer masked any human scent she could detect. Finally Semyon stood up, the knife held loosely in his right hand, turning it slowly.

'Are you accusing me of anything, officer?' he asked.

'I'm just asking questions until I know the truth and have caught whoever killed that herder.'

Semyon looked at her, the knife turning slower now. Ludmila's eyes went to it briefly. He stopped turning it.

'Like I said. It's dangerous in the forest. Especially at night. I have to feed the animals. Can I go now?'

Ludmila moved back as Semyon cut the deer from the frame and started to drag it to the cages. The tumult from the wolves rose in pitch and volume. Ludmila watched, then turned. It was time for that bath.

It took an hour before she had enough water for the zinc bathtub. Irina found her soap and a towel and, keeping her stitched hand out of the water, Ludmila was able to soak for a while in her room. She ran through her mind what she had discovered so far. It wasn't very much. She needed to probe deeper into every aspect of the case. She laughed to herself at the word 'case'. This was like no case she had ever encountered or heard about. She had to find new ways of dealing with everyone involved. A flayed corpse. An Orthodox cross. A secretive scientist. His protective daughter. A surly Georgian woodsman. Uncooperative native Siberians. Hostile tribal priest. A nocturnal assault. A tame wolf! She risked washing her hair with the crude block of pale soap she had been given, working it into a rich lather in her hands before applying it. She had kept back a large jug of clean warm water to rinse. They are all under suspicion, she reminded herself, all of them. She slid down in the bath and gave her hair a preliminary rinse then emptied the jug of water over her head.

Through the cascade of water she caught the sound of shouting from outside. She reached for a towel and rubbed her hair roughly, then she dried herself as quickly as she could, pulled on her uniform and wrapped a clean handkerchief around her hand. The shouts were from two men and they were speaking in broken Russian and then in fluent Evenk and then again in Russian. There was obvious panic in their voices. Ludmila pulled back the curtain. Irina was outside. Two Evenki men –one of them she recognised as the boy-translator's father- had ridden in to the compound on reindeer. Ludmila rushed outside, jamming her hat over her wet hair.

'What's the matter?' she asked.

'Innaksa has gone missing. He wasn't in his bed this morning and they've been searching all day. He knows the forest so he won't have got lost. They thought he might be here.'

'We'll find him. Bring your wolf,' ordered Ludmila.

'What? They've got their own dogs, they don't need Kolya.'

'You said yourself he can track ten times better than a dog. Bring him.'

'He's hurt.'

'So am I. Bring him.'

Irina angrily called Kolya over. At first he didn't move, aware of his injured leg, but after a few more pleas from Irina he came obediently over to her.

'Tell the other man to get off the reindeer. I'll go to the camp with the boy's father and organise a proper search.'

Furious on the one hand with Ludmila for her arrogance and assumption of authority and at the same time admiring her abilty to act decisively, Irina asked the other man to dismount. Ludmila grabbed the pommel of the saddle and launched herself on to the animal's back. It wasn't too happy with her amateurish riding skills. She grabbed the braided leather bridal tied to the stumps of its horns and yanked it savagely left and right. After a few moments, the reindeer settled down and allowed Ludmila control. The two men watched in amazement, as Ludmila took off in the direction of the camp.

At the edge of the camp, Irina took care to secure Kolya by his chain to a tree. Reindeer grunted and coughed in the makeshift pens, their bells jangling and tinkling. The camp dogs barked excitedly at the presence of the wolf. Ludmila headed straight for Innaksa's family tent, guided by his father. There were four or five tepee-style tents, with birch wood frames covered in part by reindeer hide and occasionally army surplus canvas tarpaulin. Holes had been cut into the coverings to allow the stove chimney through. Innaksa's mother was distraught. The shaman stood by, scowling as the young Russian woman in the military uniform pulled back the flap of the tent without permission and went inside.

The floor was covered with conifer branches as a crude but effective form of insulation. An old woman sat in the corner –presumably the child's grandmother- sipping tea from a saucer. An old man sat next to her smoking. Their faces were blank as they watched Ludmila move about in the cramped confines of the tent. It was warm and there was a smell of unwashed bodies, offset by the tea in an improvised samovar on the stove and a pan of reindeer stew bubbling next to it. The strong smell of the pine branches struggled with the more pungent odours.

Ludmila asked where Innaksa's bed was. Her father pointed. It was close to the edge of the tent. Anyone could have reached in and grabbed the child as he slept, Ludmila thought. Irina entered the tent and Innaksa's mother held the lapels of her coat and wept and shouted.

'What's she saying?' Ludmila demanded.

'She say Wolfman take our child,' said Innaksa's father dumbly.

At this point the shaman burst in and said something angrily to the parents of the child. Irina guessed it was about bringing the two Russian women here when it was no business of theirs. Ludmila turned to Innaksa's mother.

'Give me an item of the child's clothing.'

The woman looked mystified at her husband. He translated for her. Frowning, she handed over a pair of reindeer hide breeches. Ludmila snatched them and strode out of the tent straight to Kolya. Irina followed.

'Let the wolf smell this and then we follow him,' Ludmila said.

'I told you, yes he can follow a scent better even than a dog but we can't be sure he'll do what he's told.'

'I have watched how obedient he is most of the time, especially to you. Give him the breeches.'

Irina took the little boy's trousers and held them in front of Kolya's snout. He duly sniffed them but then looked away, as if he wasn't really interested. Irina tried again, urging him with a few words which she knew would be meaningless to the wolf.

'Kolya, these belong to Innaksa. You know him, don't you? We need to find him.'

The wolf sniffed them again, as if to please his mistress, then his nose went to the ground and he started to snuffle and whine. He lifted his head in a direction towards the camp.

'Unchain him but keep hold of the lead!' Ludmila shouted.

Irina unhooked the chain and was almost dragged headlong as Kolya made straight for Innaksa's tent. The dogs, held back by some of the boys, went wild and snapped and barked at Kolya. The reindeer herd rumbled frantically back and forth in their pen. The men shouted, a couple of the women screamed and the children yelled excitedly. Kolya stopped at the entrance, then went around the outside edge of the tent before setting off from the place where Innaksa had been sleeping just inside.

Irina knew she couldn't keep up with him, so with all her strength she pulled him to a standstill and took the chain from around his neck. Would he still follow the scent? Kolya set off at a loping pace completely focussed on the scent. Irina and Ludmila followed him. The shaman shouted a warning to the men of the brigade not to follow, but Innaksa's father ignored him and kept pace with the two women.

Irina watched Kolya as he followed his snout over the marshy ground. He would pause briefly, for seconds only, and then continue following the boy's scent that was only barely distinguishable from a hundred other smells. She felt a swelling pride that pricked her eyes and caused her to gulp involuntarily.

She turned to Innaksa's father as they ran.

'What did the shaman say? Why didn't he want you to follow Kolya?' she asked between breaths.

'He say wolf will take us the wrong way. Not to be trusted.'

He has a point there, Irina thought.

'The wolf smelt the child's clothes, now he is tracking. I have worked with police dogs,' Ludmila.

'He's not a dog,' said Irina again.

They ran for over thirty minutes until they came into a clearing where a group of conifers had been destroyed several years before by the predations of a tiny beetle. Giant trees lay splintered across smaller trees, gaunt spires stripped of greenery loomed over shattered stumps and the ground was churned up under an open grey sky. This was one of the ways Nature created gaps in the monotonous uniform canopy of the taiga for other species to thrive. Kolya paused here longer than usual. He seemed at a loss. He put his head down and crouched low in his haunches and moved forward. He was making for one of the larger fallen trees which had now fallen into serious decay. He stopped and pawed the ground and whined. Irina felt the heart in her chest pounding as if it would burst. The wolf had unearthed something. Irina stooped to pick it up. It was Innaksa's squirrel doll.

'Out of the way!' shouted Ludmila as she went toward the spot where the wolf was making fairly desultory attempts to remove the earth from rotten, moss-carpeted timber. With her bare hands she began to pull at the decayed wood. It came away in larger and larger pieces. There were signs of recent activity in the soil, as if someone has been digging. Irina and Innaksa's father tore at the wood and the soil, both of them dreading to think what they would find. Finally, Ludmila pulled a broad section of bark away and revealed Innaksa, staring in utter horror at them, his mouth gagged with an old rag, his hands and feet bound with cord, but alive.

His father howled like an animal and dragged the boy from under the tree. With his knife, he cut the cords and undid the gag. The boy immediately screamed and collapsed sobbing into his father's arms. His screams were high-pitched and unnatural. After a moment, he broke down into more modulated sobs as he clung desperately to his father like an infant primate. His father's face was a mask of incomprehension, relief and horror, the mouth hanging open, the crooked lower teeth protruding, the eyes staring at the ground. Kolya came and licked the boy's face.

Ludmila looked round wildly. 'He can't be far away.'

'Why would he do this?' Irina wondered out loud. She felt sick but didn't know what else to say.

'He was obviously disturbed. He didn't intend to bury the boy. He was just storing him there for later, when he would probably have skinned him alive like the other victim.'

The coolly analytical tone of the militiawoman's voice and her emotionless assessment of the situation made Irina want to hit her – not for the first time.

'It wasn't a question! It was...it was...it doesn't matter what it was! How can you stand there and be so clinical? The boy was buried alive!'

'I have to remain calm. There is no point in getting emotional. That will not catch the killer,' Ludmila replied evenly.

Irina walked over to the little boy still shuddering in his father's arms. She crouched and spoke to him.

'We will catch the man who did this, Innaksa, don't worry. You go home with your daddy and see your family again.'

'I will have to question him about what happened,' Ludmila said and immediately crouched down and placed her face close to the boy's. 'Did you see who took you? What did he look like? The man who took you. Describe him to me.'

Innaksa stopped sobbing and stared wide-eyed into the eyes of his interrogator. His father was torn between concern for his son but he was also keen to know what the abductor of his child looked like.

'Let him get home and see his mother first. Let him recover!' Irina shouted angrily. Then Innaksa pointed to the doll which was still in Irina's hand. She handed it to him, but then paused.

'Can he have his doll back or do you need it for evidence?' Irina asked with what she hoped was a withering tone.

'Yes. I need it.'

She walked over and took the doll from an incredulous Irina.

'There may be fingerprints on it. Let's go.'

With that she turned and walked back the way they had come.

The boy screamed then burst into a new round of racking, breathless sobs.

7

It took them the best part of an hour to walk back to the camp and it was already starting to get dark. The whole brigade rushed out to meet them, shouting and talking over one another. Innaksa's mother hugged the boy and wept. She screamed out something to the surrounding woods – a challenge, a curse, Irina couldn't be sure. The shaman stood to one side, not daring to usurp the mother's claim on her son. He seemed sullen and began to beat his reindeer skin drum slowly and to chant and dance in jerky little moves. Occasionally he would stop and shake the bracelets he wore on his wrists and grimace at the darkening woods around them. Irina stood at the edge of the camp with Kolya and Ludmila. The militiawoman watched the shaman with unconcealed contempt.

'He still thinks it's a spirit,' she said. 'They all do. Their ignorance is appalling and it is getting in the way of me catching this criminal. Because that's all he is. A man. A criminal. And he'll go on trial and be executed for his crime. The man who attacked us last night is the killer. He's here. In these woods. Close by. He will try and kill again. I don't know why he has chosen the herders. I don't even know if he is a herder himself. I've smelt his sweat. I've hurt him. He's real. He's human. And I will hunt him down.' She took the doll out of her greatcoat pocket and the cross out of the other. She looked at them. *What did they reveal? What did they mean?*

Her mind raced. She would stay in the camp. Wait for the next attempt. But what if they had scared him off? What if he would move on somewhere else? To another camp? Who was he? A fur trapper? A herder? A lunatic? A religious fanatic? What? What was motivating him? As she watched the shaman dance, her own brain danced with a hundred half-formed, conflicting thoughts.

Irina managed to persuade Ludmila not to question the boy further. Ludmila barely spoke as they trudged back to the field centre.

'What is the Georgian's relationship with the herders?' she asked suddenly.

'I don't know what you mean,' Irina replied, stiffly.

'Do they like him? They supply the reindeer for the wolves. He has a lot to do with them, but how do they regard him?'

'They don't dislike him. They don't like him. They don't have to like him.'

'But you try to understand them. Speak their language. Does he?'

'No. That's not Semyon's way. You've seen how he is. He is like a man from another time.' As soon as she said this, Irina wished she hadn't.

'Explain.'

Irina hesitated. Ludmila noted it.

'He's just … old fashioned.'

'A kulak?'

Kulak. That word. It meant so many things. So many dangerous things. A fist. A tight fist. A tight-fisted peasant. A peasant with his own cattle. Resisting collectivaisation. Saboteur. Czarist. Bourgeois entrepreneur. An enemy of the people. An enemy of the Revolution. A criminal.

'Semyon fought bravely against the Nazis.'

'He told you?'

'…Yes. Why would he lie?'

'Why wouldn't he lie?'

'That's a ridiculous question.'

'Nothing is ridiculous when you are dealing with people who want to destroy what we have built up.'

'You could call the herders kulaks if you wanted. But not Semyon. I've known him since I was a little girl.'

'We don't *know* anyone. Only what they *do*.'

'That's not true.'

'Do you know where Semyon goes when he is not at the field station?'

Irina was beginning to shake with fury. She had to control herself or she feared she would become incoherent.

'He goes back to his cabin. He traps animals in the forest. He drives the truck into…' She stopped.

'Where does he drive the truck to?' Ludmila stopped Irina and looked at her piercingly.

'He has days off. He drives to Lunovskoye. The mining town. Where they mine aluminium. He has friends there. Other Georgians. He gets drunk. Sleeps it off. Comes back.' Irina felt she was betraying Semyon, but was not sure how.

'When is he going there again?'

'As a matter of fact he's going tomorrow.'

Ludmila said nothing but turned and strode off across the saturated ground toward the field centre. Irina watched her go. Her instinct was to warn Semyon. But that would confirm his guilt in Ludmila's mind. Irina knew that the big bear-like creature that had attacked them was not Semyon but how to convince this automaton, this cold, beautiful monster from Moscow masquerading as a police officer?

That evening, Grigori changed Ludmila's bandage and they ate in silence. Semyon refused to join them despite Grigori's pleas. He said he wasn't hungry and left them alone. Grusha and Masha were already taking unsteady steps and investigating their surroundings. Grigori excused himself and went into his study. Irina cleared the table and washed up. Ludmila went into her room, swaddled herself in a blanket, wrote furiously in her note book and made a plan.

She slept in her uniform and loaded her pistol. As soon as light dawned, she peered through the curtains and watched and waited. Eventually Semyon strode into view, carrying a hessian sack which he placed carefully on the passenger seat. Then he kneeled in the light snow that had fallen in the night, bowed his head and crossed himself. After a few moments, he got up and began the arduous task with the starting handle. Eventually the truck roared into life. As Semyon got into the cab, Ludmila sprinted out of the cabin and keeping low to the ground, ran to the back of the truck and climbed in. She had already determined that the truck carried no side mirrors and the rear window of the cab was obscured by the high rear cargo bed. Semyon wouldn't have seen her. She crawled to the front end of the cargo bed and wedged herself in between the rolled canvas tarpaulin that occasionally covered the back of the truck.

She had no idea how long the drive would be and settled herself in for a long haul. Wisps of snow were falling and the temperature was not much above freezing. She huddled herself into a foetal position and pulled down her hat over her ears and pulled on her gloves, wincing as her stitches dragged.

The ZIS bounced and rattled and groaned over the marshy terrain. Ludmila tried to sleep but it was far too cold. Occasionally she did drift off for minutes at a time and was rewarded with her usual bad dreams. Knowing that Semyon would have no idea she was there, she would stand and watch the passing taiga through the old slatted boards. The landscape was broad and flat and monochrome where it wasn't dark conifer-green. The sky stretched endlessly pearl-grey and charcoal and now and again shot through with early winter sunlight. There were mountains capped with snow to the east. Ludmila worked out that they were travelling north east most of the time at a speed of little more –she guessed- than twenty five miles an hour.

Slowly the light faded but in the distance she could make out the gigantic sihouette of an industrial mining complex. There were huge mounds of earth, hundreds of feet of cross-hatched ironwork, belts, gantries, long processing sheds and a sulphurous smelting plant. The landscape was desolate, lunar, forests and topsoil having been cleared to begin the layer-by-layer strip mining for the bauxite, leaving a huge amphitheatre. Steam shovels pecked at the red earth like so many mechanical hens. Trucks came and went busy as ants with a constant roar and clatter. There were low concrete buildings flying the flag of the Soviet Union. Administrative offices. There was also a strong military presence. Armed soldiers and armoured vehicles. Most of the labour was provided by prisoners.

Semyon pulled up outside an assemblage of wooden huts, which had sprawled and included a few crudely marked streets. There was an open square in the centre, round which were some makeshift shops and a bar. This was Lunovskoye. The inhabitants were mainly Asian in appearance. The workers that weren't prisoners were drawn from the local population. The inhabitants of the administrative buildings were largely Russian.

Ludmila took this in and processed it as fast as she could. The smell was overpoweringly mineral, scorched, igneous. A red dust hung in the air, churned up by the unceasing movement of earth-laden vehicles.

As soon as the truck stopped, Ludmila leaped from the cargo bed and withdrew from the truck in a line with the rear before ducking into a back alley formed by the back-to-back nature of some of the ramshackle dwellings. She watched around the corner of the building as Semyon got out and took the hessian bundle from the seat next to him.

Slamming the truck door behind him, he started off at a brisk pace obviously knowing exactly where he was going. Ludmila followed him. Not once did he look round until he reached the door of a small wooden house down a side alley. Ludmila sensed that he would look round before entering, pre-empted his move and ducked back behind the corner of the building. When she looked back, Semyon was gone, presumably through the door. The light was fading now and Ludmila was able to move to the single window that looked out into the dingy side alley, which stank of cats, rotting vegetables and kerosene. She could hear singing coming from inside the house. It sounded like ten or fifteen people, adults, male and female, possibly the odd child. It was slow, intoned, religious. Some sort of hymn. Flat against the wall she craned her neck and peered in the window. A tattered woollen curtain had been drawn across but it was skimped and there was a gap through which Ludmila could see. The room was lit by candles and a group of people stood before a man who wore a cloth-of-gold stole about his neck and sported a huge bushy beard. She watched as Semyon came forward and opened the hessian sack. He took from it a golden cross. A woman came forward and draped a garland of roses around it and then Semyon handed it to the man in the stole. Gathering his hands in the stole, he took hold of the cross and held it aloft. He said something and the rest of the group responded. He said something else and again the congregation –for that's what it was-responded. It was a litany. The congregation then all crossed themselves in unison and came forward one by one to kiss the feet of the golden Christ-figure perched decorously on the ornate three-sparred crucifix.

Ludmila had seen enough. She retreated to a bar –or rather a house with an open shop-front that sold alcohol-which had a perfect view of the side street. It was a dead end, so anyone who went down would have to come back the same way.

The bar was dingy, lit by a single low-wattage electric bulb. Three customers were drinking at a table in the corner. A thin boney-faced man with hardly a hair on his head, a sullen-looking stocky man with a white beard and a buck-toothed younger man in a flap-eared cap. The overweight bar tender sat reading his newspaper behind the bar. The three looked up as Ludmila entered. They took in her militia uniform with the red star on the peaked cap, then went back to their card game.

'Tea,' said Ludmila.

The bar tender didn't look up from his newspaper.

'Didn't you hear me?' she asked, containing her irritation.

'We only have vodka,' he said.

Ludmila reached over and tore the newspaper from his grasp and flung it over the other side of the room. The three men looked up from their game.

'That is a samovar and there is tea in it, or are you blind as well as deaf?'

The fat man's neck flushed red. After a significant pause, he stretched and turned the tap on the samovar and served Ludmila her tea in a glass that was streaked and grimy.

'Two kopeks,' was all he said.

Ludmila paid and sipped the piping hot stewed black sugary tea.

She sat at a table in the window and waited. She felt the card players' eyes on her back and didn't look up as the barman retrieved his scattered paper. After about an hour, a group of people emerged from the side street and then went their separate ways. She couldn't see Semyon at first but then he appeared, carrying the hessian sack and talking to the celebrant of whatever rite she had just witnessed. The latter was smaller and rounder than Semyon, who appeared to tower over him. But both had very impressive black bushy beards. Eventually the smaller man made his excuses and left but not before Semyon had given him the hessian sack and its precious religious icon. Ludmila fingered the crucifix in her pocket.

She rose to intercept him. She would arrest him for illegally attending a religious service and possessing a religious object and take it from there.

The scene in front of her eyes –Semyon walking across the twilit street towards the bar having said goodbye to the celebrant- suddenly went black apart from a blue-white spark which shot across her line of vision. Then nothing.

8

Her mother was making blini for breakfast. She was talking to Ludmila but it wasn't her voice. It was an old woman's. Then a man she didn't know came into the kitchen and said the roof was leaking but that was to do with the time of year and that she was waking up.

'She's waking up Agneta, look. Her eyes moved. She's not dead.'

'I know she's not dead, you fool. She's been breathing.'

Ludmila's head was aching violently. With every heartbeat a sledgehammer smashed into the back of her skull. She tried to move her head. The pain was intense. She opened her eyes and saw an old man and woman in their seventies peering at her with concern. The woman was a typical *babushka*, a round rosy-cheeked face with a dark scarf covering her hair. The man was lean and whiskery with a mournful face wearing a woollen cap.

'Don't try to move, miss… officer,' the woman said.

'Someone hit you on the back of the head,' said the man matter of factly.

Ludmila put her hand to the back of her head and felt the hair matted and sticky. *Blood.*

'Where am I? And who are you?'

'We run the grocery supply shop for the mining collective,' said the woman

'How did I get here?'

'Semyon found you. He saw the men that did it but they ran off when they saw him. He's a big guy,' said the man.

'You know Semyon?'

'Yes, he—,' the woman began but the man silenced her with a look. 'We know him. He comes to Lunovskoye a lot.'

'To pray?'

'I don't know about that,' said the man.

Bracing herself, Ludmila raised herself into a sitting position. The banging in her head became almost unbearably intense for a moment, then subsided. The woman went to assist her but Ludmila waved her away. They had put her on a table in the back of their shop. There were barrels and boxes and sacks and racks of dried fish and sausage and shelves of tinned food all around her. She swung her legs over the edge of the table. She placed her legs on the floor and immediately felt the room spinning. She gripped the table as the man and woman moved to hold her steady.

'I'm fine, I'm … fine, thank you,' Ludmila reassured them.

'I will bandage your head for you if you will just sit down, officer,' the old woman offered.

Ludmila shook her head but as soon as she did realised that was a mistake. She waited for the pain to subside again. She touched the back of her neck and felt what must be encrusted blood. 'Where is Semyon now?'

'He said he would come and get you and take you back to where you are staying,' the old man said.

'Did anyone else see who attacked me?'

'I'm not sure. I think it was just Semyon. Who saw.'

Convenient.

She needed to think. Who had hit her? The men in the bar? The owner? No, it must have been Semyon. There were no witnesses. And yet she was sure she had seen him in front of her when she received the blow to the back of her head. Had he possibly given the men in the bar a signal? So why had he brought her to the shop? He could have left her. Maybe he hoped she was dead.

Semyon entered the shop, talking in low tones to the old couple. He looked at her without expression.

'You can stay here tonight. Vassily and Agneta have offered you their bed,' he said.

'I need to go now.'

'You have been injured. You need to sleep. I will take you back tomorrow.'

'I can find my own way back.'

'How? Over a hundred miles in the dark? No one goes that way except me.'

Ludmila saw it was pointless to argue and the pain in her head was making her feel nauseous. The old woman could see what was about to happen and produced an enamel bowl from nowhere and held it under her chin. Ludmila retched and vomited while the old woman held her hair away from her face. She patted Ludmila's back and shushed and stroked her. Ludmila felt her eyes sting briefly with tears. The woman dabbed her mouth with a damp cloth and gently escorted her up some creaking wooden steps to the old couple's bedroom. She laid Ludmila on the bed which smelt of violets and tobacco, gently pulled off her boots and covered her with the eider down quilt. Ludmila sank into a deep, dreamless sleep.

When Semyon roused her late the next morning, her hand automatically went to her belt and she found her pistol was missing. She demanded Semyon return it to her but he denied all knowledge of it.

'The men who attacked you must have taken it,' he said. 'We need to get back to Pustinya.'

They got into the truck and followed the road that had been specially constructed to gain access to the mine, for about an hour, then they turned off over the marshy terrain flanked by taiga forest. Ludmila felt drowsy but fought to stay awake. She filled her nostrils in an attempt to gauge if Semyon was the man who attacked her, but for once her sense of smell betrayed her. She could smell nothing. The blow on the head must be responsible. She demanded again that Semyon return her weapon.

'I told you I haven't seen it. Militia or no militia you don't walk into a bar in a mining town and expect people to jump when you say jump. You're lucky you're still alive.'

Ludmila hadn't the strength to argue. They drove in silence for over an hour. The landscape didn't change. An endless forest that broke out occasionally into broad glade. The sky was yellow-grey and threatened snow.

'When we get back to the field station, you're under arrest,' Ludmila said simply.

'For what?' The Georgian almost snarled at her.

'For attending an illegal religious ceremony, owning a forbidden religious icon and,' she paused, 'on suspicion of murder.'

Semyon slammed his foot on the brake pedal and Ludmila was thrown forward.

'You're arresting me on suspicion of murder? Whose murder?'

'The murder of the native herder and the attempted murder of the child.'

'You are insane! I rescued you from being killed, made sure you were looked after when you followed me here – where? In the back of the truck?- and you think I'm a murderer? Do you think I would have done all that?' Then he laughed loudly. 'I must be the kindest killer that ever lived!' And he carried on laughing.

He stopped abruptly and reached into his coat pocket and pulled out a hand gun: Ludmilla's standard issue 7mm Tokarev, which she had loaded herself.

'Give me my gun,' Ludmila said.

'Oh of course officer. You're arresting me for a crime I didn't commit and I am going to give you your gun so you can take me into custody. After all I am a very kind criminal so I will do what you want. Get out of the truck.'

Ludmila stared at him but did not move.

'Get out or I will kill you and bury you here in the forest. You can find your own way back.'

'You have just admitted your own guilt. Reconsider and it will go easier for you in your trial. What you are doing is completely self-destructive.'

'Why? Because I don't want you to arrest me for something I didn't do?' Semyon laughed again. 'Get out.'

Inwardly, Ludmila cursed herself for telling the Georgian she was going to arrest him.

'You will be tried in a court of Soviet law and if you are innocent you will have nothing to fear.'

The big man laughed even louder.

'Get out.'

Ludmila opened the heavy truck door and stepped down on to the oozing ground. A cold wind was starting to blow.

'I can follow your tracks.'

'If I thought you would survive to follow my tracks I'd kill you now,' Semyon said looking directly into her eyes. The effect was chilling. 'Shut the door.'

Ludmila closed the door. For the first time she felt a wave of fear engulf her. She would die out here without food or shelter. Semyon crashed the gears angrily and the truck moved away and was soon lost among the trees. The tracks the big ZIS made were clear in the mud and for a while Ludmila followed them. The light was already starting to fade and the temperature approaching freezing. She pulled her cap down over her ears and buttoned her coat to the neck. She thrust her hands deep into her pockets and felt the cross and the little boy's doll. Light flakes of snow drifted in the wind. Ludmila picked up her pace.

Her boots soon became sodden and her feet numb with cold no matter how fast she walked. The snow stopped and the sky gradually cleared. A waning moon now floated in the darkening indigo blue with some remnant clouds moving across its grinning face. Stars emerged one by one, then all at once. The cold became intense and Ludmila wanted to howl in fury at the terrible beauty of the Siberian night. She worked out that she would have to walk seventy-five miles at least. It had taken four hours travelling at what she guessed was twenty-five miles an hour. That was one hundred miles. They'd already travelled for an hour on the return journey. Seventy-five miles. With no food in these conditions was it possible? It would mean walking for twenty-five hours without stopping. It could be done. It can be done. It will be done. This was the mantra she intoned to herself.

After two hours she desperately needed to sleep. Seventy-five miles might be possible in a day but not with concussion. Her head ached and she was lifting her feet by sheer willpower. She was walking through a densely wooded section and was just able to follow the ZIS tracks in the moonlight. Whether in reality or whether her injured brain was revisiting the fears of childhood, she started to hear things moving in the trees around her. Hear was the wrong word. She didn't actually hear or see anything. She sensed movement and presence. She felt eyes watching her move through alien territory. She imagined they smelt the blood in her hair and the fear in her heart. She was wounded prey, growing weaker by the minute and the inhabitants of the taiga knew it. A wolf howled in the distance and her blood froze. It was answered by another distant howl. The powerful desire for sleep overcame all her fears and she moved a little deeper into the dense conifer cover at her side. The ground was drier, ankle deep in pine needles. She dug out a soft hollow in the needles at the base of a huge larch and curled up like an unborn creature, pulling her coat around her and her hat harder over her ears. She was shivering violently. She slid into unconsciousness. She dreamt her mother wrapped her in a shawl and called on wolves to curl round her and keep her warm. She felt their coarse fur and their sticky tongues licking her face. Her mother was singing a lullaby and the wolves nuzzled her with their snouts and broad skulls and whined in harmony with her mother's singing. She was playing in the snow with a little girl. They were playing with a large dog, or it could have been a wolf. It looked at her and bared its teeth. She felt frightened. Her mother came and picked her up. She stopped shivering and somewhere a voice –her mother's?- was telling her that this night she would die.

9

Irina placed the wreath of twigs, dried berries and pressed wildflowers on her mother's grave as she always did on the 28th September. That was the date her mother died according to the inscription on the little wooden cross. *Elena Vassilyovna Medvedenka April 20th 1905 – 28th September1930.* In the middle of the wreath was a creased and battered black and white photograph of a pretty, dark-eyed woman in her mid twenties holding a tiny baby: Irina. Grigori came and stood beside his daughter.

She asked the question she always did on this day every year since she could talk. 'What was she like? My mother?'

Grigori answered as he always did. 'She was beautiful and she loved you very much.'

Irina wept as she always did. She would leave the wreath, which she had made as a little girl, on the grave for one night and then retrieve it and keep it in her room, slowly falling to bits, till next year. Why she wept for someone she never knew, Irina didn't know. It was possibly the idea of the death of a woman who was not much older than she was now, who had just given birth to a baby she wanted to watch grow and marry and have children of her own, that made her weep.

'Do you miss her?' she asked her father.

'More and more as each year passes.'

She felt her father's warm hand on her shoulder. He squeezed it, then he pulled Irina to him and they stood there as the crows bickered across the tree tops, the wolves grew restless in their cages and the polar wind started to pierce the skin. Irina buried her face in the smell of pipe tobacco her father always carried in his clothes. Grigori looked across his daughter's head, her hair lightly whipping his face. He was looking at the monotony of the taiga landscape. Its bleakness and emptiness resonated with him. Summer was over. Autumn would be short and the winter long and hard.

The ZIS roared into the compound and came to a halt. Irina broke from her father and ran toward Semyon as he dismounted from the cab.

'Semyon! Have you seen Ludmila? '

The Georgian looked genuinely puzzled. 'Who?' She realised he didn't know her name.

'The militiawoman. She's not here. We thought she might be with you.'

'As you can see she's not. Unless she's hiding in the back. Have a look.'

He continued walking in the direction of his cabin without pausing.

'What could have happened to her? I'll go to the herders' camp and see if she's there. If she's gone after the killer on her own she's crazy.'

Irina was not sure if she was relieved that Ludmila had gone, or more disturbed by what harm she might be doing on her own. She went in and pulled on her coat.

The mood in the camp was sombre. They had arranged shifts of guard duty at night and the shaman was performing more rituals to keep the wolf spirit at bay. Irina went straight to Innaksa's tent.

The boy's grandmother was trying to coax him to eat but he didn't seem interested. When he saw Irina he looked up eyes widening and said, 'Have you brought Uluki?' That was the name Innaksa had given his figurine. It simply meant 'squirrel'. When Irina shook her head, Innaksa retreated back into himself. His grandmother pushed another spoonful of reindeer stew toward his mouth, but he turned his head away. Innaksa's mother looked up from the baby she was breastfeeding.

'He has bad dreams. Every night.'

Then she bent her head towards the baby and shifted her to the other breast.

'He doesn't cry. The wolf take his soul.'

'That's not true.' Irina crouched in front of the little boy. 'Listen Innaksa, the man who took you is not a spirit. He's a bad man. He hasn't taken your soul. We are going to find him and take him away.'

She put a hand to the boy's face and stroked his cheek with her thumb. He didn't respond, but said simply, 'Tell the soldier lady I want Uluki back.'

'I will. Has she been to see you again?' The boy shook his head. 'Not today? Yesterday?' He stared at her.

'Uluki.'

'I'll get him back, I promise.'

She rose to say goodbye, but neither grandmother, mother or Innaksa made eye contact. It's as though they're blaming me, she thought.

When she withdrew from the tent, she met the scowling face of the shaman. He spoke to her rapidly in Evenk, but Irina didn't know what he was saying but he could guess. She found Innaksa's father teaching the boys reindeer-lassoing techniques with a length of braided hide and a tree stump. She asked him if his little boy had said anything about the attack. He shook his head.

'He come to him in dreams at night. He screams, but say nothing.'

'Have you seen the soldier-woman?'

He shook his head.

Irina said they would find the killer and bring him to justice but she could hear how half-hearted her words must sound. Innaksa's father looked at her, gathering up the rope into loops, a rolled cigarette clamped and smouldering between his lips, but said nothing. Irina hated to admit it but Ludmila was right about one thing. Religion had a lot to answer for.

When she got back to the field station, Kolya ran out to greet her, his limp now barely noticeable. Semyon was busy butchering another reindeer carcass and the wolves were making their usual racket. Inside the cabin, her father was locked in his study and she could hear him typing. She always wondered what he was writing that he didn't want her to see. She typed up tables of figures and other data about the wolves they were studying. The length of ears, their colour, their weight and how different wolves reacted to the same stimuli and what that meant hypothetically. Which wolves had mated and what were the results –in terms of the behaviour of the offspring- on a scale of one to five, where one was 'amenable' and five 'completely feral'. She knew enough about the science to know that her father's work would not be popular in certain circles. In official circles. But she also understood that he was a scientist and that scientists, like -she acknowledged with a mental grimace, police officers - seek out the truth. Or at least that was the theory.

She made a fresh samovar of tea and heated some sweet rolls she had made that morning and knocked on her father's study door.

The sound of typing stopped and Grigori came to the door. Irina heard the sound of the brass key turning and the door opened.

'I thought you might be hungry.'

'Starving.'

He took the tray she offered him. He was about to close the door, when Irina heard herself ask him what he was working on.

'The usual.' He smiled.

'Can I read some of it sometime?'

'One day.'

'Is it so secret?'

Grigori looked at his daughter for a moment. Then he said, 'Come in for a moment. Have one of the rolls.'

She shook her head but accepted his invitation to come in. She felt she was seven again. Being tolerated briefly in the world of adults. It wasn't a good feeling but it wasn't wholly bad either.

Grigori pulled the paper he had been typing on out of the roller together with its carbon copy. He placed the pages in a drawer in his desk and pushed it shut.

So secret. So damned secret. Why doesn't he trust me? Irina sat in the chair opposite the desk and tried to appear disinterested. Grigori was filling his pipe. Irina watched as he lit the tobacco and the familiar rich loamy smell wafted in a blue fog toward her.

'I'm sorry I don't share some of my work with you, Irushka.' He puffed on the pipe, then gripped it between his crooked teeth and patted the bowl with his forefinger. Irina waited.

'You see, well, you know what I'm trying to do here, don't you?'

'I should do. I've been helping you ever since I can remember,'

'But there's something you might not know, something that this whole terrible business with the murder and so forth has brought into focus.'

'What?' She asked, almost involuntarily.

'Why do we study animal behaviour, Irushka?'

'Because we want to know why they do what they do.'

'And?'

'And … I suppose so we know something about ourselves.'

'Exactly! Was Mendel interested in sweet peas? Well yes, of course he was. But that was all he had to experiment with. What was he really interested in?'

'Us.'

'We can't help being anthropocentric. It's in our nature. No matter how much we try and think ourselves into other creatures.'

'That doesn't sound very scientific.'

'Doesn't it? Why not?' He started to answer his own question. He was treating her like a student in a seminar.

'Scientists look at Nature and ask 'why?' Ok, that's pure science. Knowledge for the sake of knowledge. I don't inhabit those lofty citadels of the scientific mind. I'm a scientist who wants to know why human beings are what they are, and that if that state of being is imperfect what can be done about it. That is what behaviourism is all about.'

'So where scientific enquiry becomes psychological investigation? Or politics.'

'In a way.' Grigori looked at his daughter as if not sure whether he should continue. As if he was making some shameful confession which would change their relationship forever. Then he took the plunge. 'What if there was a way to eliminate the barbarian in us completely, so that there would be no more wars, no more torture and thoughtless cruelty, no more cutting ourselves off from our fellow creatures so we could justify hurting them, demonising them, destroying them? What if, in a word, we could *breed* that darkness out of the human race forever?'

He leant back and puffed on his pipe, every inch the scientific academic in one way, but in another a wild-eyed passionate idealist.

'But dad, the authorities won't see it that way.'

'Why not? This is real Soviet science. It is about eradicating the self-serving, individualistic saboteur in favour of the altruist, the collectivist.' He paused. 'The communist. How could our system not approve?'

Again that insouciant grin, the mocking tone. Irina covered her face with her hands and shook her head, then ran her fingers through her thick hair, which she realised needed a wash. She felt like his wife or his mother. Didn't he see that his research was dangerous?

'If my mother was here, what would she have said?'

Grigori looked thoughtful for a moment, then said. 'She'd have said go where the truth takes you.' The boyish laughter was gone. The lean, intelligent face a sombre mask. He seemed lost in sadness. Irina got up and left.

She walked out into the compound. Semyon was at the edge of the forest felling and splitting birch for firewood. As soon as Irina emerged on to the porch, Kolya stopped licking his rapidly healing wound and bounded ahead of her. She needed to clear her head, to think. Her tumbling thoughts were interrupted by a shout from Semyon and a fierce growling from Kolya. He had found something in the wood. There was another sound, a higher pitched growl followed by a bestial screech. Irina ran towards the sound and followed Semyon into the wood. A few yards in they discovered Kolya in a vicious stand-off with a stocky bearlike creature with the face of a weasel. Wolverine. Irina screamed. The wolverine glanced at her for a microsecond. It crouched ready to spring at Irina. Kolya leapt at the creature ears flattened to his skull, teeth bared and eyes wide. Two gunshots went off and the wolverine fell dead. Kolya pulled back for a second then dived on the wolverine and started to tear at its flesh. The wolves in the compound yelped and howled as the scent of blood drifted toward them. Irina looked at Semyon. In his hand an automatic pistol which he quickly returned to the pocket of his coat. He then waded in to Kolya and pushed him aside - not something you did casually with a feeding wolf. However Kolya had long ago placed Semyon above him in the pecking order and he backed off. Irina knew that Semyon would be after the valuable wolverine pelt. He gutted the animal swiftly with his short, razor-sharp knife and pulled the intestines, stomach and liver out and let Kolya gorge himself. He looked up briefly from his work.

'Are you all right?' He asked her.

'Yes. Thanks once again Semyon, though I think Kolya would have got in first.'

She looked down at the wolf, his snout covered in blood, and ran her fingers through the thick fur on his neck.

'I didn't know you had a pistol,' she continued.

'I … don't use it much. It's an old army Tokarev.' A pause. 'They let me keep it.'

He went back to his work, and Irina frowned to herself as she watched him relieving the wolverine corpse of its thick dark coat. As far as she knew, Semyon had never used a hand gun.

10

There was a smell of animal pelts and frying meat. Her eyes seared with pain as she tried to open them. Someone was moving around. There was the sizzle of hot oil. A hacking cough. The creak of floor boards. It was warm, she was covered in coarse heavy blankets. Her head still ached. *Where am I?*

'Try not to move,' said a voice in heavily accented Russian. Had Semyon come back for her? She remembered she had fallen asleep under the huge pine to the distant sound of howling wolves. Then nothing.

'Where am I? Who … are you?' She managed six words, then stopped exhausted.

'I've made some soup. Here. Sit up.'

A strong arm supported her back and moved pillows so she could sit up. A rough horny hand passed her an enamel mug of hot soup. She took it gratefully and sipped, scalding her tongue.

'Careful.' The voice was deep, kind. 'I found you in the forest. You were almost dead with cold. I brought you to my cabin on my reindeer. I take it from your uniform you are military.' He stated rather than asked.

She tried to get out of bed.

'No. Don't move. I have bandaged the wound on your head. It is very bad. You must rest.'

Almost obeying his orders, she let sleep swallow her.

When she awoke again she was looking into the eyes of some sort of dog. It cocked its head and licked its chops and yawned, then padded off across the cabin to where a hunched figure of a man no more than thirty with matted blond hair and beard sat hunched next to a pot-bellied stove eating from an enamel plate. His fork scraped the last remnants of his meal and he raised the plate to his lips and drank off whatever juices were left.

'So, you're awake.' The man said.

Ludmila tried to get out of bed and discovered she was naked.

'Give me my clothes,' she croaked.

'They were wet. They are drying here over the stove. Stay where you are. I'll bring them to you when they're dry. Don't worry. You're safe.'

The next time Ludmila awoke sunlight was pouring through the window and she could hear the *pok!* of wood being split somewhere outside. The head pain was gone. She felt stiff and violently thirsty. An enamel beaker of water had been left by the bed. Ludmila gulped it down. *How long have I been asleep? What day is it?* The door of the cabin creaked open and a dog ran in and the figure of her rescuer stood in the doorway.

'Good. You found the water. I will get you more. If you need to use it the privy is outside at the back.'

He passed her clothes that had been neatly folded on an old chair, then brought a chipped enamel jug full of water to her and went out again. Ludmila frowned after him. Ludmila had never trusted unmotivated consideration. There must always be a reason why someone does something for someone else - unless it was for the Good of the People, she reminded herself quickly. So why was this man helping her?

The thought flashed through her mind that here was her killer, fattening her up for some elaborate sacrificial ritual. Too easy to kill her in her sleep. He needed to see her suffer and beg for mercy. He needed to keep her alive, like the witch Baba Yaga did in the stories. The eater of children, the bones scattered around her hut. Her mind flashed back to sitting on her mother's knee reading fairy tales about princess Vassillisa and the witch. Baba Yaga would come to her in her dreams and she would wake terrified. Her mother lying next to her would comfort her and sing to her. Her mother as far as she could remember was kind, when she wasn't locked into a deep depression. But mothers *were* kind. That was part of being a mother. It was woven into their fabric. She would sing lullabies to her terrified daughter, to comfort her, because that's what mothers were expected to do - apart from when she sat immobile in her chair staring into darkness. Then she was unreachable and Ludmila would quietly play with her dolls.

She dressed, went outside and passed the man –whom she could now see was tall, bearded, blond with rather close-set blue eyes- and used the privy. When she emerged, the man was standing looking toward her. Again, he looked concerned, genuinely concerned. She stared straight back at him.

'I need to get back,' she said bluntly.

'You are not well enough to go anywhere yet I don't think,' the man replied.

'Let me decide that.'

'You have been asleep for over forty-eight hours. You were almost dead from cold. How did you get your injury?'

'That is my business.'

'You are a police officer, militia, yes?'

'You're not Russian,' she said.

'No. From … Yugoslavia.' There was the slightest of hesitation, which Ludmila was not slow to pick up. He smiled at her, a broad handsome grin.

'I came here after the war. I am a fur trapper. That is how I make a living.'

'You are with a kolkhoz then?'

Another barely perceptible hesitation.

'Yes … of course. Not far from here. I can see you are a police officer. You ask a lot of questions.' Again the broad grin. He returned to splitting the birch with effortless precision.

'It's my job.'

Suddenly, she felt very dizzy and her knees gave way beneath her. Instantly, the man dropped the axe and caught her before she fell. Ludmila was aware of strong arms and took the opportunity to inhale his scent. Tobacco, sweat, obviously, but also an inexplicable odour of freshly baked bread. This wasn't the man who attacked her. He held her steady as the landscape tilted around her. She felt sick, but it passed and she was able to stand after a few minutes.

'You see? You're not strong enough to continue your journey.'

Ludmila shook him off irritably. He stood back and watched slightly amused as she swayed as if drunk.

'What's so funny?'

'I'm not laughing. I'm just smiling at your determination. You're tough. But you don't trust easily.'

'Why should I? I don't know you.'

'My name is Ivan Ivanovich Ivanov.' He laughed again. 'Not my real name. The Russians can't pronounce Yugoslav names. Even the Yugoslavs can't pronounce Yugoslav names! I trap animals. Sell their fur to the collective. Rescue strange women from the forest. I changed the bandage on your hand as well by the way.'

Ludmila was at a loss. She felt that it must be good once in a while to have answers instead of endless questions. Meanwhile she felt weak and dizzy. For the first time she put her hand to her hair and realised he had bandaged the wound on her head as well as her hand. She guessed she must look ridiculous.

She needed to sit down so she went back into the cabin, found a three-legged stool and shared the warmth of the stove with the dog who had crept in while his master was working. She looked at the animal. He returned her gaze and then whined and put his paw in her lap. He was needy and eager to please. Ludmila ignored him and realised she was hungry. There was a pan of stew on the stove and she found a bowl and ladled some of it in. She tasted meat and onions and potatoes and also herbs she couldn't identify. It was delicious and she was helping herself to a second portion when the man who called himself Ivan came in.

'Good. I am glad now you are eating too. Please. As much as you like. Build up your strength.'

He deposited the birch logs he was carrying in a basket next to the stove and gently shifted the dog out of the way with his boot.

'It is getting cold. Winter comes soon in these parts.' He rubbed his hands and held them to the stove. The fingers were long and thin but roughened and calloused by years of work in all weathers. Ludmila shifted a little to the left to give herself more space as he drew up a stool and helped himself to the stew. They ate in silence.

'When you are a bit stronger, I will saddle up a reindeer and take you wherever you want to go,' he said presently.

Ludmila nodded.

'My apologies, it is the only transport I have. Meanwhile,' he looked at her intently, 'it is good to have company.'

Ludmila paused between mouthfuls. It was said evenly without any discernible ulterior motive, but she knew she would have to be on her guard. She was injured, he was stronger than her. He probably hadn't been with a woman for months, maybe years. She knew she was attractive to men but didn't really care. She had had more than enough attention from drunken Red Army soldiers. Drunken men and clumsy boys. They were all the same. They didn't protect you. They used you. Still, he could have done anything while she was unconscious. He could do anything now. But he had made no move. Just looked at her kindly with dark-blue close-set eyes and a quizzically furrowed brow, which she found infuriating.

'Tell me how you came to be in this wilderness,' she said, helping herself to a third bowl.

'I was fighting. With Tito's partisans. After the War, they asked for volunteers to go to Russia. I volunteered. As a good Communist. To visit the Motherland. Contribute to her future. I like my own company. I like trees and animals. I can shoot. So …' He tailed off as if the rest were self-explanatory.

Ludmila had never heard a story so full of holes. She didn't know where to start, but *questions questions questions!* They could wait. The stew was good. She was warm by the stove. He had a kind face and he had taken care of her. Her ice-cold suspicions began to thaw and she found herself looking at him sleepily. She was vulnerable now. As vulnerable as she had ever been. But she didn't care. Or at least she felt she could put all that relentless interrogation to one side. For the moment. A short while. Enjoy the peace of the taiga, the Siberian autumn afternoon, where the last insects were humming their death-song. Enjoy his stupid boyish earnest face. *Enjoy.*

He kissed her on the mouth. Very gently, very tentatively. She felt the soft lush beard, his warm mouth. She kissed him back and he carried her to the bed.

He made love to her very gently and considerately, so much so that she wondered if he wasn't really a woman. He even withdrew as she came and held back while she convulsed, then ejaculated warmly and stickily onto her belly. No man had ever done the things to her that he was now doing, or at least not as thoughtfully, as caringly … as long. She felt pleasantly drunk, although she hadn't had any alcohol. *Perhaps it's the herbs. This male Baba Yaga has drugged me with magic herbs.* She was a little girl again. Princess Vassillisa in the Witch's hut, but the Witch wasn't so bad after all.

After several drawn-out and noisy acts of love-making – Ludmila realising she was as starved of physical affection as the Yugoslav- they lay exhausted and talked. Ludmila felt giddy, not so much from the sex or the concussion as from the sense of how exposed she was, how fragile. She imagined herself a cat, boneless, sprawled, sinuous, nine-tenths asleep, but with a secure knowledge that her velvet paws hid vicious blades that could blind and disable an attacker in an instant. She stretched and asked Ivan to tell her his real name.

'Dragan Stojanovic. Since you asked.'

'That's not so hard. It's almost like Russian. So, Dragan Stojanovic. Tell me about the partisans of Marshal Tito.'

'Even in bed you sound like a police officer.'

He meant it as a joke, but Ludmila bridled. 'I only want to know a bit more about you. I am naked with a man I have known for a couple of hours. To ask questions is appropriate I think.'

The Yugoslav held up his hands in mock surrender. 'Ok. It is appropriate. I joined the partisans in 1942 and we fought the fascists at Neretva. I was in the 2nd Proletarian Division. We not only had to fight the Germans and the Italians but the Chetniks as well.'

'Who?'

'Royalists. Reactionaries from my own country. The fighting was brutal. I was a machine gunner. I lost a lot of my comrades. My best friend.' He paused. Ludmila could sense that he was trying to steady his voice. She spoke.

'I was at Leningrad. I was fifteen. They put me in a bombed building as a sniper because I was good with a rifle. I killed nineteen Germans.'

'Congratulations. Where were your family?'

'My mother killed herself and I never knew my father. I was brought up in an orphanage. I joined the Young Communists and they taught me how to shoot.'

'Your mother killed herself? How old were you?'

'Seven.'

'That is so sad.'

'What about your family?'

'My father was a printer. My mother looked after the house. I was an only child.'

'Like me.'

'Yes.'

'They both died in the War. In the bombing.'

The silence was long and thoughtful. It was dark. Dragan got up naked from under the heavy coarse blankets and loaded the stove with another birch log. Ludmila watched his tall lean frame, pits and long white scars etched in the moonlight, almost hairless, as he padded about the cabin, feeding scraps of food to his dog.

'Come back to bed,' she murmured. She surprised herself with the timbre of her voice, deepened and softened by love-making. He did as he was asked and, sore and depleted as they were, they made love again. Ludmila knew it would take him ages this time and, with a hint of girlish mischief she had never experienced before, she smiled to herself.

Hours later, wide awake, with Dragan snoring softly beside her, Ludmila's mind began to churn remorselessly. *Why didn't she believe him? Why did his stories seem so thin?* He had gone into detail about the battle at the Neretva river. How his best friend had tried to save him and had been blown to pieces by a grenade. He showed her scars from shrapnel wounds. They shared accounts of battles. Of how she was spotted and the Germans had trained a mortar on her until it was silenced by Russian guns. His story rang true and yet it didn't ring true. He was hiding something. But what harm was he doing out here? What could he possibly be guilty of, this absurdly kind and generous man who made love like a woman? She had been told that police work is often about intuition but she had rejected that in favour of hard evidence and methodical investigation. *Bombing?* He said his parents died in 'the bombing'. What bombing? Yes, there was surely bombing in Yugoslavia by the Americans and their Allies, as far as she knew, but bombing was a word used about systematic raids on specific targets. Like the Germans on Leningrad. Like the Americans and British on Dresden. But Yugoslavia? Her brain turned and turned.

She slipped out of the bed without disturbing her lover, and found her coat and pulled it around herself. Shivering as her feet touched the cold stone, she moved over to the stove, still warm with glowing red embers. She found matches and lit a hurricane lamp that stood on a corner shelf. Outside a low wind was stirring the trees and clouds drifted across the half moon. She discovered a small room that served as a larder and storeroom for the cabin. There was an old battered chest of drawers. Gently, she opened the drawers one by one and by the light of the yellowy, flickering flame went through the contents. Tools, playing cards, cutlery, a packet of tobacco, shirts, trousers, coins, socks, bootlaces, string, rifle bullets. In the very last drawer she found an envelope stuffed with photographs. Family picnics, possibly his parents, smiling in the sunshine of another time, children, friends and then a head shot of a dark-haired handsome young man with a knowing smile and a cigarette dangling from his mouth. He was in uniform. On his collar the skull and crossbones insignia of the Waffen SS.

She turned the photograph over. There was a date '19 April 1941' and 'Jorgen' and 'Heidlberg'. She leafed through more photographs and found another with the same young man this time sitting on the bonnet of a German military vehicle, with Dragan. There was no beard, but it was him without a doubt. The same smile, the same close-set eyes, the same tall figure, his arm around the dark young man this time holding his cigarette, a little effeminately, in his right hand. She went back into the bedroom and threw the photographs on to his sleeping form in the bed.

'Who is Jorgen and who the hell are you?' She demanded.

'You have been looking through my belongings.' The voice came from behind her. She turned and found him standing behind the door, draped in a blanket, holding his rifle, pointing it at her. It was a statement. Not a reproach.

'You are a German SS officer.'

'I was. I am now a fur trapper in Siberia and we are no longer at war.'

'You lied about your time in the war.'

'Not really. I was at Neretva. I did lose my close friend. I was a machine gunner. I did see combat. I ...'

'You're twisting the truth.'

'Listen to me!' The barrel of the rifle was trained casually on her lower abdomen. 'Listen! My name is Horst Meier. I was an Oberleutnant in the Waffen- SS 7th Division. I deserted in 1943 after my best friend was killed. I am a deserter! No longer a Nazi.'

'You deserted because you knew you were going to be defeated, so what?'

'No. You're not listening. I deserted in 1943. Two years before the War ended. I'd had enough of the lies and the fanaticism. I wanted to get out. I saw my opportunity and I went. I came here to the Soviet Union.'

'Liar. You couldn't have done that without being killed.'

'I came through Turkey and the Caucasus and Ural Mountains into Siberia. The only thing I knew how to do was shoot so I became a fur trapper. I had no family. My mother and father were killed in Hamburg during an air raid. I had no ... no friends, no one.

'It was stupid to keep the photographs,' he continued, 'but without them I would have had no memories. I would have been destroyed as a human being.'

Ludmila eyed him coolly but with every nerve in her body charged with electricity, her eyes scanning the gun, his trigger-finger, his eyes, the weapon.

'I don't want to kill you,' he said, cocking the bolt on the rifle. 'You're the first human being I've been close to for five years. Making love to you, I realised just how empty I was, how hungry. For warmth, for affection, for someone to touch me in the way you did.'

He is talking like a woman, Ludmila thought.

'Who is Jorgen?' she repeated.

He said nothing for a moment but kept the weapon pointed at her, as if he knew that the question was intended to lower his guard. Then he spoke.

'Was. Jorgen was my friend. We grew up together. His parents were wealthy. He came from a 'good family'. I was radical, a socialist, like my father. But Jorgen seduced me and I joined the National Socialists.' He smiled thinly.

'He seduced you? Like a man seduces a woman?'

'You still ask questions like a police officer.'

'He seduced you like a man seduces a woman.'

'Not at first. We were just close. We had girlfriends. We laughed a lot. Then …' He shrugged.

'Then what? You had sex. He fucked you. You fucked him.'

The man's silence was conclusive.

'So you prefer men to women?'

'You must know that's not true.'

'You said you were hungry. A starving man will eat anything.'

'Jorgen was not just handsome. You've seen the photographs. He was a life-force. He had *lebenskraft.*'

He fell silent, then looked up.

'He looked after me. But I …'

'What?'

'I … don't have to answer your questions. I am holding the gun.' The smile had come back into his features. He waved it at her head.

'And he died?'

'What?'

'You said he died. He was killed in Yugoslavia.'

'Yes.'

The rifle remained lined up on her forehead, but his mind had drifted elsewhere on some unseen wind of memory.

'We were fighting a long battle to take the bridge from the partisans. We moved centimetres at a time and then fell back. With a lot of us killed or mutilated, dying. But we were the Waffen-SS. We had our motto. Loyalty to the end. Obedience no matter what. Jorgen led us against the partisans. We were an advance party. We became surrounded and we had to fight our way out. I was behind him when he was shot through the neck and he fell like a stone. Just before, he'd smiled at me and said 'You buy the beers when we get back.' He winked and then he was dead.'

'So what? You deserted? Because your lover was killed?'

'I deserted because I couldn't see the reason for what we were doing anymore. I was young. Five years is a long time. Now I am an old man.' Again the hint of a smile. 'So, what do you want to do with me?'

'I will have to arrest you.'

He laughed, a little emptily. 'Why?'

'Because you are an enemy alien.'

'Not anymore.'

'You tried to destroy the Russian people. You are here illegally.'

'I told you. I deserted!'

His face flushed with anger, but then he became calm again.

'How do you think it is for me, living here alone in this wilderness? Do you think it is something I would choose?'

'Why didn't you go back to your own country? After the War?'

'I don't know my own country. This is my country. This emptiness. This Siberia. I wouldn't choose to live here but I couldn't live anywhere else.'

'I don't understand.'

The rifle never moved from its line on her forehead.

'Before I found you in the forest, I was surviving. I was even content. When I found you I couldn't believe my luck. I had someone, another human being, to care for, and she responded to me. Do you know what that feels like? You must do. You must have felt something. Between us.'

'It felt good. It was probably necessary.'

'Nothing more?'

Ludmila looked at the tall German for several seconds. He seemed to be in pain, almost physical pain. There were tears in his eyes. She looked at the golden hairs on his thick powerful wrists. His fingers curled round the trigger were very beautiful. His eyes were a dark cobalt blue. And they never wavered. One squeeze of the forefinger and she would be dead. She could see that he was unhappy and capable of doing something extreme. She knew she had to talk to him, like she would talk to any desperate, dangerous lunatic on the streets of Moscow - before subduing and apprehending them.

'You must have loved this Jorgen very much. Is that why you are so unhappy? Why you stay here? Why you can't go back?'

The tears were thick and glutinous, lensing his eyes like spectacles. He gulped and sniffed loudly. He was becoming vulnerable. She had lowered her voice and softened it deliberately so that he would respond just as he did. It was necessary. He had the power to kill her. If she was to survive, she had to do this.

'You loved a man who you had grown up with. A beautiful man. Inside and out. A man who could lead but also look after his men. An attractive man, I can see from the photographs. And you were special to him. But you found yourselves in a war, in a unit that despised weakness and certainly the love that you had between you. You found yourselves among fanatics and became fanatics yourselves. All that mattered was your love, your bond. You would have followed him anywhere. To the ends of the earth.'

She looked at him directly, as unwaveringly as he looked at her. In situations like this, she became cold and focussed. She stood outside herself. She believed it was what made her a good police officer. She tried to understand what he was feeling. Despite what she said, she couldn't feel it herself. She knew that was what people in these circumstances wanted to hear. Some compassion. Some understanding. It weakened their resolve somehow, this acknowledgement of their feelings. She had seen it with suicides and wife-beaters and self-pitying, violent drunks. It was working now with Ivan … Dragan … Horst … whatever his name was. She could still feel his warmth and stickiness drying on her belly. She had been vulnerable. She had allowed him to take her over completely. Cover her like a stallion covered his mare. Fuse, merge, lose her identity, relinquish control. His penetration was total. Not just her pleasantly bruised vagina, but her whole being. She had wanted to sob loudly when she came, and probably had. Making love with him had unlocked something inside. Just as it had with him. She had been temporarily released from bonds she didn't even know were holding her. But now, in an instant, all that was gone. She was Lieutenant Ludmila Sirotovska, orphan, with no patronymic, of the Peoples Militia East Moscow District. She was facing an emotionally disturbed male who was holding a gun to her head and the only weapons she had at her disposal were her tongue and her brain.

'If you put the gun down, I promise we will sit and talk about this, calmly. I will listen and maybe we can work something out…' It was weak but she needed to keep talking or die. He interrupted her. She looked at his tobacco-stained, even teeth, his full lips, the blond fringe of moustache and beard as he spoke.

'Stop. You're talking like a police officer. A few hours ago, we were lovers. You gave yourself to me totally. I to you. It was beautiful. I could hardly bear it. I was… I was eviscerated. It was beautiful. It was beautiful.'

Ludmila lifted a hand towards his face, but the look in his eyes made her abort the gesture.

'Horst, Horst, ssh, we can talk. If you feel anything for me, take the gun away. Please.' She found the pleading, tearful tone from somewhere.

'Do you love me?' The gun still pointed, the voice echoing her pleading tone. 'Do you?'

Love him? She didn't know what that meant. All she knew was that it meant a lot to him. It meant everything.

'Yes,' she said, as sincerely as she could.

He looked at her and shook his head.

'Yes, I do, really. I love you.' He was going to kill her.

He shook his head again sadly, then inhaled through his nostrils, exhaled, turned the rifle on himself and pulled the trigger.

Ludmila screamed involuntarily as the blood and lumps of brain spurted from the other side of the German's head and he fell backwards. He was dead immediately, his bloody mess of a face staring sightlessly at some point on the wall opposite.

Ludmila stood up, then sank down again, her head reeling from the shock. She felt nauseous and was shivering and sweating. She pulled the coat around her and looked at the dead German, her lover, her enemy.

When the sick feeling had passed, she stood up and took the bloody rifle from his dead hand and put it against the wall. She found her notebook and in the flickering lamplight immediately wrote down everything that had occurred, leaving out the intimacy. She wrote it in the third person, the better to give her some distance on events. She made clear that she was in fear of her own life and had tried to talk to the man but that '*he was obviously disturbed by his past and that the isolation of his existence had further upset the balance of his mind.*' What would she do now?

The dog had begun a frenzied barking at the sound of the shot and he was now scrabbling at the door of the cabin with his paws, yelping and whining. Ludmila ignored him, slowly got herself dressed and then opened the door. Before she could stop him, the dog raced in and over to his master, alternately sniffing at the blood and brain matter and nudging him with his snout. He howled long and plaintively and Ludmila stared in wonder at this dumb animal's desolate show of grief.

11

Irina trudged through the taiga as the autumn rains churned everything into thick mud. It was raining as she walked, a cold, stinging rain, turning to hail and blown from the north and east, signalling winter. She had visited the herders to see if Innaksa was any better but she found him still clingy and barely speaking. His father had carved him another squirrel and painted it in bright colours, but the boy had shown no interest in it. When he saw Irina, he brightened a little as he always did but his face fell in disappointment when she admitted she still didn't have Uluki.

She had no fear as she walked through the forest because she knew Kolya would protect her. His wound was pink and healing and he no longer limped. She looked down and smiled as he panted through the mud, long tongue hanging from slightly open jaws. She was taking a different route back however, one that circumvented the deepest part of the taiga and went along the edge of a broad lake. As she emerged from the trees and saw the lake pockmarked with rain and whipped up into white-topped grey-green lumps by the wind, she heard singing. She recognised the voice as belonging to Semyon, deep and resonant. It was a hymn or religious song that she had heard before, but what was odd was that Semyon could be seen standing on the shore of the lake, partially hidden by tall reeds, holding out his arms and lifting his face into the pelting rain.

She ducked back into the trees to watch him. What was he doing? Praying? It was certainly magnificent whatever it was. The water seemed to carry the sound for miles. Then as she watched, she saw him make the Sign of the Cross, reach into his pocket and pull out the hand gun he had used to kill the wolverine.

'Semyon, no! What are you doing? Stop!'

The wind carried her light voice away and Semyon didn't hear her. She ran toward him and as she did so, she realised that he wasn't going to fire the gun, but held it by the barrel and was about to throw it into the lake. He paused briefly when he realised someone was coming towards him, but then quickly hurled the weapon into the middle of the lake. His face was red and contorted in fury as Irina came up to him.

'Semyon, what are you doing? Why are you throwing the gun in the lake?'

He looked at her as he tried to gain control of his temper.

'It was useless. Everything had seized up. It was dangerous. A piece of crap.' He turned away and Irina knew he was lying.

'It's not yours, is it? Is it, Semyon? I've seen that gun before. It belonged to Lud --- to the militiawoman. Didn't it?'

Semyon said nothing but just stared across the water, the wind flapping the skirts of his big coat, the thick dark hair plastered to his head.

'I found it.'

'Where?'

He shrugged. 'In the forest. She must have dropped it.'

Irina couldn't believe what she was hearing. 'Why didn't you say anything? She's been gone for days. She could be injured, dead.'

Semyon turned to her slowly and looked at her. The expression said everything.

'Whether you liked her or not – whether I liked her or not – isn't the point. We'll have to look for her.'

'She should have told us where she was going. It's stupid to go into the forest on your own.'

'We're going to have to let the authorities know.'

'It's pointless. She's dead.'

'Semyon, she's a human being!'

The big man said nothing. Irina turned on her heels and called to Kolya who had run off to the other side of the lake in search of any stray water fowl.

'Leave it be, Irina. You don't want more militia crawling all over the place.'

Irina paused and turned to him slowly. 'Why Semyon, what are you afraid of?'

He looked at her from under his unkempt eyebrows flecked with grey and said nothing.

A thought as cold and uncomfortable as the hailstones stinging her face, entered her head and made her shiver. *What if the killer is you, Semyon?*

She dismissed it as soon as it materialised, but it had made a tiny imprint on her mind and it wouldn't go away. She headed back to the field centre. She would go to Sobol Cherny on foot and radio the militia in Krasnoyarsk.

Arriving at the cabin, she found her father quickly but methodically filling a metal trunk with documents and canisters of film.

This was not an unusual occurrence. It signalled the arrival of an official from the Peoples Commisariat, Department for the Mobilisation of Scientific Forces. The

Russian Academy of Sciences was obliged to report to this department on a regular basis. Field Study centres could be inspected with minimum notice, their files opened, data studied, scientists interviewed and requests for detailed activity reports demanded.

The rug had been pulled away from the stove revealing an open trapdoor which hid a timber-lined hole no more than two feet deep.

An open letter lay on the kitchen table. Irina looked at it. The date on the letter was three weeks ago, the postmark the same.

'I picked it up at the kolkhoz today. It only arrived yesterday,' her father said, placing another thick wad of files into the trunk.

Irina studied the letter. It was from a Major Second Rank Petrenko. Peoples Commissariat. Scientific Department.

```
To: Comrade Professor Medvedenko
Concerning: Domestication of the Siberian
Grey Wolf
Reference: 70947/C/Narkom

Please prepare all materials relating
to the above project for the scrutiny
of my officials and be available for
interview 3rd October 1948.
```

There was more in the letter about what details would be requested from specific experiments with a sheet outlining them in duplicate which required both Grigori's signature and the Commisar's. She put the letter down and went to help her father load the files into the trunk.

'Dad,' she began.

'Remember, try and not read anything or look at anything too closely. Answer his questions. Don't elaborate.'

He stood and went back into his study to the tall metal locker, to which only he had the key, to collect more documents.

It was disconcerting but she felt she was becoming infected with Ludmila's innate suspicion. There was something in her father's tone that didn't match what he was saying. But to suspect your own father of lying to you, no, that wasn't right. He was her father after all.

She was placing the small canisters of film into a neat cylindrical tower in a corner of the trunk when she noticed the title on a scrap of white paper gummed to one of them: 'Wolf Sisters Expt. 1924. (4)'. She frowned. What on earth was this? Impulsively, she put it into the pocket of the coat she was still wearing. Again, she asked herself why as soon as she had done it. It was wrong. It was disloyal of a daughter towards a father. She was about to put it back when Grigori re-entered with another armful of documents.

'This is the last lot. Have you got everything in?'

'Yes,' she said, her heart beating rapidly. Her father must be able to see she was blushing surely? 'Let me put those in.'

She took the grey cardboard files, stuffed with typewritten pages and reams of data in the form of graphs and tables, and bound with string. She placed them in the trunk. Grigori then closed the trunk and locked it with a padlock from the bunch of keys on the lanyard around his neck.

'Right, let's get this put away safely and then why don't you bake a cake for Comrade Commisar … Petrenko?' He grinned at her like a mischievous little boy.

As she stirred the flour and reindeer butter and sugar in the big bowl and cracked eggs into the mix, Irina gradually began to put her thoughts and feelings into some sort of order. The wooden spoon gradually churned the ingredients from a floury lumpy unmanageable mass into a smooth sweet yellowy cream. She made a mental list. There was still an insane sadistic killer on the loose; Ludmila had gone missing; Semyon was trying to dispose of her gun; they were being inspected by the authorities; little Innaksa was traumatised by his ordeal at the hands of a killer; she had stolen a canister of film from her father. She hadn't mentioned to him about the gun and her intention of contacting the authorities in Krasnoyarsk about it. She put in dried fruit and continued to stir. She felt suddenly calm and resolute. She laughed at herself. If only baking a cake could solve all the world's problems!

She placed the cake in the oven and told her father she was taking Kolya for a walk and to take out the cake in forty minutes. She set the timer on the old alarm clock she kept by the stove because she knew he would never remember.

Kolya bounded after Irina as she set off briskly east toward the fur farm at Sobol Cherny. The sky was full of yellow-tinged clouds and the hail was now turning to very fine snow which wouldn't stick. She rarely visited the farm because she hated to see the endless rows of cages with miserable sable and fox standing cramped on wire floors in their own excrement, or racing round and round in a mania of despair, waiting to be slaughtered and skinned. But they had a radio and it was the only means of communication with larger centres like Krasnoyarsk.

She hadn't gone more than half a mile when she heard the rumble of a diesel engine and, when she turned, she could see Semyon driving as fast as the ZIS would go, toward her. The truck bounced in the rutted ground and churned up thick mud and marsh grass. Within minutes he had caught up to her. He stopped with a crash of gears and a squeal of brakes, then jumped out of the cab. Kolya growled and started to bare his canines in a rictus. Irina quietened him down with soft words and a gentle stroking between his ears.

'Where are you going?' Semyon demanded.

'I told you. I'm going to contact the authorities in Karasnoyarsk about Ludmila.'

'No. You can't go. There's enough attention here already. You know there's a Commisar from Moscow coming. Your father just told me.'

'Yes of course I do but that doesn't matter. We can't pretend nothing's happened. She's been gone for days.'

'I told you, she's dead.'

'You know that?'

'Not for sure, but she's not used to the forest. She wouldn't know how to survive.'

'She seems pretty tough to me.'

'In Moscow maybe. But not here.'

'Someone needs to know.'

'I won't let you go.'

Semyon stood in front of her to make his point. Kolya began to growl again, sensing tension.

'Let me past, Semyon.'

The Georgian shook his head. 'Get into the truck. I'll take you back.'

'No.' Irina moved to go round him. He moved in front of her again. She didn't know whether to laugh or to be afraid. Kolya's growling grew deeper and developed into a menacing, grating canine purr.

'Semyon. This is wrong. Don't do this. You're going to upset Kolya which isn't a good idea. Now, move out of the way.'

Semyon looked at Irina his face with its thick pock-marked flesh creased into a hundred lines of fear, desperation and -finally- decision. He turned to the truck and with his head lowered, supported himself against it on two powerful arms. Then he turned.

'She followed me. To the mine. She was spying on me. She was going to arrest me. She was attacked. I looked after her. She was going to arrest me. I took her gun.' There was a long pause. 'I left her in the forest'.

Irina's mind was reeling from the information delivered staccato, but she picked up on the last item first.

'You left her in the forest? That's days, nearly a week ago! Semyon! What were you thinking?'

'She was going to arrest me. She thought I killed the Evenk and kidnapped the kid. What do you think would have happened to me if she'd taken me back to Moscow? I'd be a dead man!'

His eyes were wide, vulnerable, pleading. Irina suddenly felt pity for the giant, his arms hanging by his side, hopeless.

'Take me to where you left her,' she said finally.

12

Major Second Rank Nikolai Sergeivich Petrenko felt the cold muddy water seep between the stitches of his thin Muscovite shoes, lined with two sheets of cardboard. They'd warned him it was Siberia and that in Siberia winter is even earlier than in Moscow. *I should have brought galoshes.* He stood looking at the compound of the Pustinya Field Study Centre. *Pustinya.* Wilderness. He heard –and could smell- the wolves. Wolves! They figured in every nightmare he'd had as a child. Not even Pioneer Peter's victory over that symbol of untamed nature, the Wolf, in Prokoviev's opera -which he had attended as a dutiful Pioneer himself-could console him. He always woke up screaming as the wolf opened its jaws to devour him. Who had he offended to get this assignment?

He shivered in his thin overcoat and pulled his fur hat –something that he had had the foresight to bring- over his ears. Two and a half days on a train on wooden seats surrounded by screaming children, poultry and, at one stage, a goat. Then he'd had to bribe two bargemen to ferry him up the Yenisey. He'd sat on sacks of potatoes in a boat that stank of the dead animals whose fur was taken back down the river. He'd disembarked in some godforsaken little town on its banks and from there on reindeer back –reindeer back!- to the Pustinya Field Centre. The bones in his groin were raw and bruised.

In the cabin, Grigori had finished packing the trunk. He closed the trap door after packing the top of the trunk with layers of sacking to deaden any change in reverberation on the floorboards. He pulled the rug back in place and looked out of the window and lit his pipe. He was shocked to see the tall figure of a young man in his mid- to late-twenties in a grey belted overcoat, wearing a fur hat and holding a bulging briefcase in one ungloved hand and a cheap-looking suitcase on the ground next to him. He was dancing from one foot to the other as he seemed to be making his mind up about whether to enter the compound or not. Grigori pulled on his jacket and went out to meet the man from Narkom, the People's Commisariat.

Petrenko sipped the hot sweet tea and dried his wet feet by the stove. He had finally stopped shivering. The professor had offered him an extra woollen vest but the commissar had declined, feeling he was being made a fool of. Grigori quickly recognised the young man's prickliness and determined to tread very carefully. He had asked how long he would be staying and the thin, beak-nosed official had merely replied 'As long as it takes. I trust you can accommodate me.' Grigori had replied that he was welcome to stay as long as he liked. Petrenko then asked him about his work generally and how it was progressing.

He sat forward in his chair fixing Grigori with a startling blue-eyed stare. The pupils of his eyes were fixed dots and made him look like a predatory seabird. Grusha and Masha were exploring his damp socks with their snouts. Petrenko pulled his feet away from them and tried to tuck them under him - just like a bird might do.

'Don't worry about them, Major,' the professor laughed. 'They're just our latest clients. Two wolves, same womb, completely different personalities.'

Losing interest, the cubs moved away and the Commisar relaxed a little and put his feet gingerly closer to the stove.

'You talk about them as if they were human.'

'Granted, but we can learn much from them. Look at Pavlov. He has learned a lot about us from his mutts.'

'Please try to be more scientific in your language, professor.'

Grigori nodded and made a mental note to use the language of scientific papers. 'From what I can ascertain, the wolves showing the highest amenability of temperament, on the scale I have devised, show certain physical characteristics, which must owe something to Mendellian genetics…'

The stare became harder. 'Really?'

Grigori held up his hand and smiled. 'However, I would say ninety percent of high amenability of temperament is *acquired*.'

'So, what happens to the animals that are least amenable? Can they be trained?'

'Unfortunately, not. They are destroyed or released back into the wild.' Grigori felt himself sweating. He re-lit his pipe to deflect attention. The interrogation had begun in earnest.

'Our fairy tales are full of stories about wicked wolves and, of course, loyal dogs. It is probably something that has been known since man first watched the wolf hunting and wondered how or if he could harness that energy, that ferocity and skill for his own use.' He felt he was blathering but puffed blue smoke from his pipe to -he hoped- convey gravitas.

Commisar Petrenko maintained his seagull stare. He obviously wasn't satisfied. Grigori decided to blunder on.

'Ideally, I have thought that perhaps one day any illumination my work may shed to benefit of the Soviet Union would be welcome, but for the most part I observe, record and publish. It is for others more visionary than I to apply those observations.' He cringed inwardly at this blatant display of false modesty.

'Ideals are a remnant of a bourgeois age, as I'm sure you know, comrade Medvedenko. We had idealists before the Revolution, now we have only realists. We make something real, something of material good, from the hypotheses of science. Otherwise what is the point of it?'

Grigori didn't want to answer this because he knew he would be caught out. He signalled his assent with a solemn nod and the tiniest of apologetic smiles. He was being gently rapped on the knuckles by an ideologue and wished to demonstrate his submission. They were two animlas sniffing round each other. Was he being invited to show his loyalty, his dedication to the Soviet project? He decided to take a risk and become more expansive.

'Imagine a world,' he began. He re-lit his pipe and puffed. Once, twice, three times. He shook the match and tossed it into the ashtray. 'Imagine a world without crime. Without psychopathology. Without the destructiveness wrought by self-willed, self-serving individuals. Despite the best endeavours of our psychologists, our Pavlovs and so on, we have still not emptied our prisons nor our mental hospitals. Suppose science found a way to do just that. To eradicate crime. Because what is crime, but the exertion of the individual will without regard for morals or ethics of any kind? Just animal self-interest.'

'I believe you are falling back on to idealism, comrade professor', Petrenko said in a dangerously low murmur as he stared into his tea.

'No, on the contrary, comrade Petrenko. The research I am doing is yielding very real results, as you will see when you examine my work more closely.'

He sat back and eyed the commissar through clouds of blue smoke.

Petrenko coughed. He didn't smoke. 'And this has nothing to do with genetics, you say?'

'Not in any substantial way, no. Genes do exist, of course. Where else would we get our mother's eyes or our father's hairline? But they are limited in number. I am going beyond genetics. Genes can be changed. And like musical notes they can produce infinite results. My work on the wolves has shown that over –now- fifteen generations their genes can be changed and changed again by acquiring traits and then passing them on by example to the next generation.' Again he cringed inwardly. He didn't believe a word of what he was saying. This was chess. The wrong move now and the game would be up.

Grigori knew exactly what the game was. The geneticists were on the run. Stalin had no time for the existence of genes and the idea of mutation and evolution of species over vast tracts of time. Genes limited human possibility, human perfectability. If generations could take on the best traits of the previous generation and then hand these on to be enhanced by the next, and the one after that, and so on, then human evolution aspired to the stars and not to some bestial dead-end here on earth. Geneticists had been dismissed, exiled, shot and disappeared for making a case for Mendel and Darwin. The Leader wanted optimism, a positive mind-set, hope. He did not want the pessimism of an era of liberal bourgeois thinkers. Therefore anyone walking in the genetic field had better tread carefully.

That was the game.

13

'Talk to me, Semyon, talk to me.'

She was determined to break his silence. She stared hard at his profile as he crouched over the wheel and peered through the hail as the truck churned through the increasingly muddy terrain.

In the end, he broke.

'She thought I'd killed the Evenk. She thought I did *that!*' He punched the wheel and the truck swerved violently. 'And kidnapped the little boy and buried him alive. She said I'd done *that!*' His voice rose. He was almost in tears. Then the whole story came out. How she'd followed him to the mine, how she'd been attacked, how he'd rescued her –he exclaimed bitterly at this huge mistake- how he'd had no choice but to leave her in the forest. It was either him or her.

'Is there any chance she's still alive?' asked Irina quietly when he'd finished his story.

No reply. The big man resumed his vow of silence.

'You know it's right that we look for her, Semyon. Don't you?'

A few moments passed.

'If we don't find her and we assume she hasn't … survived, will you tell the authorities?' he asked eventually.

'Semyon … Semyon, I don't know. If I said yes, would you leave me in the forest too?'

Semyon continued to squint past the absurdly flapping and useless windscreen wipers.

'If we don't find her, Semyon, then no I don't think I could tell the authorities. Other than she went into the taiga alone and against our advice and wasn't seen again.' *What am I doing? I'm protecting a man who has admitted he has left a woman to die. I am protecting someone who may have killed others.* She looked through the filthy glass, bouncing with hard white pellets. Semyon brought the truck to a stop with a squeal of brakes.

'Is this where you left her?'

'Yes.'

Irina looked round. To anyone else it was just another piece of featureless forest, but not Semyon. He had lived here most of his life. Accused of White sympathies by the Red Army as a young man in Georgia, he had spent several years in a labour camp in Central Siberia. When he was released, he stayed. He had turned up at the field study centre while out trapping for the kolkhoz at Cherny Sobol and asked Grigori for a job. That was in 1933. He'd been at Pustinya ever since. Irina had been nine years old and she remembered how he would throw her into the air, give her great bear hugs, how he taught her to trap animals, to forage for mushrooms, cut down trees, watch birds on the lake and then shoot them, name the flowers she picked, giving them the Georgian names. There were more flowers in Georgia, she realised, more everything. Sunshine, the sea, mountains, forests, birds, animals. Semyon had always made it sound like a fairy tale place, though he never showed any inclination to return. He was part of her life. To give him up because he tried to save himself would be the real crime. Still, they had to make the effort to find Ludmila.

Irina released Kolya from the back of the ZIS. Then she had a thought. If Ludmila had hid in the back herself, then her scent would be on the rolled-up tarpaulin. It was worth a try. She persuaded Kolya to interrogate it. Immediately he jumped from the cargo bed and proceeded to head down back the way they had come. Semyon and Irina looked at each other and got back into the truck. Semyon turned it round and followed the white wolf. They drove for about three miles, when Kolya stopped and then went deeper into the taiga. Irina followed, with Semyon reluctantly behind her. At a large spruce tree Kolya was finding the scent very strong. He looked up at his mistress but didn't proceed any further. Irina looked round the base of the tree. The needles had been disturbed and there was evidence of reindeer hoof-prints. Semyon found something. It was a button made of cheap base metal to look like brass. It was from Ludmila's great coat.

'So she made it this far. But where did she go next? The reindeer tracks lead away and to the east. Do we follow them?'

'Why?' asked the Georgian. 'They're just reindeer tracks.'

'But what if she was found by herders and they took her to their camp?'

'There aren't herders this far east at the moment. They're all bedding down for the winter.'

'Look, Semyon, she was here. That's clear enough. There's no body but there are tracks. I say we follow them.'

Semyon said nothing but turned back to the truck and took out a rifle and an army rucksack filled with essentials like a knife, axe, matches, a water canteen, dried reindeer meat, and a blanket he kept ready in case he was stranded anywhere. He shrugged it on to his shoulders. Irina looked at him sadly. She wanted to hug him but she knew that would be the wrong thing to do. The hail had eased off but it was turning to light snow. If they didn't go now they would lose the tracks.

'How far do we follow them?' was all the Georgian said.

'Till they run out – or until we find her.'

They set off into the taiga as the light slowly began to fade.

The tracks were not hard to follow and they did seem to be a single reindeer. Soon they discovered a dog's footprints and when it became less muddy, they made out what Irina was sure were boot prints.

'A man, his dog and a reindeer. And Ludmila?'

Semyon shrugged, expressionless, and they continued on. Night came down suddenly but the snow stopped and the sky began to clear. Semyon hacked branches for a shelter and Irina built a fire. They boiled water for tea and chewed on the salty meat, throwing a little to Kolya. The temperature was dropping as the stars and moon came out. Wolves howled in the distance. Kolya, snout down along the ground half asleep, twitched his ears but didn't bother to raise his head or answer. He had no tribe. His pack were the light-voiced bipeds who fed him.

Semyon had made a floor of larch branches under the shelter and he gave Irina the blanket and hunched into his woollen coat. The wolf curled round her and she offered half the blanket to Semyon.

'It's only fair as I have my own personal fur coat,' she laughed. He accepted shyly and turned on his side.

'Good night Kolya. Good night Semyon.'

No reply came from either of them. Irina lay on her back looking at the stars winking between the crossed branches of their shelter and wondered briefly before she fell asleep if her father had remembered to take out the cake.

She awoke to Kolya nuzzling her face. His hot stinking breath made her push him away with a half-laugh, half-groan. She got up to empty her bladder only to discover Semyon with his trousers down crouched beneath a tree grunting and straining. A loud fart like a gunshot made her stifle a giggle and she quickly went the other way to relieve herself. It was cold and low grey-yellow clouds had blown in over the taiga and promising more, heavier snow. She walked a little deeper into the forest to see if she could find any edible mushrooms, but was out of luck. Kolya followed her. Occasionally he would lift his snout and smell the air. He was hungry.

When she got back to their little camp-site, Semyon had revived the fire and was boiling water for tea. He shared out the last of the dried meat, with some for Kolya which was gone in an instant. He licked his chops expectantly. Semyon quickly packed up and stamped out the fire.

'So what do we do?' he asked.

'There are still tracks. We follow them before the snow obliterates them.'

Semyon looked at the sky and she knew he was praying to his Old Russian God for a blizzard.

'Come on.'

They moved through forest and then across several wide clearings and back into forest again. Snow threatened but never arrived. They moved fast to keep warm and must have walked for four or five hours before Irina pointed to smoke rising above the treetops.

'What do you think, Semyon? Trappers? Herders? A house maybe?'

'Let's find out,' was all the big man said.

Another half hour brought them through a particularly dense section of forest to another clearing. Standing in the clearing was a wooden cabin and some small outbuildings and a paddock. In the paddock was a reindeer. The clearing had been created presumably by the owner, as evidenced by the scattered tree-stumps. It was a typical trapper's cabin. Skins of sable and mink hung on wooden frames. An axe lay against one of the bigger stumps used as a chopping block. There was a covered log-stack full of birch and conifer. The chimney that protruded from the roof was narrow, capped with a conical hat, and made of rusty iron encrusted with jet-black resin. Various outriggers had been added as afterthoughts to the main cabin: a porch and small veranda, the log-stack, a lean-to roof, some sort of store-room on stilts a couple of feet above the ground. It was carefully situated on a natural mound so it wouldn't flood and faced south for maximum light. In front was a mound of earth and a shovel.

Irina called out. But there was no answer. Kolya began a low growl and his hackles rose. He bared his teeth. Suddenly, there was a fierce barking and out of nowhere a huge dog, a Siberian husky, flew at Kolya. Kolya met his attacker in mid flight and the two animals tore into each other with vicious snarls and yelps. Irina saw blood on Kolya's white coat as they went for each others' throats, but before she could tell whose blood it was, there was a loud rifle shot and the two combatants immediately separated. Another shot deterred them completely. Irina looked up and saw Ludmila, clad in an oversized fur coat and fur hat, a rifle in her hands.

'I have three more shots and I never miss. Give me your rifle and get inside the cabin!'

Semyon handed over his rifle and they obeyed her command. Kolya had fled and the big husky had disappeared.

Once inside the cabin, which was warm and stuffy, Semyon and Irina stood and waited to be told where to sit. Ludmila ushered them to a wooden bench against the far wall with a movement of her rifle. With one hand she emptied Semyon's weapon, withdrew the bolt and pocketed it. She took off the fur coat and hat and hung them on the back of the door. Semyon and Irina watched her in silence.

'Ludmila,' Irina began.

'No talking. Except when I ask you a question. Understood?'

She glared at them, her eyes moving slowly from one to the other. They nodded.

'How did you find me?' she asked.

'We followed your trail. It wasn't hard,' Irina answered.

'What trail?'

'We went to where … to where you were left and Kolya picked up your scent. Then there were footprints.'

'To where you abandoned me.' Ludmila directed this at Semyon. He simply stared back at her without blinking.

'Did you think I would die out there, kulak?' She sneered.

'I am not a kulak.'

'You're a kulak and a murderer.'

'I am not a murderer. I saved your fucking life.' Semyon flushed angrily, breathing hard through his nose.

'You tried to kill me and make it look like you saved me. You're a liar as well. I'm taking you to Moscow where you will face trial.' She glanced outside. It was starting to snow. 'We need to get back to the field station. How far is it?'

'It's seven hours walk to the truck at least. It's dark and snowing. We wouldn't make it.' Irina looked at Ludmila directly.

Ludmila seemed to be making a decision. Finally, she said, 'All right. We will go tomorrow as soon as it's light. First put these on him.'

She handed Irina the set of black steel handcuffs that hung from her belt. Irina shook her head and said simply, 'No.'

Semyon roared, 'You cannot do this to me! I have done nothing wrong!'

'Be quiet. Put them on him please. Hands behind his back.'

Irina looked at Semyon apologetically. 'We have to do what she says.'

The Georgian looked at Irina like a beaten dog, then put his hands behind his back. With some difficulty Irina fastened them to his thick wrists. Ludmila came over to check them.

'I can see you've worn manacles before. There are scars on your wrists. You are a convicted criminal.'

'I took my punishment and served my time. I was released.'

'Where were you and why?'

'It was a mistake. The Reds thought I was fighting with the Whites, but I wasn't. I was with the Bolsheviks. It was a long time ago. I was exonerated. That's why I was released.'

Ludmila said nothing, but yanked on the cuffs and went and took her seat. 'You could cook us a meal,' she said to Irina.

Irina seized on this as a way of breaking the tension. She stood up and looked around the cabin.

'Whose cabin this is? When are they coming back? How did you find it?' she asked.

'It belonged to a German. He brought me here. He's dead. Now you know. So prepare supper.'

Irina found her way around the kitchen and the stove and the tiny larder. She cut a haunch of reindeer into slices and fried them in some congealed yellow fat. She found a wilted cabbage and some soft, sprouting potatoes and did her best with them. Ludmila sat with her rifle pointing languidly at Semyon as the food was cooked. Irina realised how hungry she was. She boiled up a samovar and found some unlabelled green bottles. She uncorked one of them and found it was a dark home-brewed beer. She offered one to Ludmila, who shook her head. She offered it to Semyon. The dead German who made it must have traded some of his furs for hops and barley. Semyon drank it while Irina held the bottle and he didn't stop till the bottle was empty.

'Can I … can I ask how he died, this … German?' Irina asked tentatively.

'He shot himself with his own rifle. You can still see the blood. I couldn't clean it all off. There.' Ludmila pointed to faint brown stains on the wall below a picture of a German Alpine scene cut from a magazine and framed. Ludmila had cursed herself for not noticing it when she first arrived. It was out of place in this Siberian wildness.

'Is that where you tried to bury him, outside?'

'Yes. It's shallow. The ground is hard. I couldn't leave him as he was. The dog was howling. Now he seems to have forgotten him. Speaking of which, you will have to keep your animal away from my dog.'

'Your dog?'

'He seems to think he belongs to me now. I tried to get rid of him but he keeps coming back. I will have to shoot him before we leave.'

Irina shook her head and continued preparing the food. *Siberia suits her. She is as cold as ice.* She tried to make eye contact with Semyon, to let him know how sorry she was that he had brought him here. That everything would be all right. He didn't look up.

They ate their meal in silence. Irina fed Semyon as best she could. The snow fell thickly outside the cabin. Tomorrow would be a struggle through the drifts. Ludmila planned to take the reindeer and they would take it in turns to ride it. She threw Semyon and Irina blankets, then settled herself facing them. The dog had returned and settled by the stove. There was no sign of Kolya.

Semyon was soon asleep and snoring. Irina, though dog-tired, lay and tried to think what they ought to do. Semyon mustn't go back with Ludmila. Whether he was guilty or not he would be executed. He had no chance.

In the morning the snow had stopped and the trees glistened in the deep-gold dawn light. The sky had cleared and was almost cloudless. They finished the remains of the supper, pulled on their coats –Semyon hadn't removed his– packed a rucksack with food and emerged from the cabin into the blue-white glare of the snow.

Ludmila called the dog to her and walked a little way into the forest. His trust was heart-breaking. They heard a shot and Ludmila returned alone.

14

Ludmila had made Irina show her how to saddle the dead German's reindeer. They would take it in turns to ride the beast, apart from Semyon who would be tethered walking behind it. Irina persuaded Ludmila to allow Semyon to be cuffed with his hands in front of him.

Irina took the saddle first and they set off through the snow which was knee-deep in places. Ludmila walked at the side, the loaded rifle her only encumbrance.

The reindeer's hooves spread the load and he at least found no difficulty moving, but the going was tortuously slow.

Yellowing clouds to the north threatened more bad weather later. The air was raw and an icy breeze tore at their cheeks and stung their eyelids. The light of the sun bounced off the snow causing them to screw up their eyes against the glare.

Kolya joined them later, kept at a distance from the nervous reindeer by Irina.

After two hours, Ludmila took Irina's place on the hard leather saddle. Irina cast glances at Semyon who said nothing put plodded stoically behind the grunting, coughing animal.

They stopped after four hours to eat. No one spoke. It was enough to find the energy to move.

Irina's mind raced. She couldn't allow Ludmila to take Semyon back to Moscow. That was out of the question. She knew the same thought was in Semyon's mind. But for the moment there was nothing they could do.

Finally, nine hours later, as dark grey clouds blanketed the endless forest and an icy wind whipped up the now powdery snow, they stumbled on the ZIS, dustjacketed in white. After allowing Semyon temporary release from his handcuffs to use the starting handle- they drove into the Pustinya Field Centre.

Grigori herded them in to the warmth of the cabin, his face a mixture of concern for his daughter's absence and surprise at the manacles on Semyon's wrists. The reindeer was wide-eyed with terror as the wolves started baying when they caught his scent, but Grigori managed to guide it into a makeshift paddock at the other side from the wolf compound.

Commisar Petrenko was visibly disturbed by the intrusion of the three. Grigori demanded to know why Semyon was handcuffed and Ludmila told him in her usual abrupt manner.

'He's under arrest for murder, attempted murder and kidnapping.'

She then insisted that the Georgian be held in one of the wolf cages under lock and key. Irina and Grigori protested vehemently at this but Ludmila made Grigori open one of the cages at gunpoint and hustled Semyon in. The three occupants were well known to the burly human who fed them and they approached him like pet dogs.

'He'll freeze to death out here,' Irina said. 'How can you do this?'

'He seems to be friendly with the wolves. They'll keep him warm,' was all she said as she turned the key in the padlock and then pocketed the key.

Grigori had made a stew loaded with dumplings and potatoes and spiced with paprika and they sat down and ate it hungrily, Ludmila taking a bowl out to Semyon - though only at Irina's furious insistence.

Commisar Petrenko decided to take charge of the situation. He observed that the militia woman was only a lieutenant and he considerably outranked her. He demanded to know what the Georgian was being arrested for and what a Moscow officer was doing so far from home.

Ludmila, making frequent use of her notebook, gave Petrenko a respectful if staccato report about the whole situation. Grigori was open-mouthed at the news of her abandonment in the forest by Semyon and his arrest as the supposed wolf-man terrorising the herders. He made to protest but was told by Ludmila to keep his objections to himself. She then asked for any weapons to be handed over to her with ammunition. Irina and Grigori handed her their rifles and several boxes of cartridges. She removed the loading mechanisms from both rifles and put them in the pocket of her tunic. Then she spoke to Petrenko.

'Commisar, I respectfully request a conversation with you in private.'

Petrenko turned to Grigori. 'Comrade professor, is there anywhere ---?'

Grigori pointed to his study door without a word. Irina took her father's hand and began to stroke it. He glanced at his daughter but again said nothing. She could read anger, confusion, even despair in his features.

Ludmila closed the study door behind her and spoke very quietly.

'Comrade commissar, may I ask precisely what your work is here?'

'You may ask and as a higher-ranking officer of Narkom I don't have to answer you, lieutenant, but I will. I am here to monitor the work being carried out at this field station by professor Medvedenko. I will go through his work files and write out a report for my superiors in Moscow.'

'Is there anything suspicious about his work here?'

'Suspicious? In what way?'

'Are his working methods in any way unorthodox?'

'By which you mean anti-Soviet, comrade lieutenant?'

'Of course.'

'As far as I have been able to assess from the data he has shown me, I have no concerns in that direction. Why do you ask?'

'Comrade Commisar, I have been here -or rather in this area- for over two weeks now. I have made an arrest for the killing of a local reindeer herder and the kidnapping of a child. The man I have arrested also tried to leave me in the forest to die. I will take him back to Moscow for trial.'

'You are doing your duty, but I fail to see …'

'A moment, comrade Commisar. I have had the opportunity to observe the behaviour of the father and his daughter and I find it … suspicious. Especially him. He is secretive and I started to have my doubts as to the exact nature of his work. Also, he plays jazz records.'

'And this made you suspicious? Suspicious enough to observe him unawares.'

'Of course.'

Petrenko thought for a moment. What the militiawoman was saying certainly chimed with his experience of Medevedenko. He was flippant, ironic, a 'cosmopolitan', and there was a sense that he was hiding something under the casual bonhomie. True, jazz was disapproved of and in effect illegal. However, the commissar could see no objection to the man as a scientist. Despite his mocking tone, he had a strong sense of the application of his work to Soviet society.

All this went through his mind as he looked at the attractive –no, despite her abundant unwashed hair, the lack of any eye make-up-*beautiful* woman in uniform. Her mouth was full and an arousing shade of pink, her teeth straight and white, with only a small gap between the top incisors. Her eyes green, her body small and petite but wonderfully curved –as far as he could tell – beneath her tunic. But it wasn't so much what she looked like that drew him, but the animal heat she gave off. It was vulpine in its intractability and self-sufficiency and sheer feral magnetism. The man who was afraid of wolves was being drawn inexorably to this female of the species.

Ludmila could read all of the commisar's thoughts, from his avoidance of eye-contact to the fidgetting in his chair as an erection started to shift the topography of his trousers. It wasn't unusual for men to feel like this when they were alone with her. As the young Narkom officer squirmed and his ears and neck reddened, he managed to retain enough professionalism to resist Ludmila.

'Comrade lieutenant,' he began. His voice was an octave higher than normal and he coughed to lower the register. Ludmila simply stared at him, her head to one side. 'Comrade lieutenant, what do you expect me to do? The professor is working on a government project with exemplary thoroughness and application.'

Ludmila drew up her chair so that their knees were touching. Petrenko pulled away in alarm. She laid a hand on his thigh and looked directly into his eyes.

'Professor Medvedenko must be thoroughly investigated. I haven't the authority, but you have. Demand to see all his files.'

Her hand was warm on his thigh. His breathing was fast and shallow, his heart pounded. His erection was now almost painful.

'Comrade lieutenant, this is most irregular', was all he could say as he gulped and tried to gain control of his breathing. But the militia woman stared into his seagull's eyes and stroked his thigh and squeezed it now and again. Commisar Petrenko had never had this much attention from a woman before. He tried to project himself out of the scene to see it from the point of view of an observer who might come in at any minute. The militia woman, her own cheeks flushed, her pupils dilated to black, was practically kneeling in front of him as her hand crept higher and higher. Not once did she look at her hand but stared at him unblinking. Her breath was sweet and warm on his face she was so close. For her part Ludmila was fully aware of herself as predator, a cat with a mouse, a dog with a ball, a wolf with a petrified rabbit. It was something that had got her out of trouble before, something that soothed male aggression with a subtle female aggression of its own. Her hand had found the buttons on his fly. The heel of her palm rubbed against his erection. He pulled back in his chair but Ludmila gripped him hard and forced him forward. The moment was on a knife-edge. The moment passed, the knife-edge tipped in her favour. Her hand found its way into his underwear and grasped the warm hard flesh of his penis –as slender as she had expected it to be- and immediately began to knead and throttle it. Petrenko lifted himself off his chair and gasped. In seconds he had spurted hot semen all over himself and her hand. She laughed quietly, triumphantly, then withdrew her hand, all the while staring into the rabbit's appalled and grateful eyes. He leant forward -to kiss her?- his mouth half open and his eyes closed so that he looked idiotic, but she pulled away.

'Now... if you would, commissar.'

She stood and opened the door into the living room. Petrenko sat back, stunned. He rose, adjusted his wilting, sticky member with a hand inside his pocket, then left the study.

In the living room, Irina played absently with Grusha and Masha. Grusha bared her tiny fangs and snapped at her while Masha allowed her head to be fondled and scratched and she licked Irina's face.

'What are we going to do?'

'About what?'

'About Semyon.' She replied with some exasperation. Her father didn't appear to be that concerned with the fact that his helper for nearly twenty years was locked up and accused of murder.

'There's nothing we can do. She's the law. And besides there's comrade Petrenko to think about ...'

'How long is he staying?'

'Till he's finished.' Grigori dismantled his pipe and started cleaning it.

Irina lowered her voice. 'Have you ... is everything hidden that needs to be hidden?'

'Yes, don't worry. He's only seeing what he needs to see.'

'This is like a bad dream. I wish we'd left her to die in the forest. I wish ...' She changed tack. 'What are you going to do with all your research if it won't get official approval? You can't just keep it in a trunk.'

'No, Irushka …no, you're right.' Grigori said and blew through the pipe stem to clear it.

'What do you think they're talking about in there?'

'Irushka, listen to me.' Grigori leant forward and spoke in an urgent whisper. 'My work will never get approval. I've had contact from other scientists in my field and they are telling me that people are being sacked from their posts, worse, disappearing all together to God knows where. We – you and I- we will have to leave.' He paused, fussed with his pipe, didn't light it.

'Leave? Leave Pustinya? Leave Siberia?'

'Leave Russia.'

The door to the study creaked open. A flushed Petrenko stood in the frame adjusting his tightly knotted tie and smoothing his hair like someone in a comical film. He seemed to be making great play of fastening his jacket so that the folds drew across his groin. He straightened it, cleared his throat, then entered the room. Ludmila was close behind him, her face passive, her eyes ferociously alive.

'Comrade Professor,' said Petrenko, 'I must insist on seeing *all* the data you have collected for your experiments.'

Grigori's heart pounded. 'I don't understand…'

'I have reason to believe that you are not being candid with me, and if you do not willingly give me access to all your work and we discover that you have been hiding anything, anything at all, it will go very badly for you.'

And then Grigori did a very stupid thing. Almost beyond his control, with an instinct to check that what he had hidden was hidden successfully, his eyes moved to the threadbare rug by the stove. Petrenko didn't notice it. The hormone surge he had recently experienced was still in the process of subsiding. But Ludmila noticed it. She moved in quickly. She shooed the two wolf cubs out of the way and grabbed an edge of the rug. Irina glanced at her father in terror. Again this did not pass unnoticed by Ludmila, She yanked the rug and pulled it away from the stove. The makeshift trapdoor was unmistakeable. She looked at Grigori.

'Open it.'

'It's just storage space ...' Grigori stuttered, unable to think of anything else.

'Obviously. Open it. Please.'

Grigori was paralysed.

'Then let me,' said the militiawoman. She inserted her fingers into a narrow slit between the boards and pulled. The section of flooring came away easily. She put it to one side and pulled out the blankets, revealing the battered metal chest.

'Commisar Petrenko, if you would help me...'

As Petrenko went to help Ludmila lift the trunk out of its hiding place, Grigori found his voice. 'Look, you must understand, this is inconclusive stuff. I ... I put it there to avoid confusion. More work needs to be done ...'

'Stay back,' Ludmila warned.

When they had succeeded in extricating the trunk, Petrenko held out his hand.

'The key please, comrade Professor.'

Slowly, Grigori handed his bunch of keys to Petrenko.

'Which one?' asked Petrenko.

'Stop this playacting and show him the right key!' Ludmila snapped angrily.

Grigori pointed to a small brass key on the bunch. Irina groaned inwardly. An ice-cold wave of terror swept through her. Her despair was complete.

15

More snow fell.

Semyon huddled between the three animals who were now his bed-fellows. He had always been careful when bringing meat for certain of the animals, to keep the best part for himself, usually the liver, and deny it to the wolves. This way he maintained his position as alpha male, at least with these three amenable Siberian Greys. He would never have tried it with Ivan the Terrible, for example. He was a class-1 alpha male, completely untameable, unamenable and highly dangerous. The three, whom Irina had named Mitya, Aloysha and Vanya after some characters in a book he had never heard of, licked Semyon's mouth with sticky foul-smelling kisses and Mitya even rolled over to play like a puppy. Occasionally he had to growl warningly as one of them became too rough and he would pinch the soft skin of its belly till the wolf squealed and backed off. He had eaten the stew the militiawoman had brought him and made sure none of the brothers got a sniff of it. Now all he had to face was the dropping temperature and his own dark thoughts.

He had no intention of being taken to Moscow and his instincts, like those of his wolf companions, were of escape and survival. He got up and paced the cage. He had built the cages himself from heartwood-rich pine poles, hammered two and a half feet into the ground, and sheets of military wire mesh, proof against rot and the persistent gnawing of powerful canine jaws. The militiawoman had kept his hands manacled in front of him. He growled in frustration. *I should have killed her. I should have put a bullet in her in the forest and buried her body as I threatened.* He shivered and convulsed, more with fury than from the plummeting temperature. Somewhere a wild wolf howled and the pack responded. The three took up the call and soon all the caged wolves were one howling, demonic chorus. He shook the mesh and roared out into the freezing Siberian night.

In the cabin, Ludmila had supervised the laying out of the contents of the trunk. She delegated Petrenko with the task of making sense of the contents of the various documents. He had suggested they arrange all the material by date. She had agreed but insisted that the film canisters be placed separately and had Irina bring in the projector from the study. Grigori sat mute and helpless, a condemned man. Irina willed him to sit up and speak to the material spread out on the floor, sniffed at by the curious wolf cubs. He could make a case surely for results of his work. He had always been able to reconcile it with the prevailing orthodoxy. A succession of Narkom officials had left satisfied with what he was doing and approved a continuation of funding. So why was he now so paralysed, just answering yes or no to Petrenko or Ludmila's questions? She listened to the wolves howling outside and heard Semyon's desperate roar and she railed inwardly at her own helplessness and her father's apathy.

Finally, Ludmila ordered Grigori to begin showing the films. She had closed the shutters and now she turned off the single electric light, leaving only a kerosene lamp burning low and yellow in a corner of the room. Sluggishly, Grigori spooled the first film. Then he ran the braided brown cable to one of the two sockets that were connected to the petrol generator outside. The bulb flickered into life. The projector faced a blank wall of the cabin. Grigori asked Irina to adjust the focus of the lens. The films were three minutes long and the subjects were exclusively wolves. Wolves in groups, wolves singly, wolf cubs, suckling, playing, wolves being measured, tagged, wolves squabbling, eating, mating. Ludmila watched without a flicker of interest. Petrenko, hunched forward, took notes in a cheap notebook.

They came to the last three canisters. Irina saw her father stiffen.

'Run the film, comrade professor. What are you waiting for?' Ludmila asked sharply.

Grigori seemed to sigh as he opened the first of the last three canisters. He spooled it and sat back. The projector whirred and flickered. On the screen not wolves this time but human beings -a small dark girl and a slightly taller fair-haired girl. They were aged about three years old. They were climbing a small birch tree in what was recognisably the front garden of the cabin in which they were all sitting. The tree was still there, Irina noted, as she watched these two infants, one of whom she recognised as herself. But who was the other girl? As the four adults watched, the girl on the ground then found a long branch and tried to push the other girl off the branch with it until a young woman rushed into the frame and dragged the child away angrily. Petrenko wrote furiously. The film flapped out of its spool and ended.

'Next,' said Ludmila.

Grigori spooled the next film. In this one, the same two girls, this time at a child's party. A cake was flung to the floor by the smaller girl and she then pounced on the other child and the same pretty young woman pulled them apart. The film ended.

'Next.'

Grigori threaded the last film. The same two girls playing in the snow with a large dog. The fair-haired girl is hanging round its neck affectionately while the darker-haired girl lashes the dog with a switch. The dog flinches and backs away. On the snow the shadow of an adult figure, presumably the camera operator. The smaller child is remorseless in her assault on the dog –a grey and white Siberian husky- until it finally snaps and bites the child, gripping her head in its jaws. There is a flurry of incoherent images of snow and sky as the operator presumably puts down the camera and separates dog and child and … the film flaps free of its spool. Ludmila snapped the overhead light back on.

'Explain. Please.'

'What do you want me to explain? They are films of two little girls getting up to mischief.'

'Who are they?'

Yes. Who are they? Irina was burning to know. She was sure that the fair-haired girl was her, but she had no recollection of any of the events on film. Why had her father filmed them? And who was the other girl? And there was the woman. Was she her mother? It certainly looked like her from photographs. Despite her fierce curiosity, for the moment she decided to say nothing.

'The fair-haired girl is Irina, the young woman is my late wife. The other little girl was from the daughter of a colleague of mine who was staying with us. I used the camera to film the children playing.'

Ludmila was incredulous. 'Playing? The small child is putting herself and the other little girl in danger and you are filming them?'

'My wife was standing by. She made sure they were safe.'

'Really? You call one child pushing another out of a tree safe? Taunting a dog, safe?'

Irina broke in. 'Dad, when did you film this? I don't understand. Why haven't you told me about these films?'

Grigori took his pipe apart and proceeded to clean it. His jaw set, his face reddening.

'Dad!'

Then Petrenko joined the conversation. 'Professor, is there any documentation to go with these films? Maybe that would shine a light on what you were doing?'

'Yes, there are notes … somewhere. And … yes, it is more than a family movie. I was interested in children's behaviour. I filmed them as a father, yes, but also as a scientist. I was curious about how two similar children could behave so differently.'

'In what way similar?' Petrenko fixed him with his seagull stare.

'They had similar backgrounds, stage of development, similar education … Look, I am a scientist. A behavioural scientist. I have spent my life investigating animal behaviour and the way that can be extrapolated to human beings. It is a respected line of inquiry. A scientist will often start with experiments on himself or … or those close to him. It's all in the search for knowledge.'

He found himself standing up, raising his hands, looking round. He met the various gazes of the other three occupants of the room. His daughter straining to make sense of what he was saying, Ludmila coolly assessing everything he did say, Petrenko's gaze forensic, a man in his element. Grigori sat down again and opened his tobacco pouch with shaking hands.

Ludmila spoke first. 'The commissar will go through all your documents to confirm everything we have seen and everything you have said. As a police officer, I am concerned that you have gone beyond what is normal for a parent and you have been experimenting on children…'

'I wasn't experimenting on anyone!' Grigori blurted out. 'I was observing them. There's a difference!'

'Comrade professor, please calm down.' Ludmila stared directly into Grigori's eyes.

Grigori sat down in exasperation and put his head in his hands. Irina touched his shoulder but he didn't respond. Her feelings were confused. She felt betrayed and excluded but at the same time a deep sympathy for her father.

Ludmila broke the silence. 'Are there any other films? And I warn you I will find them. Better you show them to me now.'

Irina was torn, but then she rose and went to her coat on its wooden peg on the cabin door and took out the canister of film she had retrieved from the chest. She handed it to Ludmila without making eye contact with her father, even though she could feel him look up from his hands and watch what she was doing. Ludmila took it.

'Why have you got this?' she asked.

'I helped my father pack the trunk. I … I kept this back.'

'Irushka, why?' Her father's furrowed brow and anxious stare confronted her.

'I was going to put it back, but you came in and I didn't know what to do. I … I was curious too, I suppose.'

'Run the film.'

Grigori got to his feet wearily and once again spooled the film as Ludmila turned off the light. He ran the projector.

The same two little girls, this time rolling on the ground fighting like cats. The lighter-haired girl -Irina- was being having her head banged on the ground by the other girl. The camera shook and was moved away from its subject by someone or something. The earth, a man's shoe, the sky and then the figure of a woman -the same woman- again coming to separate the girls. The dark- haired girl was pulled out of the frame. The camera stayed on a sobbing Irina whose face was scratched and bleeding.

Irina sat back in her chair, at a loss, and stared at the floor. She couldn't make any sense of it. What was her father doing? Why did he film those horrible things? Who was her tiny tormentor about whom she could remember nothing? And what would Ludmila and this Narkom official do now?

The first thing Petrenko did was gather up the material carefully and put it back into the trunk. He then dragged the trunk into the study. His head was still reeling from the summary attention paid to him by the militiawoman but this twist in his investigation gave him something else to think about. He asked that tea be brought into him, excused himself from the company and closed the study door. As he sat down to unpack the trunk again, he couldn't get rid of all the feelings Ludmila had left him with. The only thing he wanted at this moment was her. Her hand on him. Her mouth on his. The smell of her hair. The soft pressure of her body. He groaned softly. He began to read: Outline of Working Hypothesis Concerning the Behaviour of Wolves and its Relation to Human Behaviour ... With admirable self-control the commissar read on.

In the main living space, the three listened to the howling of the wolves. Ludmila stood up with irritation.

'What is wrong with those animals?' she demanded. The question remained rhetorical as Irina and Grigori stared blankly into space, neither would look at the other. 'Tomorrow, you will show me how to get to the fur trapper's kolkhoz and I will contact authorities in Krasnoyarsk who will contact Moscow. Local militia will take the Georgian into custody. As for you, well that depends on what the commissar discovers in the professor's work.' She sneered at the word 'work' like it was something revolting. The films had aroused something in her which she couldn't explain. The fact that someone could film small children like that without any sense of responsibility offended her sense of what was right. This scientist Medvedenko was a cold monster. No father could treat his child as if she were a laboratory animal, nor any child for that matter. Suddenly she asked, 'Who was the other girl? The smaller, darker one?'

It was something Irina wanted to know. She sat up and stared hard at her father's downcast head.

'Dad?'

Grigori's head rose slowly as if being wound by invisible threads. He looked confused for a moment. Ludmila watched him closely, her head cocked like an animal.

'She was, as I told you, the child of a colleague.'

'Her name?' Ludmila snapped.

'I really can't remember.'

He's lying, thought Ludmila. 'You can't remember a childhood friend of your daughter's? The child of a colleague? Try a little harder.'

'Her name was Marya. Yes, that's right. Her father was professor of human biology in Moscow. Dmitri Versov. He's dead now. Killed in the war.'

'How very convenient.'

'I would say how very sad.' Some of Grigori's sardonic tone was returning.

Ludmila ignored it. 'And his family?'

'All dead too. The little girl died in a car accident when she was only seven I think. Long before the war. Tragic.'

Irina looked at her father. He seemed genuinely moved. He choked a little as he finished speaking. His eyes glistened with tears.

'This can all be checked out. You will write down everything you can remember.'

'Of course.'

Grigori was beaten, defeated. Irina felt his pain, helplessly.

Outside the howling suddenly stopped. All that could be heard was yelping and crashing and shouting. Semyon was struggling with someone or something and shouting and roaring incoherently. Ludmila grabbed the rifle next to her and ran outside, followed by Irina and Grigori. In the study, Petrenko heard the commotion but decided to stay where he was. It involved wolves and therefore it didn't involve him. Continuing to sift the papers into categories of his own making he kept one ear on what might be happening outside.

When they got to Semyon's cage, it was all over. Alyosha, Mitya and Vanya were pacing restlessly, sniffing but not crossing the open cage door across which Semyon was lying. He was bleeding. Grigori got him to his feet and he and Irina dragged him to the house. Ludmila saw that the lock had been burst open. The wolves curled their lips, snarled and bared their canines but kept their distance. She was ready to put a bullet into them if they came any nearer and the wolves seemed to sense it. She dragged the damaged gate shut and fastened it with some old rope that lay near by. The wolves rushed at the gate and tore at the steel mesh with their teeth, then turned on each other yelping in a frenzy of fear, aggression and frustration.

In the cabin, they laid Semyon on the old cracked leather couch. Grigori was assessing the damage to his hands. He demanded that Ludmila take off the handcuffs. Grigori asked Irina to fetch hot water and tear some clean sheets into strips. Semyon was in considerable agony, his top lip curled and his teeth clenched, but he made no sound except for the odd animal grunt and snort of pain. Petrenko came to the study door and watched as Grigori bandaged the Georgian's hands. Semyon's nose had been broken and Irina gently eased his head back and held a strip of cloth to his nose. She cleaned the blood from his face and tentatively explored for any other wounds. His hair was matted with blood.

'What happened?' barked Ludmila.

'Let him recover! He's in a lot of pain!' Irina cried.

'How did you open the gate?'

Semyon struggled to answer her. 'It was the killer. I heard him … sniffing round … the wolves heard him … he broke the lock …didn't know I was there … we fought … he had a knife…' Semyon let his head fall back on the worn cushion, his face screwed up with pain.

'Who?'

'The killer … the one you should be looking for … the killer …'

'There was no one there. You broke the lock. You injured yourself.' Ludmila was outraged at his play-acting and deceit.

'Why would he do that?' asked Grigori.

'To make us think there was someone else of course! That he isn't the killer. If he'd just escaped I would have caught him, but he is making out that he was attacked. It's obvious!'

'His hands have been lacerated with something sharp. He was defending himself as best he could with his hands manacled.'

Semyon struggled once again to speak. 'He was big … stank like a mating wolf … you can smell him on me …'

'You smell of wolf because you've been in their cage! This isn't going to work. The handcuffs will go back on him when you've finished.'

'You bitch!' Irina screamed at her. 'You heartless bitch! Have you no feelings at all?'

Ludmila was unperturbed. 'He is a prisoner of the Soviet state. He is under arrest and under my authority. Give him some morphine and he can stay here for the night – in handcuffs.'

It was too much for Irina. She burst into tears. 'Semyon, Semyon, I'm so sorry, I'm sorry! This is all my fault!' She repeated, sobbing, over and over again.

Grigori finished bandaging him and gave him a shot of morphine. Semyon was soon fast asleep, emitting what sounded alarmingly like a death rattle. Ludmila ordered Irina and Grigori to bed and Petrenko back into the study. She helped herself to tea from the samovar and sat with the rifle on her knees as the hurricane lamp dwindled and went out.

The animal –was it a tiger? A wolf?- had her in its jaws, its teeth gripping her skull, biting down, the pain was intense. Everyone was watching and pointing. No one helped. Not even her mother. She just looked … mournful, as if her daughter were already dead. Ludmila awoke with a shudder. How long had she been asleep? The cabin was completely quiet. There was no sound outside. Snow was falling heavily, blanketing everything. Semyon snored like a tractor. A thin yellow strip of light could be seen under the study door. Petrenko was still working. Ludmila got up stiffly, stretched, shook herself and knocked on the study door. She had no idea what time it was. Petrenko came to the door. His heart began to pound rapidly in his chest as he let the tousle-haired, sleepy-eyed militiawoman into the study. His eyes were red and swollen. He had been reading in the poor electric light. Papers were scattered all over the floor and on every flat surface. He tried to keep his face expressionless but could feel a smile quivering the muscles of his mouth. Why is he looking at me like that? Ludmila wondered. Is he smiling? Or is he going to cry? She looked down. The reason was obvious from the set of his trousers. She smiled inwardly. She had no idea what men saw in her body which made them react so. All she knew was it happened regularly. Women –mostly disinterestedly- had told her she was attractive. Men –mostly with ulterior motives- had told her the same. As for herself, she couldn't see it. Her face was a face. Her breasts, breasts. She enjoyed the pleasure sex gave her and marvelled at the way men devoured her like hungry animals and women tasted and appreciated her like sophisticated sommeliers. It never occurred to her that her own disinterestedness, her own disembodiment, might be seen as something profoundly attractive.

Ludmila took in the scattered papers. Petrenko closed the door behind her. He stood close to her, breathing in her scent - animal, female, overpoweringly pheromonal. He felt himself trembling and clenched his fists. He looked at the nape of her neck and felt emboldened to breathe on her skin and move the fronds of her hair. She looked round sharply in annoyance. He pulled back, as if scalded.

'What have you discovered?' she asked.

Petrenko cleared his throat. 'There are reports which relate to the films. I cross-referenced from my notes and from the labels on the film canisters …'

'And?'

He almost groaned it was so unbearable. To be alone with this creature in a room at night, a woman who had caused him to ejaculate while looking at him with such profound desire. *She couldn't possibly leave it there, could she?* He had no experience with women, and even if he had he doubted such a full-on assault as hers would leave any man unscarred, not wanting more …

He collected himself as best he could. 'These notes here'– he gestured to a pile of typewritten notes on the desk- 'outline his hypothesis and how he intends to make his observations. By filming the children as they play, as they interact with each other. He details at length how he chose his subjects. He refers to them as A and B. He never mentions that one of them is his daughter, which I find highly unusual as it is obviously relevant …'

Ludmila was quickly growing impatient. 'Yes, but what about the legality of what he is doing?'

Petrenko paused and looked at her. 'Strictly speaking, he has done nothing illegal. His peers would only want to know what conclusions he came to, what he actually proved. They wouldn't be too concerned with his methods.' Her cheeks were flushed and her eyes wide and dark. She was a fiercesome interrogator and he was her pliant suspect.

'Never mind his peers,' she snapped dismissively. 'What about you? What about Narkom? What about the Party? Isn't there a case to be made against him there?'

'Well …' he paused, vaguely aware that it might be in his interest to be evasive and to see how she would react. His interest. Testosterone made him fearless. He moved toward her, took her face in his hands. They were cold, the nails seemed to claw her neck and throat. Swiftly, in one powerful movement, with both hands she batted his hands away.

'Comrade commissar, you are behaving inappropriately!'

Petrenko almost laughed. *Inappropriate? After what she had done?* His underwear was still damp. He still itched from the ejaculate drying on his penis - *on his penis* which she had caressed and pummelled! He wanted her. He wanted her to suck him till she drew blood and he screamed for mercy. He wanted her to claw the meat out of his back as he fucked her like an out of control mechanical thing. He wanted her. He found the strength to grab the lithe little militiawoman and throw her to the floor. They wrestled and scuffled for a moment in silence. He tore at her tunic but it wouldn't open. He scrabbled for her trousers and having more luck there, ripped them below her buttocks. He frantically opened the fly of his trousers while she writhed and kicked... suddenly she went very still. In the dim light, her dark eyes stared at him, lifeless as a doll's, her lips parted. Her submissiveness brought Petrenko to a halt. She smiled. He could feel the fleshy warmth of her naked belly, her thighs slightly parted but still constricted by her uniform trousers. They panted in each other's faces.

'All right, comrade commissar Petrenko, if this is what you want. You don't have to take. I will give. With one condition.'

Nearly out of his mind, his voice strangled with lust, Petrenko said, 'What is it?'

'That you bring a case against the professor for his unethical scientific practice and offence against the children of the Soviet Union.'

'Yes, yes – anything!' his breath came in huge gasps now. He pressed his forehead against hers. 'Anything!'

He hissed into her ear, mindful of three other people asleep in the cabin.

'Good. And if you don't carry it through, I will arrest you for rape.'

This would have chilled a man to the bone in more normal circumstances. But these weren't normal circumstances for Commisar Petrenko. A man who had never had sex with another woman, a virgin brought to the peak of absolute arousal by this beautiful she-animal, at once submissive and completely in control. What man could resist? What man could say no to this bucking, thrusting, squirming half-naked police officer who offered him the glories of her body for one simple promise? What man? He felt her pull down his trousers over his gaunt hips, then she shuffled hers to her ankles and spread her legs wide. Everything was achieved in an intense whispered silence. Her smell was intoxicating. As he was about to come, she stopped him. Obediently, but with great reluctance, he withdrew with a gasp and came over her stomach. Ludmila smiled to herself. A predator in complete control of her prey. Now the cat had her mouse, the she-wolf her buck rabbit.

16

Ludmila barely slept as she kept watch over the comatose Semyon. Petrenko had slept in her bed –his entreaties for her to sleep with him had been curtly refused and he had had to make do with furious masturbation as he inhaled her scent on the sheets. As the yellowy, snow-reflected light began to filter into the cabin, she roused Semyon roughly. He grunted and staggered to his feet and looked at Ludmila with dark, wide-irised eyes. He retched violently but could bring nothing up. Irina came into the living room still dressed, her hand brushing back her unkempt hair as it fell across her face. Her eyes were red and puffy from crying.

'What are you doing?' she demanded.

Ludmila looked at her briefly. 'I am taking him to the herders' encampment to show them that I have their killer and that he is no spirit.'

'I'm coming!' She ran back into her bedroom and emerged minutes later fully dressed and struggling into her coat.

Ludmila meanwhile had ushered Semyon out into the snow and towards the truck. She made Semyon climb onto the cargo bed and ordered Irina to tie him to the metal rail across the top of the cab. She checked the knots and jumped down. Irina stayed on the cargo bed with Semyon.

'Get down,' the militia woman said. 'Now.'

Irina descended reluctantly and got into the driver's seat. The useless wipers at least removed the thick layer of wet snow from the windscreen. Not having Semyon with his injured hands to start the truck, Ludmila took the handle herself and with determined effort, and several turns, managed to start the engine. Her face was flushed as she climbed –with a triumphant nod towards Semyon- into the cab.

'Drive,' was all she said. Irina drove.

She drove through heavy snow which was melting as the sun grew stronger. The ZIS was built for these sorts of conditions and moved easily through the drifts.

As they pulled into the camp, the herders came out of their tents, chimneys already smoking as the women prepared the first meal of the day. The children ran alongside, pointing and shouting at the burly manacled Georgian. He stared ahead, his mind elsewhere, barely comprehending what was happening to him. Blood was soaking through the rags bound round his hands but he felt no pain as the morphine still held sway in his system. He looked like a captured animal, a circus bear whose bid for freedom had ended in ignominy and defeat, a broken clownish Christ on a mechanical donkey.

Irina pulled up in front of Innnaksa's tent. His father stood and watched, his face a subtle mix of impassivity and curiosity. He smoked the last of his tiny, grubby cigarette, spat and came forward to greet Irina. He nodded upward at Semyon and frowned. Innaksa ran out of the tent and clung to his father's leg.

'Where is Uluki? Tell the soldier woman I want Uluki back!'

His father growled at him to be quiet but the boy became more and more frantic and repeated 'Uluki! Uluki!' over and over again. Only when his father struck him hard across the back of his legs, did Innaksa calm down.

The shaman had emerged from his tent and he approached the truck, watching Semyon intently. He rattled out question after question in Evenk without waiting for an answer.

'What is going on? Why is the big Russian tied to the truck? Why have you let the Soviet bitch back into our camp?'

Ludmila stepped forward, her boots creaking in the snow. 'Here is your killer. I've brought him to show you. He is a man. Someone you know. Someone you deal with every day. He is no devil! Look!'

The herders seemed stunned for a moment. All were silent apart from the still-ranting shaman.

'This isn't the killer! This isn't the murderer! You are being tricked by this uniformed whore from Moscow!'

Irina watched Semyon closely, her eyes filling with tears. This was so wrong, so cruel, but there was nothing she could do. Semyon hung his head low, looking at the herders from under his thick unruly eyebrows.

Innaksa's father picked up the little boy and pointed to Semyon.

'Is this the creature who took you, Innaksa?' he asked in Evenk.

The boy said nothing, still smarting and sulking from the blow he had received from his father.

'Innaksa! Talk to me! Iş he the one who took you?'

'What's he saying?' Ludmila demanded of Irina.

'I think he's asking Innaksa if Semyon was the one who kidnapped him.'

Ludmila looked at the boy. 'Well? Is he?'

'Will you give me Uluki?'

Ludmila looked at the boy, then nodded.

His eyes brightened. He pointed at Semyon. 'Yes! Yes! He took me! He is the wolfman!'

Ludmila took the carved squirrel from her pocket and gave it to Innaksa.

'I will need a statement from the boy,' Ludmila said to his father.

Just then, a stone came out of nowhere and struck Semyon full in the face. Then another. And another. The children started it and then the women followed. A lasso flew from Innaksa's father's hands and landed around Semyon's neck. It tightened and the Georgian's eyes bulged and his whole bloodied face became discoloured. Semyon was pulled forwards over the cab but held back by rope that secured him to the truck. Two other men grabbed the lasso and started to pull with Innaksa's father. It was as if they meant to execute him there and then.

'Stop them! Stop them!' shrieked Irina.

Ludmila fired her rifle in the air and the men stopped pulling for an instant and the women and children ceased their hail of missiles.

'Let go of the rope and stop throwing stones or I will use my weapon on you.' Ludmila spoke with deadly quiet.

Irina could only watch Semyon as his head rose slowly and he coughed and choked and shook his crimsoned head to loosen the braided leather rope. It didn't work and Irina leapt on to the cargo bed and loosened the rope herself. Then Semyon did something that Irina found completely incomprehensible. He howled. He lifted up his shaggy bearded head and howled. Immediately the wolves miles away in the compound took up the refrain and howled with him. Again and again he howled. The shaman gaped as the rest of the herders drew back. Semyon had a powerful voice that paralysed.

'We're getting out of here now!' Irina shouted and dived into the cab. Ludmila followed, training the rifle all the while on Innaksa's father and the shaman by turns. Irina gunned the truck into reverse and pulled away from the camp. Semyon continued to howl. The hail of stones resumed. The truck gathered speed, screaming in low gear. Ludmila pulled the rusty door of the truck shut and Irina turned and slammed the gears into first and drove as fast as she could from the camp, snow and slush spraying from the tyres and tracks as they accelerated.

'What did you think you were doing giving Innaksa the doll?' Irina shouted over the din of the truck. 'You knew he would say yes – just to get it back!'

'I have a positive identification from a victim of the assault,' Ludmila replied evenly.

'But what about fingerprints? You said the doll would have fingerprints of the killer!' The truck lurched and bounced and swerved.

'That would prove Semyon wasn't the killer!'

Ludmila didn't respond. Semyon continued howling as they fled toward the field centre. Irina stamped hard on the brake and stopped the truck.

'What are you doing?' Ludmila demanded.

'I'm going to see Semyon. He was hit with stones and nearly strangled – or hadn't you noticed?'

'Keep moving!'

'No!'

Irina jumped from the cab. She didn't care whether Ludmila shot her, she had to get to Semyon, still baying like a wounded animal, flung about by the jolting of the fleeing vehicle, manacles stripping the flesh from his wrists. She climbed back on to the cargo bed. When Semyon saw her he stopped his howling, then slid to his knees, muttering repetitively. Irina sensed Ludmila behind her.

'Take off the handcuffs and untie him, you vicious cow! You heartless fucking psychopath!' The anger arose somewhere in her belly, erupted from her throat and tore the freezing air. It was a ferocious living thing apart from herself and would tolerate no resistance. Ludmila took all this in, like a fighter weighing up an opponent's ability to cause serious harm. She blinked with slow deliberation, untied the rope and unlocked the cuffs.

Semyon was by now too weak to stand, let alone fight back. His eyes were still opiate pools of ink but he allowed Irina to attempt-unsuccessfully- to staunch his bleeding face with a handkerchief. He continued muttering what Irina guessed were prayers.

'You drive the truck back. I'll stay here with Semyon. You *can* drive can't you?'

Ludmila again refused to answer but jumped down from the truck and took the wheel. The ZIS lurched and almost stalled and then picked up again and kangarooed for a few yards with a cruel wrenching of gears. Finally, Ludmila gained control of the unfamiliar vehicle and they drove back to Pustinya. On the back of the truck, Irina cradled Semyon's head and stroked his hair while he continued his desperate litany.

Commisar Petrenko hammered out his report on the old Underwood Cyrillic typewriter. He had discovered at least three incriminating, but as yet unpublished, scientific papers by Medvedenko which correlated to the filming. In them, the comrade professor had made it clear that he was studying two three-year old girls, A and B, to determine differences in their behaviour when interacting at play or in other social and family situations. Petrenko quoted at length from them in his report, having first filed them in grey-green cardboard folders.

'… whereas girl A showed every sign of responding to reward or sanction in any given situation, girl B responded little if at all to anything but her own needs and wants. Girl A and girl B are similar in every way and yet they behave completely differently. Girl A is socially amenable but girl B is violent, abusive and destructive despite her very young years …'

The paper concluded:

'… The purpose of this article is to demonstrate that just as in the animal kingdom, identical animals can show differing behaviours as regards empathy, intelligence and amenability to human beings, so too in the human sphere, we have 'wolves' amongst us. This has implications for our justice system and the well-being of law-abiding peaceful citizens …'

Petrenko sat back. This was the woolliest paper he had ever read. Identical? In what way identical? He could find no other information to enlighten him. And to carry out a study on just two people and draw such far-reaching conclusions! Certainly scientists in Soviet Russia were encouraged to outline the practical implications of their findings for the betterment of the Soviet peoples, but still … What finally incriminated him was the following paragraph in the third paper entitled: "Intrinsic and extrinsic factors in behaviour from a

group study of the Siberian Grey wolf
(Canis lupus lupus)". It read:

'… the conclusion this study draws is
that the intrinsic factor, that is to say
the overwhelming genetic component for
the propensity towards amenable or non-
amenable behaviour, is clear. Wolves are
born either 'wild' or 'tameable' to use
layman's terms. By comparing studies on
wolves and children, it can be
extrapolated that exactly the same
intrinsic factor is present. Wolves are
born not made. Criminals —the deliquent,
the murderer, the thief, the unfeeling
psychopath-are born not made.'

Intrinsic? *Intrinsic?*

Petrenko pulled the paper and its carbon skin from the
machine. All thoughts of the ravishing Ludmila had been put
to one side as he went through the professor's papers. But
now the itch was returning. The thought of her spread out
before him, offering herself, -all that gorgeous flesh!- caused
him to harden uncomfortably. He adjusted himself in his
fortunately roomy, chest-high trousers and suppressed an
urge to run out into the snow, sprawl on the ground and
extinguish the fire in his testicles. Instead, he summoned
Grigori into the study.

Grigori came in at a shuffle. In the space of a few hours
he had aged twenty years. His face was grey, his cheeks
sagged and his eyes had a dead look. He was a condemned
man and he knew it. All his work of the past two decades,
which he had tried to keep secret because it would incur the

wrath of the Soviet scientific establishment, and which he had been saving for a time when he might gain a sympathetic hearing, had vanished like melting snow.

Petrenko gestured to him imperiously to sit down. He arranged the folders on the desk in a neat pile and then looked at Grigori with his pitiless avian stare.

'So, comrade professor, I would like to hear your explanation,' he began.

'I'm ... sorry? My explanation ... for what?' Grigori slurred his words as if he had been pole-axed by a stroke.

'For a series of experiments involving children, for making completely unscientific claims about human psychology and for asserting the supremacy of genetics. The last having been completely discredited in the aftermath of the Great Patriotic War against the fascists in Nazi Germany.' Petrenko was growing pompous and verbose as he warmed to his subject.

'I went where the findings took me. As I told you before, I was searching for a way of eliminating crime. Is that so wrong?'

'Your brief here was to study the domestication of wolves. Where do you have permission to exceed your brief, comrade professor?'

'Nowhere,' Grigori mumbled wearily.

'Exactly. Nowhere. You realise of course that certain bourgeois elements in the world of Inheritance Studies ...'

Grigori was suddenly jolted into life. 'Inheritance Studies?'

'Inheritance Studies. Yes. What used to be called Genetics. You must keep up, comrade professor. There is no such thing in Soviet Science.'

'Since when?'

'Genetics has been discredited as I said. It is a fascistic pseudoscience promulgated by bourgeois saboteurs in the scientific community, many of whom are being rooted out and re-educated as we speak. Science is at the service of the people of the Soviet Union. We exist to do their bidding.'

Grigori could see no point in saying anything more. This ideologue would stonewall anything he could come up with. Across his own desk, the scrawny bureaucrat was gloating, looking down on a corrupt bourgeois intellectual, a traitor to the Soviet project, with undiluted contempt.

The behaviourist academic lowered his head into his hands, took off the steel-rimmed glasses and sank thumb and forefinger into his eye-sockets, then replaced the spectacles. Petrenko could smell victory, he could taste his opponent's defeat. He presumed he could see into the rotten soul of this vile academic who had experimented on children and interpreted his findings along lines outlawed by the Party. He launched into a preening obloquy.

'Who are you, a complacent bourgeois,' he began, 'to tell the Russian people that their lives should be circumscribed by a clutch of acid and sugar molecules? How dare you limit the potential of a pioneering society by separating them into wild beasts on the one hand and pet animals on the other! The presumption! You are privileged, sneering and most emphatically wrong.' He came from behind the desk and stood over Grigori. 'If you were correct, how did I, Nikolai Sergeivich Petrenko, the son of a Sverdlovsk cobbler rise through the ranks to become a Commissar? We are only one generation from a crucible that burnt away all the old values and gave the ordinary working man and woman freedom and hope! One generation, comrade professor. And we will pass all our knowledge, our bitter experience on to the next generation. And so on to the next and the next … and the next. We are not trapped in a cage of genetics, but released into an infinite blue sky by Soviet science!'

As Petrenko, fangs bared, hackles raised, howled truimphantly over the bowed and submissive scientist, he was not aware of a deeper emotion stirring in Grigori, a punishing sense of failure as a man, a scientist, a husband and a father.

In a little while, Ludmila, Irina and Semyon returned. Semyon was now singing some religious song in between howling and laughing. Ludmila frog-marched him stumbling and laughing into the wolf compound and locked him in the cage with the brothers Karamazov.

Ludmila re-entered the cabin, taking in the defeated form of Grigori on the broken-backed sofa being comforted by his daughter, and the pert, flushed, expectant Petrenko, gazing at her like a dog that is proud to have pleased his mistress. He gestured with a wave of his hand across the neatly filed documents and over to Grigori.

Ludmila gave a muffled grunt of approval and then addressed herself to Irina. 'Where is the radio transmitter you talked about? I want to contact my superiors.'

PART TWO

1

The train from Vladivostock to Moscow was barely three thousand miles into its 5700 mile journey when Colonel Dmitri Alexeivich Volkov, personal assistant to Marshal Stalin, received a message.

The radio operator, a blond youth with unruly hair and acne, handed it to him with a shrug. Volkov took it and read it carefully:

Message received: 14th October 1948. 7.04am Moscow time.

Message reads: Suspected serial killer arrested by Moscow militia officer. Also arrested scientist suspected of anti-Soviet genetic research. Pustinya. Central Siberia. 57N91E. Narkom Commisar Petrenko also of Moscow has full report. Request permission to escort suspects to Krasnoyarsk and on to Moscow.

'What has this got to do with us?' growled Volkov, his florid jowls chafing against his military collar. He flipped the transcript on to the radio operator's desk.

'Evidently someone in Krasnoyarsk had seen the newsreels and thought it was significant. Possibly they knew Marshal Stalin would be visiting Krasnoyarsk on his way back to Moscow,' the radio operator said, with another shrug. 'How would you like me to reply, Colonel?'

Volkov thought for a moment, chewing his moustache. He knew that if he didn't show the message to Stalin and it later proved important, he would be shot. On the other hand if he showed it to the Marshal at the wrong time and it proved to be unimportant, he would be shot. He was getting too old for this. Long in the tooth, like an old wolf. He had fought tsarist Cossacks, White Guards, and Nazis, but surviving the strategies and manoeuvres of Stalin's inner circle was proving tougher than anything this old warrior had had to face. At least fascists put a bullet in your heart and not the back of your head. He made a decision. 'Give it to me. I'll take it to him.'

The radio operator handed him the transcript, his face expressionless, but Volkov could read it with ease: *Rather you than me, comrade colonel.*

The old soldier pulled his greatcoat around him and moved painfully through the swaying, rattling carriages.

The radio room was five carriages up from the Marshal's distinctive bright-green private carriage. Heavily armed soldiers filled the compartments. A machine gunner nested on the roof of the rear carriage. Such was their leader's paranoia that he would only travel through Russia in this bullet-proof train, the wooden sides of his carriage replaced with half inch steel plates. He never sat in the window but sequestered himself in a corner, facing backwards.

Volkov had been in attendance on his leader for the interminable trip to the ends of the earth on this rattling heap of shit. We have aeroplanes comrade Marshal. They fly very, very fast. We could have been in Vladivostok in twenty four hours instead of twenty four long days. You could have spoken to your precious scientist with his great plans to feed the Russian people, in comfort. But no, the aeroplane is dangerous. It can be shot down - and secretly you're shit-scared of flying aren't you, comrade Marshal? I really am getting too old for this.

So ran the colonel's thoughts as he stumbled and cursed his way down the train, stepping with effort from one carriage to the next. Finally, he reached his destination.

He peered through the small round window of the carriage door. Marshal Stalin was out of his line of vision, huddled he knew with his back to the wall on his left. He could see who was sitting opposite him quite clearly though. That opinionated arsehole with the rock-hewn face and arrogant blue-eyed stare. That self-promoting sycophant with hair slicked flat to the head, side-parted and shaved like a Nazi: Trofim Denisovich Lysenko.

Volkov knew his history and he knew that Russia had always thrown up its saints and mystics, its charismatic heroes who had the ear of the current tsar and who could manipulate him like a string puppet. Those peasant-priests who came out of the steppe, like Rasputin. It's no different now, thought Volkov, trembling inwardly at his own lack of loyalty and ideological rectitude. This buffoon Lysenko has the ear of our leader. A Rasputin for our own times.

Volkov coughed and entered the carriage. A couple of junior officers playing cards opposite Stalin and Lysenko looked up, then stood to attention, stubbing out their cigarettes. Volkov waved them at ease. He looked across at the Russian leader and the scientist. They were playing chess, Lysenko staring hard at the remaining pieces on the board and Stalin sitting back smoking his pipe in amusement. The bleak Siberian countryside unfurled inexorably outside the steel-grilled window.

'Check mate, I think, comrade Lysenko,' murmured Stalin.

Volkov looked at the board. A veteran chess-player –and military strategist of considerable skill- he could see a way out for Lysenko's king, courtesy of a rook lurking behind the lines but with a clear line of attack on Stalin's besieging bishop-knight alliance. Lysenko could see it too but had the sense to topple his king in surrender and sit back shaking his head in wonder at his Leader's superior intellectual powers. He pulled a tobacco tin from his breast pocket and took out a cigarette. He snapped it shut without offering it to Volkov and tapped his cigarette on the tin before putting it away. He lit the cigarette and, almost insolently, blew the smoke in Volkov's direction.

Prick, thought the colonel.

Stalin was more welcoming. 'Colonel Volkov, sit down, have a drink,' He motioned to the nearly full bottle of vodka on the table. The Marshal was drinking less since his stroke. Volkov declined politely. The junior officers sat down and resumed their card game.

'So, where are we? I seem to have seen that birch forest before. Are we going around in circles do you think?' Stalin laughed loudly at his own joke. Volkov, Lysenko and the two officers joined in, no one wanting to be the first one to stop. Stalin waved them all silent.

'Krasnoyarsk is our next stop Marshal,' Volkov said. 'We are meeting a delegation from a forestry collective eager to learn from comrade Lysenko's experiments with the oak forest plantation.'

Volkov had been told this was not going well. The plantations were designed to act as windbreaks to the flaying polar winds. The planting was based on the idea that trees grown in clusters will co-operate and produce 100% viable oaks. As someone who came from a long line of woodcutters and charcoal burners, Volkov knew that this was nonsense. Trees competed, they raced each other for the sun like arboreal athletes, deprived each other of light; they stole water from one another and strangled the life out of each other with their anarchic, self-seeking tangled root systems. Trees were at war and the best tree won. But he couldn't say this to the great Lysenko, whose Soviet trees showed only the valour, team-spirit and self-sacrifice of elite Red Army warriors. He had picked up that many of Lysenko's oaks were dying precisely because of the way he planted them and precisely because of his crack-pot mystic ideas - ideas that had the full support of the Soviet leader. Rasputin to his Nicholas.

Lysenko drew complacently on his fat Sobranie cigarette and smiled.

'I will be more than happy to meet this delegation, Colonel Volkov. The more we spread the word over the whole of Soviet Russia about our agrarian revolution the better.'

'It is a miracle to think that the wastes of Siberia, the tundra and the taiga could be transformed by your work, comrade Lysenko,' Volkov said without a hint of irony.

'We will grow lemons in the arctic and harvest wheat all year round! Famine will be banished forever. Isn't that right, Lysenko?' Stalin looked hard and almost imploringly, Volkov thought, at the agrarian revolutionary.

Basking. The bastard is *basking* in the Leader's sunshine. He could not quite believe that Stalin, a man so intelligent, so well-read in the arts and the sciences, so astute about the motives of others to the point of paranoia, could be taken in by this mystical buffoon, this shaman. Stalin and Lysenko had embarked on an epic trek to the other end of the Soviet

Union to gather information and to spread the word about the New Agrarian Revolution. Lysenko had discovered the key to how things grew. He had turned his back on the pea-counter Mendel in favour of an holistic view of Mother Nature whose offspring were the product of her union with a Life Force which, when fully understood by man and Soviet Man in particular, would demonstrate that gene theory was false and that the good that was done in one lifetime could be passed directly to the next generation. There was no place for Darwin's evolutionary brutalism or the misguided views of genetic scientists like Vavilov, and those other heretics, who believed in the bourgeois-capitalist view of survival of the fittest. They did not have to wait millennia for the perfectabilty of Man. The future, as it always is for political leaders and some starry-eyed scientists, was now.

Despite his failing health, Stalin had accompanied Lysenko on various stages of this pilgrimage by the 'Barefoot Professor' -as the newspapers were dubbing him. Lysenko had convinced him that the whole land-mass of Russia could become a granary, a vineyard, a boundless, bountiful forest.

Volkov passed the folded radio message transcript to Stalin. 'This may or may not be relevant comrade Marshal, but it was received today from Krasnoyarsk.'

Stalin frowned and took the note. He fumbled for his spectacles, put them on and read the transcript. He peered at Volkov over the rim of his spectacles.

'What is this?' The tone was dangerous, but Volkov had committed himself.

'In the light of your and the comrade professor's journey and the fact that by happy coincidence we will be stopping at Krasnoyarsk, I thought that you might like to look into the circumstances surrounding the message. It seems an arrest has been made of a professor of genetics...'

Lysenko spat and picked a flake of tobacco from his lower lip. Volkov glanced at him briefly and continued:

'… and given your mutual interest in the matter, I wanted to make sure you were given this message.'

Stalin stared hard at his trusted aide de camp.

'Comrade Colonel Volkov,' Stalin began with an ironic sneer to his voice combined with a strange warmth designed to charm and draw the victim closer, 'I am privileged to be the leader of over 200 million people' –160 million at the last count, thought Volkov, I have seen the figures, the census was a farce - 'am I supposed to deal with every saboteur and crank, with every crime that is committed in Mother Russia?' Stalin re-lit his pipe and sat back and stared at his uncomfortable assistant with venomous amusement.

Lysenko cleared his throat and turned towards his leader, moving his elbows toward him across the table. 'Pardon me, comrade Marshal, but do we know the name of this *geneticist*?' He emphasised the last word with profound contempt.

Volkov was relieved to find the barefoot clown intervening on his behalf, though he knew full well that this was not Lysenko's intention. He clearly had the confidence of the Leader and felt sure enough of himself to ask the question.

Stalin seemed to growl before laying down his pipe and taking up the transcript. 'There is no name.'

'I can find out for you, comrade Marshal. It will not take long,' offered Volkov eagerly.

'What difference does it make who he is?' asked Stalin.

Lysenko smiled and replied, 'In the long run, no difference. They all must be banished from the laboratories eventually, but I am interested to know what this so-called scientist thinks he is working on and what findings he thinks he has made.' He tapped the ash from his cigarette into the brass ashtray fixed to the table, then put it back between his lips and inhaled, his eyes half-closed.

Arrogant fucker. 'Comrade Marshal, what would you like me to do?'

Stalin stared coldly at Volkov and said, 'I wish you hadn't brought it to me in the first place, Volkov, but now that you have be a good chap and find out who this fellow is that is being arrested. Comrade Lysenko would like to know. We could maybe even meet him over a glass of tea.' He laughed and Volkov, Lysenko and the two officers laughed with him. A moment of tension, among many moments of tension, had passed.

2

In the thin dawn light, across ragged clouds, a skein of geese honked and hooted as they rowed south on powerful wings, guided by instincts hundreds of millennia old.

Semyon was the first to wake, the three brothers Karamazov curled around him. His head pounded and the wounds on his hands throbbed painfully. What had happened yesterday? They had taken him to the herders' camp in the truck, bound like an animal. They threw stones at him. He remembered that. There was dried blood encrusted on his face and in his hair. He remembered it happening but it all seemed distant, as if it had happened to someone else. Then as the shrouds of sleep fell away, he remembered with a nauseous wrench in his guts that he was a prisoner, a condemned criminal. He groaned and one of the wolves, Mitya, whined and shoved his snout into his face and licked at the blood. Semyon pushed him away wearily. His right ear was toward the ground and that was when he felt the reverberation of heavy vehicles moving steadily closer.

Irina woke at the same time. She was dreaming of a party where all the guests turned on her and were laughing maliciously at something she'd said. She was still fully clothed and curled like a foetus under a single blanket on her bed. She shook herself out of her nightmare and woke into another. The bitch Ludmila had radioed for assistance to arrest them all and take them to Moscow. She pinched herself hard, like a little girl would, but this nightmare wasn't going away. Her body ached. Her mind reeled at the implications of everything that had happened. They would be put on trial. Semyon would certainly be found guilty of murder and executed. Her father would be found guilty of crimes against the state and would spend the rest of his life in a labour camp, as would she. She retched violently and vomited into the enamel chamber pot at the side of her bed. As she spat the last of the bilious fluid from her mouth, she heard the rumble of diesel engines.

The same sound woke Grigori, like Irina still fully clothed and curled up under a single blanket. Like her, he awoke from one nightmare –he had been escorted into a dark room and made to face a Nameless Horror- into another. He was sure he had cried out in utter despair 'No! No!' but couldn't be sure if that was in his dream as the Nameless Horror revealed itself. He asked his wife and daughter for forgiveness and even started to mutter the remnants of some prayer his mother had taught him as a child.

Petrenko woke in Ludmila's bed for the second morning running. He inhaled her scent on the sheets and masturbated furiously, clenching his teeth as he came. When he raised his head from the pillow, panting and groaning, he heard the rumble of wheels.

As soon as she heard them, Ludmila threw off the blanket and leapt, rifle in hand, off the couch. The sound could only mean one thing. Her call had been answered and she could take her prisoners to Krasnoyarsk and on to Moscow.

The heavy military lorries –three of them- pulled up outside the compound and armed soldiers surrounded the field station. The wolves set up a demented howling and flung their powerful bodies time after time at their cages. A fourth vehicle pulled up close to the field centre gates. Ludmila watched as the driver leapt out and opened the rear door. Three figures emerged: a white-haired military man, a civilian in a fur hat and thigh-length leather coat and a moustachioed seventy-year old in a military great coat but without a hat, his grey-streaked black hair swept back from his face. Ludmila felt herself sway in the doorway and she clutched hold of the frame for support. *Marshal Stalin? Here? In Siberia? Impossible!*

But as the figures drew closer she saw that it was indeed Stalin. She buttoned and straightened her uniform blouse, put aside the rifle, checked her hair briefly in the cracked mirror, bunching it up and tucking it under her cap. She remembered her empty holster and pushed it back out of view, then stood to attention and saluted. When they got close, Stalin drew back and allowed Volkov to talk to the militiawoman. Ludmila could hear movement in the cabin behind her. A yelp from Petrenko told her that the commissar had realised who the visitors were and she could hear Irina and her father talking in hissed undertones.

'Identify yourself, comrade.' Volkov's tone was official, military but carried a certain warmth. Ludmila's looks worked their usual charm.

'Lieutenant Sirotovska Moscow East Militia, comrade Colonel.'

'And you are responsible for this radio message?' He handed her a folded piece of paper. She took it tentatively and opened it and read it.

'Yes, sir.' She handed back the paper.

'Is the officer going to invite us in?' Stalin's tone was neither warm nor friendly but heavy with sarcasm and barely-controlled impatience.

'Please, Marshal, forgive my lack of manners. I had no idea that you would be coming here in person.'

'Why? We were passing and my colleague comrade Lysenko insisted we share a glass of tea with you.' His smile was wolfish, mirthless and creased the corners of his mouth but not his eyes.

They entered the cabin and were met with a trio of gawkers. Petrenko looked like he had wet himself and was visibly shaking, tail between his legs, tongue slavering in excitement. Irina and Grigori stood close together and stared in disbelief at the men who had entered the Pustinya Scientific Field Centre. Ludmila demanded that Irina prepare tea and hot food and Volkov made the introductions. Lysenko held out his hand to Grigori with a smirk.

'So, you are the professor of genetics we have heard so much about?'

Grigori had no choice but to take his hand, which was boneless, limp and damp.

'Forgive me, comrade Lysenko, but I am not a professor of genetics but of animal behaviour.'

Stalin had collapsed into the heavy armchair and was fascinated by Grusha and Masha, the former keeping her distance and emitting a low muzzle-wrinkling snarl, while the latter licked his hand and allowed him to fondle her ears.

'Really? The message stated quite clearly that your work involved genetics in relation to the domestication of our iconic Siberian wolf.'

Volkov found a wooden chair near the door and watched the interactions with amusement. Look at the prick preening under the gaze of his alpha-male protector and toying with the vulnerability of other people, so confident is he of the Georgian tsar's patronage. And his Leader he knew would be following every word and noting every gesture, every look and body movement despite being ostensibly occupied with charming the two wolf cubs. And who were these others? The commissar, a fawning bureaucrat with flushed red cheeks and a permanently hungry look. Someone who bares his arse to his superiors and his teeth to his inferiors. One of a multitude in government at all levels. The professor looks terrified and clung to his daughter – out of protectiveness or out of a desire to be protected? Hard to tell. The girl –Irina?- busily and nervously putting together the ingredients for blinis and lighting the flame under the samovar, shooing away her father, who is now wretchedly answering that shit Lysenko's questions.

Petrenko had heard his cue and immediately presented Lysenko with the file he had created on Professor Medvedenko. He offered to turn pages like a demented pianist's assistant and point out passages of interest but Lysenko waved him away as if his breath was rotten. Lysenko read through the report slowly, snorting occasionally and smirking, while Stalin, tired of playing with the cubs, got to his feet and began to look through Grigori's record collection. Ludmila saw Irina freeze in terror and Volkov sat forward as his Leader drew forth a disc and very carefully examined it. He then moved to the gramophone, wound the handle, removed the bakelite plate from its sleeve and placed it on the turntable. The room was regaled with the sound of Bessie Smith singing 'Nobody Knows You when You're Down and Out'. Volkov stared in disbelief as Stalin stood and bobbed his head to the singer's blue-black tones. Irina allowed a plate to crash to the stone floor then bent hurriedly to pick up the pieces. Grigori looked at the Soviet leader with something approaching wonder. Ludmila and Petrenko had similar expressions of shock on their faces. Lysenko conducted with one hand as he continued to read. The disc crackled to its conclusion. Stalin took it off the turntable and replaced the record in its sleeve.

'Do you like Blues and Jazz music from the Mississippi Delta, professor?' Stalin asked benignly.

Irina stood snapshot-still over the skillet, as her father tried to compose an answer.

'I made a collection of Negro music as part of my research into the cultural behaviour of other oppressed proletarians globally. You will see references to it in my papers, if the commissar has included them of course.'

'That wasn't my question. I asked if you liked it.' The tone was now more dangerous.

'I neither like it nor dislike it. It interested me as a scientist.'

A loud guffaw from Lysenko caused everyone to turn in his direction. He looked up innocently.

'I wasn't laughing at you, professor, just at something you wrote.'

'What would that be?' Grigori's voice was starting to shake. He cleared his throat.

'Just one word. *Intrinsic*. Coming from within. Without external influence. Spontaneous. Do you think that everything we are is within us from birth and that no matter what we do or what happens during our lifetime we will always remain the same?' He tutted theatrically. 'Such a pitifully bourgeois notion, wouldn't you say?'

'Comrade Lysenko,' Grigori began, having no idea what he was going to say next, but his scientific pride getting the better of his discretion. 'Comrade Lysenko, my studies with wolves have demonstrated that there are animals who are ripe for domestication and there are wolves who will never ever be tamed.'

180

Lysenko turned on Grigori with less urbanity now and almost snarled at him. 'Did you not think to create a control group to test whether or not the so-called wild animals would respond to training and then pass this on to the next generation? After all, you have been working with them for twenty years. In wolf-terms that must be what? Four or five generations?'

Despite the absolute terror that he felt in his situation and with the added torture of the Soviet Leader's ears –if not his eyes- on him, Grigori could not help rising to a scientific challenge. He was in his element. 'Comrade Lysenko, yes indeed I have bred five generations of wolves here at Pustinya. My findings are there in the research data kindly put together by the People's Commisar Petrenko. And yes of course I created a control group. I'm a scientist not … a bloody witch doctor!'

Grigori could feel the temperature of the room fall. Had she been holding a plate, Irina would have dropped it a second time. Instead she froze again. Stalin, too, became immobile, in the same way a cat becomes immobile before it pounces. Petrenko's seabird eyes bulged from their sockets and there were webs of saliva in the corners of his mouth. Ludmila and Volkov looked on disinterestedly, waiting to see what the response would be. Lysenko himself became apoplectic.

'How dare you! How dare you sneer at me, you fucking bourgeois! You parasitic worm, you saboteur scum, you smug complacent … Darwinist! So what did you find in your control group? Did you test to see whether offspring took on the traits of their parents and that these offspring passed these traits on to their offspring? Or did you ignore this completely and set up experiments to prove that you and the sainted Charles Darwin and the hundred other reactionaries in the field of genetics were right all along?'

Grigori sprang to his feet and confronted Lysenko, standing above him quivering with rage. The wolf cubs rolled in a furry tumble around the cabin, clearly excited by the animal electricity in the room.

'Yes, of course I did, Lysenko, and do you know what I discovered? Nothing! Absolutely nothing! You can put a domesticated parent in with a wild offspring and nothing changes! The wolf stays a wolf. He does not become a dog and he certainly does not pass any acquired characteristics on to his offspring, precisely because … precisely because he hasn't mysteriously *acquired* any characteristics worth mentioning in the first place!'

Grigori stopped. He realised he had taken his pipe from his mouth and was pointing it stem-first at Lysenko. His face was flushed and he seemed to be crouching ready to spring at the barefoot scientist's throat. For his part, Lysenko gripped the arms of the chair so that the tendons of his hands stood out white and his nails clawed the battered leather upholstery. A tense silence hung in the air.

'Here before witnesses, comrade professor, you have incriminated yourself.' That was all Lysenko said as he sank back into the chair and lit a cigarette.

Irina's voice rang across the room. 'Dad! That's enough!' She turned to Stalin who was observing the spat between the two scientists with something approaching amusement.

'Comrade Marshal, my father has been under a lot of strain recently. His work is exhausting and sometimes he says things he doesn't mean.' Stalin's eyes turned their attention to this placating female. He raised his eyebrows encouraging her to continue. 'My father is a man of integrity, a true scientist. He has made the study of wolves his life's work. I have helped him every step of the way. He is not a reactionary. What he does, he does for the love of the Soviet People. He wants to see a better life for them in the future. He wants to remove, if you like, the wolf in all of us …'

At that moment the wolf cages erupted in a cacophony of howling and snarling. A shot rang out. Stalin visibly quailed and looked at Volkov. Volkov rushed to the door and ran out into the darkness.

'What's going on? Who fired that shot?'

A soldier replied but what he said was inaudible. A moment later, Volkov returned, a little out of breath.

'What is it, Volkov?' Stalin asked, an animal fear clearly discernible in his ageing features.

'Nothing, Comrade Marshal,' Volkov replied as he closed the door. 'One of the soldiers thought he saw movement at the edge of the compound. Most likely an animal. He also said that there was a man locked in one of the wolf cages, with three wolves. What is the explanation for this?'

Ludmila stepped forward and explained to the Colonel why Semyon was imprisoned with the animals.

'So, lieutenant Sirotovska, you are saying that the man in the wolf cage is a murderer?' Stalin looked at her from under dark, grizzled eyebrows. 'Is that right?'

'He's not a murderer, comrade Marshal,' Irina cut in before Ludmila could reply, 'I can vouch for him. He fought with the Bolsheviks against the Whites in the twenties, he is a loyal Communist, he is a Georgian like you---'

Ludmila cut across her. 'He's a loyal Communist who sneaks off to a mining town to worship God. He is a reactionary Old Believer who tried to kill me because I had identified him as a murderer. He butchered a herder and then kidnapped a child, intending to do the same to him. We intercepted him and prevented another killing. I want to take him to Krasnoyarsk to stand trial.'

Volkov stroked his moustache and watched. He was intrigued to know what would happen next in this absurd domestic drama thousands of miles from civilisation. *What on earth are we doing here?*

The two women stood glaring at each other. Grigori sank on to the couch and buried his head in his hands. Lysenko watched them, amused but also with a sense of triumph. Grigori was one of yesterday's men. Scientists who came of age under the Tsar and who had dominated Soviet science until their wrong-headedness and conservatism had sealed their fate in numerous unmarked graves and gulags all over the Union.

A terrible silence fell on the group as they waited for Stalin to say something. He was scratching the head of Masha and laughing at the agitated Grusha who snarled at this old man who smelt of weak urine, human sweat and strong pipe tobacco.

'Comrade professor,' he began. Grigori looked up. 'Comrade professor, what do you think the Soviet Union will look like in 50 years time? Where will we be?'

Grigori wasn't sure if this was a rhetorical question so he kept silent.

'I'll tell you. We will be the most powerful nation on earth. We will have spread the word of Marxist-Leninism to many countries across the globe and they will be rising up and creating their own communist societies under our beneficent umbrella. We will be self-sufficient in oil and gas and minerals and wheat. We will be armed against aggressors and we will be reaching for the stars. I can see it here in my mind's eye. And who will create this future? Not the politicians or the bureaucrats or' –he cast an amused glance

184

at Volkov- 'the military, but the people. The ordinary people. And they will be guided by the discoveries of our brilliant scientists and engineers. Their hands, your brains, professor.'

Lysenko started forward in protest at the geneticist being included in the pantheon. Volkov smirked inwardly. Stalin put up his hand for him to be quiet. 'I have great faith in Science and in scientists. You have done wonders in the last thirty years to drag us out of the dark ages imposed on us for so long by the tsarist tyrants. Now' – he leant forward in his chair. His old leather boots creaked and Masha sprang away timidly at the sudden movement. Grusha snarled and yapped. Stalin wheezed. 'Now', he continued, 'some of our best scientists have seen fit to go against the will of the people and propagate theories that are profoundly negative and do not encourage the vision of the future that I have just outlined. They peddle pessimism and outright lies in order to help our enemies.'

Stalin paused and then he stood and surveyed the people in the room, all of them waiting expectantly for what he would say next.

'And who are the worst offenders? I'm sorry to say it is those who hold on to outdated theories about how human beings evolve and change and adapt to their situation. The glorious Red Army thundered into fascist Germany to free that country from her oppressors. They opened up the fetid death camps and exposed the corruption of the Nazis' foul philosophy to the world. They broke into their laboratories and found children and the sick and the weak and vulnerable being experimented on because they believed that genetics held the key to human nature, because they believed that what we are born with and what we pass on through our genes is all there is to the human soul.' He paused again. He was used to holding an audience captivated. 'Now, you may think that is a reactionary term, *russkaya dusha,* the Russian Soul as our poets called it. But I believe in the Russian Soul comrades, because it is very much a materialist phenomenon as opposed to a Dostoevskian, a Tolstoyan religious fantasy. It is the spirit that moves the People, that gives them the strength to repel the armoured might of the fascist armies from our borders with nothing but their bare hands and to build and create the future on a massive scale never before seen in history. It is a spirit born in one generation and passed on to the next.'

Ludmila felt a growing warmth in her belly. Volkov was grudgingly impressed. Grigori and Irina were chilled to the marrow. Petrenko was trembling with excitement. Lysenko merely smiled complacently. Their Leader was making a speech on a battered leather couch in lonely cabin in the middle of a wilderness. *For them.* Stalin was coming to the crescendo.

'So, when I see the Russian Soul denigrated by squabbling men in white coats, when I see the vision of a great future spat on and ridiculed by so-called men of science, I am deeply, deeply disappointed, comrades. I could weep. Fortunately, our revolution has thrown up men of vision who share my hopes for the future. Comrade professor Lysenko here,' -Lysenko looked modestly to the floor, fingers steepled- 'Comrade Lysenko has opened up a world of possibility to the Soviet people. These barren wastes that make up eighty percent of our Union, will one day bloom with winter wheat, arctic lemons, Siberian tropical fruit, apples, bananas, grapes. Not just reindeer but cows and sheep will roam the tundra, having been transformed from feeble creatures of the temperate zones to hardy milk- and meat- producers capable of surviving in sub-zero temperatures – are you all right Volkov?'

Volkov had burst into a fit of coughing so violent that Irina ran to give him a glass of water. He took it gratefully. Recovering, he apologised profusely as his Leader glared at him. The vision of a tropical paradise in Siberia had inexplicably made Volkov erupt into laughter, which he had diverted into a random coughing fit in the nick of time. Arctic lemons? Bananas in the taiga? Siberian cows? What garbage had Lysenko been feeding him? If I was alone with you Lysenko and my revolver, you would have six bullets in your insolent, cretinous face…!

Another shot rang out and the already febrile group reacted as if they had received a charge of electricity. A soldier –a sergeant- burst into the cabin barely able to speak he was so terrified. Volkov, glad of the diversion, grabbed him and shook him.

'What's the matter, sergeant? Speak clearly or I'll have you court martialled!'

The man calmed down and said that the prisoner in the cage had managed to break out and had run off into the forest followed by three wolves. They had followed him but, and here the man began to retch. Irina found an old bucket and he promptly threw up into it. This made Volkov furious and he slapped the soldier twice across his vomit-stained mouth, sending strings of bile everywhere. There was a commotion outside. A lot of shouting and confusion.

'What the hell is going on?' demanded Stalin, visibly frightened. Ludmila sprang to his side and cocked her rifle, ready to defend her Leader to the death. The sergeant slowly came to his senses and told them that one of the soldiers who had been patrolling the perimeter of the station had gone missing. He –the sergeant- had found him, and the man gagged again, strung naked between two young birch trees. He had been castrated.

3

Private Ivan Petrovich Kozlov, aged 18 from the Perm *krai*, more specifically from the city of Berezhniki at the foot of the Ural mountains, stamped his felt-clad feet in the low-grade leather boots and blew on his bare hands. Proud to be part of the unit guarding his leader, he was none the less freezing his balls off in the middle of nowhere. They call this place Pustinya. Wilderness. What the fuck are we doing here? What is so special about the place with its caged-up wolves and shit? He had written to his mother a couple of days ago and told her he was on his way home and that he would have some leave and be able to visit them. She was glad he had escaped working in the coal mines like his father, glad that he had survived the War unlike his two older brothers, both killed invading Germany with the Red Army. He missed her cooking, missed his father's worrying cough and sarcastic comments. He wanted to share a Zhigulevskoye beer with his dad, tell his mother about the girl he was going to marry: Marya Andreevna Stepanova from nearby Solikamsk. She was small and plump and blonde with a wide mouth and a dirty smile which contrasted with his skinny frame and hangdog expression.

As he peered at the black line of the taiga ahead of him, the thought of Marya caused an ineffable stirring of the heart and a very effable stirring of his loins. She made love like a wild cat. Noisy and greedy, her nails clawing his back as she bucked under him, forcing him deeper. Other times she would straddle him and slide herself back and forth along his hard belly, something which made her shriek with abandon, and him groan with pleasure at the sight. He adjusted his stance and wondered if he dared risk masturbating. There was only him within fifty metres of the next sentry. A patrol had been set up in twenty-minute intervals. But for the occasional glimpse of the moon as the clouds parted, it was dark. Christ, he groaned inwardly, she was a proper animal and already pregnant. Which was why a wedding was necessary before anything showed. He rubbed his prick through the coarse woollen trousers and then couldn't stop. His hand went into his underwear and he throttled his organ violently as he imagined her on top of him, her small plump breasts shaking madly as she tightened on him and forced him deeper into her … A braided leather rope tightened round his neck. Both hands went automatically to tear it away. He felt a huge body –man? animal?- pull him backwards. The creature's stench was overpowering. Ivan kicked and thrashed in a desperate panic. The ligature grew tighter and tighter as whoever it was pulled it around his neck. He felt his eyeballs bulging as he struggled to breathe. He struggled with all his strength but without a sound. His windpipe was being crushed. He could see the clouds sailing across the moon. He could see Marya. She was smiling, naked. He wanted to breathe, shout out her name. His mother. He wanted to call her, he wanted to say, 'Mother, help me!' but nothing came out. His lungs were bursting, the ligature was biting deeper, his head was pounding with a sound like a steam hammer … then everything went black and private Ivan Petrovich Kozlov was dead.

He never felt the creature drag his skinny, hairless boy's body into the forest. He didn't feel it being spreadeagled between two birch trees. Nor did he feel his woollen trousers and his underwear being pulled from his hips and the creature cupping his testicles in his hand then stuffing the whole scrotum into his mouth tearing it from his body. The creature spat the fleshy sac and the two rubbery eggs bloodily on to the snow, said one word –'Bolshevik!'- then lifted up his face and howled at the bashful moon, before running deeper into the black and silent taiga.

As Ivan was urgently pulling himself toward a climax, Semyon was scrabbling at a weak point in the mesh in a cage two hundred yards behind him. The Georgian was able to pull a small section free where it overlapped with another. The wolves sniffed at what he was doing then started to dig themselves. They had often searched for such a weak point but had never found it, now they were ecstatic with the thought of freedom. They whined and whimpered and dug furiously. Semyon let their powerful adamantine claws tear up the black earth in clods, his own hands too bloody and raw, wrists choked by Ludmila's steel manacles. Soon he was able to peel back a section large enough for a man to get through. The brothers Karamazov didn't stand on ceremony and slipped like eels through the narrow gap. They ran silently across the snow with Semyon in stumbling pursuit. He heard a shout and a thud as something slammed into the ground beside him quickly followed by a loud report. Someone had seen him. He picked up his pace and dived into the trees as the shouts of soldiers faded behind him. He felt he could run like the wolves now because his life depended on it.

Ludmila accompanied Volkov to where the still-traumatised soldier led them. One of the trucks bathed the scene in the full glare of its headlights. She could see the body of young private Kozlov hanging between the birch poles. Another soldier was being sick. Volkov ordered them back to their posts with a roar and strode over to the grisly installation. Who the hell had done this? He wondered. It was barbaric. More to the point, how had they done it? An armed guard ringed the place with a frequent patrol. And yet someone had got through and done … this. He looked at the young private's bloated face and touched his cheek, tenderly. He watched as Ludmila combed the ground for clues. She checked footprints, but tutted irritably at the churned-up snow caused by the other soldiers' boots. However, a clear trail was visible leading inevitably into the forest. She examined the prints. They were large, hobnailed. The same footwear the Georgian prisoner wore. Then she peered at the bloody debris in the snow. She teased it with her finger and grimaced.

Stalin walked into the pool of light cast by the headlamps. He was flanked by a bodyguard of soldiers whose eyes darted everywhere but were inexorably drawn to the mutilated body of their comrade. Petrenko, Lysenko, and finally Irina and Grigori brought up the rear. Stalin stared at the corpse. Irina clung to her father.

'These don't look like they have been cut off. The flesh is ragged and torn.' Ludmila said almost to herself as she examined the young man's discarded genitals

'Bitten.'

Ludmila looked up at the sound of the only other female voice.

'Why bitten?'

Grigori intervened. 'It's what the herders do to certain male reindeer. They castrate them with their teeth. It's an honour usually given to the women.'

'You're saying a woman did this?' Ludmila asked incredulously.

'I'm not saying that. I am just telling you the custom. Male herders do it too.'

Stalin watched the two women and Grigori closely. He was shivering. Volkov wondered whether it was just the cold. He took off his own greatcoat and offered it to his leader. Stalin shook his head.

'Is this some ritual killing of one of our soldiers?' he asked.

The question was addressed to no one in particular.

'No, comrade Marshal. It is obvious who has done this.' She looked up from her crouched position and made eye contact with Irina and then Grigori. 'The escaped prisoner.'

At that moment a howl rang out across the frozen snow. A single howl that wasn't this time picked up by the caged wolves. A howl that had something choral, something of the high-domed church about it.

More snow fell, obliterating tracks. A search party was despatched in one of the vehicles, its young occupants eager for revenge if slightly unnerved by their mission. They checked and re-checked the latest automatic rifle they had been issued with, the so-called AK-47 developed by the gunsmith Kalashnikov, and felt a little more reassured.

4

Ludmila returned with the group to the compound. Together they examined the gap in the fence. Irina told her that the wolves had done it. It would have been impossible for a man, especially with hands as injured and restricted as Semyon's. Nor could he have killed a man, she concluded.

'The victim was strangled by a powerful man and his genitals torn off by teeth. It is precisely how a man whose hands were bound would have killed someone,' Ludmila retorted without pausing for thought.

Irina shook her head in despair and led her father into the cabin. She politely ushered Stalin, Lysenko and Volkov back into the warmth. Only Volkov acknowledged her gesture with a nod and a brief smile.

Irina brewed more tea and served it to her guests. It was a hospitality as automatic as breathing, despite the leaden hopelessness she felt. She pretended not to overhear as Volkov, Stalin and Lysenko became engaged in an increasingly vocal argument. Lysenko was frantic with fear after what he had just seen and Stalin was agreeing with him and saying they should go. Volkov however was making a plea that he remain with a few hand-picked soldiers and try and catch the murderer of private Kozlov. With a petulant gesture of his hands, Stalin made a decision. They would leave and Volkov would remain with the search party. The killer would be hunted down and captured in 72 hours, after which time Volkov would return to his duties at the Kremlin. The change wrought in the old soldier was rejuvenating. The years fell from him, the rounded shoulders straightened, the jowls disappeared, the eyes sparkled. He shook Stalin warmly by the hand and embraced him, kissing him on both cheeks. He promised to have the killer in custody, his wretched carcass thrown bound and gagged at his leader's feet. Stalin pushed him away and taking a final gulp of tea, nodded to Ludmila only and strode out on to the porch. As Volkov issued orders to his subordinates and vehicles were started up and mobilised, Stalin called Ludmila over to him.

'As a Soviet law-enforcer, I expect you to be at the Colonel's right hand all the time. That killer must be found and dealt with. As for the professor and his daughter, make plans for their deportation to Moscow to stand trial.' Stalin was silent as the body of the young private, bundled into a military tarpaulin, was being loaded into one of the trucks.

Petrenko sidled up to them and said, 'Comrade Marshal, I will see that the report on the professor's crimes is on your desk and the desk of comrade Lysenko within the week.' Stalin turned and looked at the eager flushed face of the people's commissar. After a pause in which he seemed to be assessing Petrenko's significance, Stalin nodded and replied, 'Good work, comrade commissar. You are to be highly commended.' Before Petrenko could fawn any further, Stalin walked to his waiting armoured car, hurriedly followed by Lysenko, who acknowledged no one.

'We have done great work today, comrade Sirotovska,' said Petrenko, waving inanely at the departing giants.

Ludmila looked at him coolly. 'My work isn't over, comrade Petrenko,' she said and turned on her heel to re-enter the cabin. She turned back to him. 'Remember what I said. You make one move toward me …' She left the rest unsaid.

Petrenko almost whimpered as he watched the snow begin to fall.

Semyon kept running for an hour. The brothers Karamazov slowed so he could keep up, sometimes shunting him with their snouts, at other times snapping at his heels. Semyon was astounded that they would stay with him. He thought they would have left him long ago and joined whatever pack they could. Perhaps the professor was right and that some wolves were dogs after all? But further reflection ended there. He was simply glad of their company and their warmth as they settled down to sleep beneath one of the million larch trees in the taiga. He cleared snow from the roots of the tree and exposed a bed of damp needles. He took off his coat and lay on top of it and the brothers curled round him in a foul-breathed, furry embrace. Mitya licked the blood that still oozed from the lacerations he had received. Semyon accepted his ministrations gratefully. They seemed to ease the pain -whether in reality or just psychologically it didn't matter- and he fell into a deep sleep. As he drifted off, he thought he was at war again and could hear the shouts of dying men.

A great weight had been lifted from Volkov's shoulders. He felt he was twenty-five again. In effect he had been down-graded to the rank of corporal in charge of five private soldiers armed with light machine guns, but he felt he could storm ramparts. The arthritis melted from his joints as he sat on the battered leather couch and asked if there was any vodka, or better still any French brandy, wine or –not to seem unpatriotic- Russian champagne? Irina found him a bottle of Georgian red wine and a glass and he toasted her several times. He invited Grigori to share the bottle with him. Grigori pulled himself out of his despondent torpor and agreed to drink with him. Recklessly, Volkov asked to hear another jazz record and pleaded graciously with Irina for a cooked meal. Petrenko and Ludmila exchanged glances. Volkov noticed.

'While the cat's away –is that what you're thinking? Eh, commissar? Don't worry, the Marshal himself played the forbidden music. Who am I to question his taste? If it comes to that, who are you?'

He laughed a laugh so liberated it was infectious. It made Irina think their plight was not so grim. It even made Grigori smile. He rose to choose another record. He returned Bessie Smith carefully to her sleeve and pulled out Glenn Miller's band playing String of Pearls. Volkov couldn't contain himself and pulled Ludmila to her feet and asked her to dance. She responded stiffly and held the colonel at arms length as if his breath repelled her. Volkov didn't notice. In fact he seemed to be revelling in embarrassing these two figures of totalitarian authority. He ordered Petrenko to dance with Irina, who tried to excuse herself on the grounds of preparing a meal. Petrenko, never one to disobey an order, meekly pulled Irina on to the floor and danced clumsily and self-consciously with her. Volkov laughed and stamped his feet, out of time with the music.

Ludmila had never felt so ill at ease. What does this senior military figure, personal aide to our Leader no less, think he was doing? Her arms were draped about the colonel's stout, compact body, her feet moving deftly away from the clumping military boots. She knew he wasn't drunk yet. She could not understand where his exuberance was coming from. But then she had never really tried to discover where another's behaviour originated unless it involved a crime. She knew why criminals did things. She knew their motivation. They stole what they couldn't buy, cheated those they couldn't trust, raped those they couldn't control, murdered those they couldn't tolerate. It was fairly simple. It was their actions she responded to not their innermost thoughts or complex emotions. She could never instinctively feel the needs of someone else, much less put their needs before hers.

Irina could make little sense of the change in mood of the colonel either. There was obviously a release of tension at the departure of the most powerful man in Russia. They all felt that. But there was something else and she could only presume that the old man was in some way liberated far beyond the absence of a boss but in his whole spirit. He was like a little boy, doing something forbidden, enjoying the perturbation and disapproval of authority figures. And now he had made her dance with this reptilian commissar who even now she could feel was aroused by her closeness. His breathing was heavy and his nostrils flared trying to inhale as much of her scent as possible. It was what Kolya did to her crotch on occasion and she shuddered at the thought.

Finally, when the music stopped and the disc revolved scratchily on the turntable, Volkov allowed them all to sit down. Irina was aware of Petrenko's hungry eyes upon her. She was aware of her father sinking deeper and deeper into depression. She asked him to help her peel vegetables. He rose sluggishly and hauled a hessian sack of potatoes from the larder, took a knife, sat on a low three-legged stool and began to peel. Volkov found another bottle of wine, opened it and thrust a glass at her. She had no choice but to accept and take a drink. Volkov nodded in approval, handed the bottle to Petrenko and began a conversation with her father.

'Tell me, comrade professor, in language a simple peasant-soldier can understand, what is Lysenko's … *difficulty* with you and your work here in the wilderness?'

Grigori looked at the old soldier and his thoughts raced. Does he want me to incriminate myself further? Is it an innocent enquiry? What happens if I refuse to answer? He decided it would be prudent to offer some reply.

'Professor Lysenko …' he began, but Volkov cut him short.

'Professor? Professor of what? Planting trees?' He guffawed. 'I planted more trees than him with my old man when I was a snot-nosed kid of ten! He's no more a professor than those spuds you're peeling! In fact I'd sooner listen to a potato than that prick Lysenko. Don't you agree? Professor?' He roared with laughter.

'Do I agree …?'

'That the man's a complete cunt. Yes or no?'

Grigori was looking for a trap, but the man was so exuberant, so expansive, that he took him at his word and replied, 'He is certainly unqualified in a professional sense, but he can talk to the workers on the land. He understands their language, he …'

Again Volkov cut him off. 'He talks shit. He talks like a stupid bone-headed peasant cunt. He's an idiot who's been promoted to a celebrity by our Leader, am I right Commisar?'

He turned and jutted his chin at Petrenko and challenged him to reply in the affirmative.

'Comrade colonel, I don't think it's my place to pass comment on a man so highly regarded by our Leader.'

'Good answer,' Volkov responded urbanely. 'It's easy to see why you rose in the ranks. What about you, militiawoman … what's your name?'

'Sirotovska, colonel.'

'Comrade Sirotovska, what is your opinion of the great Lysenko?'

'It is not my place to have opinions, colonel. I just enforce the law.'

'Another good answer.' Volkov grunted ironically and took another large gulp of wine. 'You'll both go far. You have the measure of the machine.'

As Irina chopped the onions and dropped them hissing and spitting into the pan of hot oil, followed by cubes of reindeer meat, potato, carrot and swede, she wondered where the colonel was going with his questions.

Volkov took off his boots and leant forward to Grigori. 'So what are you two fighting about?' he asked quietly. He opened a cigarette case and took out a thin ready-made, hand-rolled cigarette, lit it and inhaled deeply, snapping the case shut. 'Why is our esteemed genius so pissed off with you? And your wolves?' He leant back and waited for a reply, his eyes narrowing as he drew deeply on the cigarette.

Grigori looked at Irina who shook her head imperceptibly. Grigori looked at her as if to make it clear he had no choice but to answer truthfully, then he said, 'Colonel do you mind if I smoke?'

Volkov gave a dismissive wave of his hand and shrugged. Grigori took out his pipe and lit it.

'Comrade Lysenko does not believe in what I believe in, essentially. It's complicated ...'

'Too complicated for a simple military man, eh?' There was no malice in the question, just charming self-deprecation. 'A pity our Leader appears to agree with Lysenko and not with you.'

Volkov contuniued to quiz Grigori about his work and seemed to grasp exactly what the issues were, Irina thought, as she listened to their conversation about genetics and wolves and inherited characteristics and Lysenko's influence over Stalin. The whole scene observed from her position at the stove was becoming more and more unreal. She and her father were essentially prisoners in their own home while outside a group of soldiers was pursuing Semyon in the belief that he had killed and mutilated their comrade. She watched Ludmila and the ferrety Petrenko following the conversation with, she felt, some unease on their part. It was free and open and the colonel seemed genuinely interested in what Grigori had to say.

Occasionally, Petrenko would look in her direction. He was leering at her, she was sure. She felt she was going insane. She had to get out and breathe some air before she suffocated.

'I would like permission to use the privy,' she blurted out. They could hardly deny her that.

Ludmila looked up and said, 'I will come with you.' She started to rise, but Petrenko interjected and said, 'No, officer Sirotovska, you need to hear what the professor has to say. I will accompany her.' He smiled a ghastly smile at Irina and rose and waited for Irina to move away from the stove and past him.

'I am quite able to use the privy on my own, thank you,' Irina managed, but Petrenko interrupted.

'Have you forgotten there is a killer on the loose outside the cabin?'

'No, I have not forgotten, comrade commissar.' She looked at him wondering what use he would be against a man who could kill and castrate another man in minutes and hang him out to dry. And she definitely didn't like the way he was looking at her. Grigori then offered to go with her himself. Ludmila, alert to any possibility of her charges escaping, said that was out of the question - though how she thought they would escape and last half an hour in those freezing temperatures was a mystery to father and daughter. In the end, Irina nodded her reluctant assent and went out into the night with Petrenko.

The air was savagely cold. Irina hugged herself and marched quickly to the wooden privy. She told Petrenko to stand several yards away from the door and he did as he was told. She slammed the door shut.

A low wind was moaning through the trees and the sky was heavy with snow clouds. Thick flakes of snow played on Petrenko's face as he stood in his thin city shoes and shivered. But the shivering was not so much from the cold as from an almost overwhelming sexual desire. A desire that had been blocked by Ludmila with a threat he was sure she would have no hesitation in carrying out. He moved nearer the leaning wooden shack. He could hear the young woman pissing volubly and copiously. His nostrils flared. He could smell the urine as it was expelled from her body. He clutched himself and almost howled in delicious agony. The smell of ammonia and the mental picture he had of this beautiful young woman crouched half-naked was acting like a powerful aphrodisiac and he was beside himself with lust.

The badly-fitting door opened with difficulty and Irina grunted with the effort of forcing it open. She looked up to discover Petrenko standing over her, quivering with desire. He was breathing heavily and leaning towards her. Irina wanted to scream but a cold hand was clamped over her mouth as she was pushed back into the privy. She sat back on the seat and started to kick with her legs, but the people's commissar found strength from the surging hormones in his bloodstream and he forced her legs down. 'Lie still and don't say anything about this or it will be worse for you and your father!' he hissed at her in the darkness. He groped under her thick woollen skirt for her underwear.

A low growl came from somewhere behind him, then a powerful force gripped the back of his neck and he was pulled backwards. He yelped in pain and fear as Kolya dragged his body through the snow, shaking him like a plaything. He could feel the animal's teeth sinking deeper into his neck and the foul breath of the wolf filled his nostrils. Petrenko screamed out in abject fear as inscisor and canine went to work on his thin flesh. Irina screamed too.

'Kolya, no! No!' The animal paused and looked at his mistress, his alpha-female, in puzzlement. Irina took hold of Kolya's powerful neck and physically pulled him from the throat of the commissar. Kolya's jaws had unlocked momentarily and he allowed himself to be torn from his prey, who by now was stinking of urine and faeces. Petrenko had soiled himself. Such a powerful odour of fear and submission would normally have sent the wolf into a killing frenzy, but his mistress clung on to his neck with all her weight and there was no way he could break free without hurting her, and this he could not do.

Ludmila emerged from the cabin alerted by the commotion, quickly followed by the others.

'What is going on? What has happened to the commissar? Did your wolf attack him?' Ludmila demanded in rapid fire.

'The animal tried to kill me!' wailed Petrenko. 'I demand he be shot this instant!'

Ludmila caught a whiff of Petrenko's stench. She winced. 'Is this true?' she asked Irina.

'Kolya thought the commissar was attacking me.'

'And was he?'

There was a short pause.

'Shoot the beast, now! Give me your gun. I will do it!' shrieked Petrenko hysterically. 'It tried to tear my throat out!' Blood oozed between the fingers gripping his neck.

'If he had wanted to do that you would already be dead,' said Irina flatly.

Ludmila repeated her question to Irina. She was a police officer. It was second nature. 'Did he try to attack you?'

Irina looked at Petrenko lying on the ground and made sure he had her full attention.

'Kolya was only doing his duty, comrade commisar. He should not be shot for that.'

I'm keeping quiet for the wolf's sake, not yours, her expression said quite clearly – at least to Petrenko.

Petrenko understood. He said, 'Very well. He is a guard animal and perhaps he did mistake me for some sort of intruder, so …let him live.'

'That is exactly what happened. Kolya mistook the commissar for an intruder and acted true to his nature,' Irina stated woodenly.

Ludmila eyed her steadily, then said, 'Move away from the animal.'

Irina screamed, 'No!'

Ludmila raised the rifle and aimed it at the pair. 'Move!'

In what seemed to be a single movement, Irina shouted at the wolf to go and dived toward Ludmila, knocking her sideways. The rifle went off, firing harmlessly into the air. Kolya vanished into the dark.

Ludmila scrambled to her feet and retrieved the weapon.

'That was a stupid thing to do', was all she said, but glared furiously at the other woman. She looked round at the group. Grigori had rushed to Irina and was helping her to her feet. Volkov stood to one side stroking his moustache, his emotions unclear.

'Commisar Petrenko get yourself cleaned up as best you can,' Ludmila said, taking charge. 'The rest of you, inside.' She added a 'please colonel' as she acknowledged Volkov's presence.

Grigori put his arms around his daughter's shoulders and leant his head into her. She refused to meet his questioning gaze as they went back into the cabin.

Ludmila stood a moment staring into the darkness, as the remaining wolves whined and fretted in their cages.

5

Dawn broke, pale and bleak. Semyon stirred. One of the wolves grunted and snuffled. The pain in his hands and wrists was almost unbearable, despite the attention of his comrades. He got to his feet, slowly and painfully. Away from the warmth of the animals' coats, the air was bitingly cold. The other wolves woke, immediately alert and looked up at him, awaiting orders. There was something about the early morning air that wasn't normal. The screams in the night? Had they been a dream or had they been real? To his left, crows had gathered in their hundreds and seemed to be more than usually raucous. He gathered snow into his inflamed palms to try and ease the pain. As it melted he put some to his lips, then followed the sound of the crows.

He soon discovered the reason for the corvids' excitement. In a clearing made by several windblown pines, five soldiers lay staring beatifically at the washed-out sky, their throats cut and their bowels glistening and bloody in the snow. The wolves ran past him. There was nothing Semyon could do to stop them as they tore at the intestines of the men and buried their snouts in the viscera, rooting for liver and lights. Ribs were demolished with a terrible cracking sound and the wolves' fur was spattered and smeared with blood as they gorged on the remains of the young soldiers. Each animal had his own carcass. There was no need to wait as the pack-leader took the most nutritious organs or the tastiest joints from a single kill. There was plenty for all.

Semyon watched, revolted and relieved. These men had been sent to capture him after all. He looked around for their weapons but couldn't see any. Whoever had done this had taken them. *Whoever had done this.* For one, gut-chilling moment he thought that maybe *he* had done it. That what the militiawoman believed was true, that he was the brutal killer who had butchered a herdsman and kidnapped one of their children. *And now this!* The crows were wheeling about the clearing or perching on adjacent trees. A few buzzards and jays kept a safe distance, mewing as they drifted in the milky air. Some of the crows descended on to the bodies ignored by the wolves and began to feed. They bickered noisily, aware that soon there would be others, opportunists and scavengers like them, who would catch the scent of fresh kill on the wind.

Semyon walked further on, following the tracks in the snow where the men had been dragged. It seemed as if the killer had picked them off one by one in the darkness, murdered them swiftly with a knife and then painstakingly laid them out in the clearing and disembowelled them. Semyon wondered at the brute's power. Was he even human? He dismissed the thought and walked on. There was no sign of the vehicle. This was no surprise as the trees were too close together to manoevre a truck and they would have abandoned it hours ago and continued their search on foot. Semyon grunted at the stupidity of trying to track him at night. Five inexperienced soldiers in terrain they didn't know. He thanked the Lord God for his deliverance and then laughed that the agent of his deliverance seemed to be the devil in bestial form. He knelt in the snow and joined his injured hands in thanksgiving, bellowing out the Lord's

Prayer and weeping at the same time. Fully in the moment of prayer and salutation, he gave no thought to his own continued survival in this unforgiving - but by no means Godforsaken- wilderness. He sang a hymn of joy and endurance and laughed as the crows mocked him and the Brothers Karamazov howled in harmony.

At the Field Study centre, Volkov was also feeling a *joie de vivre* he had not felt for decades. He had slept on the couch wrapped only in his greatcoat and but he had risen as fresh as any twenty-year old. He outlined a plan of action with the militiawoman. His men had not returned. They would have to go after them, regroup and search for the killer.

Grigori had bandaged Petrenko's neck and given him some of his old clothes. Irina refused to wash his soiled clothes and they were burnt in the stove. He was still asleep as the rest stood in consultation around a map spread out on a rickety card table.

At first Ludmila had objected to the inclusion of Grigori and his daughter, but Volkov had pulled his considerable rank and insisted that local knowledge was always the best in any plan. They would need to enlist the help of the herders. Volkov had gleaned that Irina especially was trusted by the Evenk.

Grigori drove with Volkov beside him. Ludmila kept careful watch over Irina in the back of the truck. The old ZIS made slow progress through the fresh snow. As they travelled Ludmila sat hunched with the rifle across her knees. She looked at Irina without blinking for a long time. Irina pretended not to notice and stared out through the slats, the icy wind whipping the hair across her face, her cheeks bruised with the cold. After a while Ludmila spoke.

'What you did was really stupid and you will have to answer for it when the time comes.'

'What did I do wrong? I tried to save an innocent animal from being murdered,' Irina said evenly, not looking in the other woman's direction.

'You obstructed an officer in the lawful exercise of her duty.'

'Do you know how pompous you sound, Ludmila?' Irina turned to look at her. The contempt was clear in every muscle of her face.

'I don't care how I sound to you. Your opinion as a traitor to the Soviet People is of no consequence.'

'Do you know that commissar Petrenko tried to rape me?'

'I don't believe you.' She did.

'Why do you think Kolya attacked him?'

Ludmila shrugged. 'Because he is an animal. A wolf. And that is what wolves do. Attack people. Which is why they should be shot.'

'Petrenko tried to rape me and he would probably have succeeded if Kolya hadn't dragged him off!' Irina's frustration with Ludmila's obtuseness made her want to scream.

'You are accusing an officer of the state, a People's Commisar, of a very serious crime. It is obvious why. You hope that it will deflect me from your own situation and your father's.'

Irina knew she wouldn't get any further with her. 'Kolya is a good and noble animal. He looked after me. Whereas you and that People's Commisar' –she spat those two words- 'are little more than savage beasts! You hide behind your uniforms and your pompous legal language and your titles but underneath you are animals, worse!' She stopped abruptly. 'What are you doing?'

Ludmila had pulled her notebook from her coat and was writing with a stub of black pencil. 'I am writing down everything you are saying. For your trial.'

'You bitch!'

Ludmila wrote that down too and looked up at the other woman as if to ask her if she wanted to say anything else. Unwisely, Irina continued.

'You fucking cold-hearted bitch! My father is a good man. All he wants is the best for his country. He didn't hurt the ... the girls in the film. He didn't hurt *me*! He was carrying out a scientific investigation into ... into how people behave. It's not wrong if it is seeking after truth and... and for the betterment of people in our country, if not the whole world! Stop writing, you fucking cow! Stop it!'

Irina made a grab for the notebook but Ludmila snatched it out of her reach and planted her boot in Irina's stomach pushing her back against the boards. Then she trained her rifle on the now sobbing woman.

'Listen to me. You are guilty of aiding and abetting your father in a crime against the state. You will be taken into custody, tried and most certainly convicted. Get in my way and you will be sorry! Do you understand?'

By this point she had thrust her face close to Irina's and her fury was ice-cold. She repeated her question, as Irina curled tighter into herself weeping uncontrollably. 'Do. You. Under -stand?'

Irina nodded and her whole body shook. She had a curious feeling that this cruelty had been visited upon her a long time ago by someone else. Images, smells, sounds flashed through her brain. The feel of a birch switch across the back of bare legs, locked in the dark unable to breathe, something clawing her face, dizzying heights, a sense of falling, an animal fear surging through her whole body.

Or perhaps it was the film of those two little girls. The words pounded in her ears. *Do you understand?* She felt she wanted to be sick. For her part, Ludmila felt something similar in the sense that this was a place she had been before, but the complete reverse of what Irina was feeling. She only felt satisfaction, a sense of power and the ability to control another human being, of curiosity as she observed the tears and the blood and heard the screams and the pleading.

The toxic bond that the moment created was gone in seconds. Ludmila pulled away from Irina and sat back against the side of the truck, aware of a slight pulse and dampness between her legs, as if she had been somehow aroused by the whole thing. Irina remained curled in a foetal ball, silent now, cocooned in fear and revulsion for her tormentor.

6

Their arrival at the herders' encampment caused a stir. The children rushed up as the white-haired man in the soldier's uniform got out of the cab. Innaksa's father came forward, with Innaksa next to him, clutching Uluki and smiling now for the first time. The shaman hung back and glowered as this symbol of godless Soviet power looked around at the wary faces of the herders. Ludmila had alighted from the truck and stood at the Colonel's side.

The shaman finally lost patience –or his fear- and stepped forward. He spoke fast and dismissively, spat, then walked back to his place.

'Who is this clown?' Volkov asked.

'The local shaman. They only listen to him. He believes it was a wolf-spirit,' said Ludmila.

Volkov pulled back his substantial shoulders and spoke. 'Listen. I want your help to capture this murderer, call him a spirit, call him what you like. But the killer has escaped from us and killed one of my men and I mean to hunt him down today. I can only do this with your help. You know the terrain. You can help me. Translate this for me somebody.'

Innaksa's father spoke. 'I understood. I will tell them what you said, but we want something in return.' He looked steadily at the colonel and drew on his thin cigarette.

'What's that?' Volkov asked, his face hardening.

'You tell Moscow people, we want to be left alone. No collectivization. No kolkhoz. Reindeer herders free people. We follow herds.'

'I will get that message to the authorities in Moscow,' Volkov said fully intending to do it but also knowing it would have no effect whatever. 'Anything else?'

Innaksa's father looked at him suspiciously, then shook his head. He shouted to the other herders and they began to move about the camp, one releasing the dogs, another saddling reindeer, the women fetching coats and parcelling up food for the men. As Irina slipped her arm through her father's and clung to him, they watched as Innaksa's father selected five or six men to be the hunting party. Innaksa himself sidled up to Irina. She ran her fingers through his hair and put her free arm around him. A reindeer was prepared for Volkov and he leapt into the saddle with the agility of a man thirty years younger. He felt alive trying to gain some control as the disgruntled animal underneath him protested at his weight. He was a soldier, a man of action, and action was what he missed.

'Officer Sirotovska, you stay here with the prisoners. We will call at the field station compound so the dogs can get a scent of the quarry.'

Seeing that she was about to protest, he silenced her with a look. 'Your job is to guard the people you have arrested. I know you will do an excellent job. We will have your killer back by nightfall – alive or dead.'

Irina shuddered as Ludmila acquiesced with a solemn nod to the old soldier's commands. They watched the search party leave and turned back to the truck.

7

When they got back to the field centre, they found Petrenko had gone mad.

Bare-headed and bare-footed in the snow, dressed in Grigori's ill-fitting shirt and trousers, he was poking a birch pole into the wolves' compound and screaming and even growling at them. The wolves snarled and bit at the stick. Sometimes they gripped it and pulled the skinny commissar toward them. He frantically tore it from their jaws and moved on to another cage and repeated his attack, screaming curses at the bemused and excited animals. The bandage around his neck was soaked red with new blood, but he didn't seem to notice. Ludmila ran up to him immediately and slapped him hard across the face, once, twice, three times. Petrenko fell backwards and held his forearm across his face. He whimpered and howled and then burst into tears.

Irina could feel little pity for him as Ludmila ordered her and her father to help Petrenko back to the cabin. They almost had to drag him there. Irina saw his feet were raw and swollen and painfully cold. His face was purple and his teeth couldn't stop chattering.

Eventually they got him inside and Irina found a blanket for him. He wrapped it around himself, shivering violently. He wouldn't look at her but stared straight ahead of him like the madman in the Gogol story, Irina thought, rocking and shaking and talking complete gibberish. Ludmila ordered him to go to bed and demanded that Grigori change his bandages. But Petrenko would let him nowhere near him. Instead he blundered into Ludmila's bedroom and lay curled crosswise at the bottom of her bed.

Irina made more tea and all three sat in silence around the tin trunk filled with the incriminating documents and cans of film. Each one of them was preoccupied with their own thoughts. Grigori was becoming almost torpid with despair. He had the sensation of being wound into some giant cocoon by skeins of sticky thread. He was beginning to doubt the reality of his situation. Is this how it ends? All my work? Everything I've done? Other thoughts pushed these aside, as he experienced gut-wrenching feelings of remorse for what he had drawn Irina into. In Moscow she would have been safe, away from this, studying hard, finding someone to share her life, working in some laboratory, thinking about a family. Instead she was here and he had incriminated her.

Ludmila stared at the trunk with resentment. She would have preferred to have been hunting down the man she had arrested for murder. But that honour would go to Volkov. Then again, she would have the greater honour of taking in two political criminals now that Petrenko had apparently lost his mind. What to do with him? He was a burden, a nuisance. She dismissed these thoughts as secondary and became aware of Irina's large blue eyes staring at her like a silent predator. Implacable.

Irina's thoughts had hardened into tempered steel. She hated this woman who had brought destruction into their lives. That she, Irina, had brought her in only increased the burning anger she felt. The woman was supposed to have caught a vicious murderer but all she had done was mercilessly hunt down an innocent man and arrest her and her father - *for what crime*? For investigating wild canines in the middle of a barren wilderness?

She continued to stare with the mindful presence of an animal even when she knew Ludmila was aware of her. Ludmila stared back and then sipped her tea and turned away. Irina continued to stare.

'What is on your mind comrade Medvedenka?' Ludmila asked.

Irina said nothing but continued to stare.

'If you commit a crime, you must pay the price. It is simple. You look at me as if you would like to kill me, but it won't change anything.'

Irina said nothing but her gaze remained fixed on the other woman.

Swiftly and without warning Ludmila struck Irina across the face and sent her reeling backwards. Grigori leapt to his feet and protested, at the same time struggling to help Irina up. He could see there was blood on her lips. He took out a handkerchief and gave it to his daughter. She took it, wordlessly, and resumed her penetrating examination of the militia woman.

Ludmila shrugged. 'All right, you may stare at me for as long as you wish. It will change nothing. As I said.'

She sat back and wondered what success the search party was having.

Volkov felt every inch the Russian hero though he knew he must look pretty absurd mounted on a protesting reindeer he barely knew how to handle. He watched the other herdsmen and picked up quickly the best way to control the animal but it was hard going. He felt no tiredness however, only a surge of animal energy. He didn't feel the cold either, just the bracing tonic of the clear, silent air.

They had called at the field station and found an item of Semyon's clothing which they had allowed the dogs to examine. The dogs knew what was required of them. All the human beings needed to do was follow them as best they could.

Volkov jabbed the reindeer's flanks with his heels and forced it into a faster and faster pace. His thick hands were burning with cold but he ignored the growing numbness and pain. He was determined to find the brutal killer of one of his men. Every nerve in his body, every chemical, every drop of his military blood was engaged in that single objective.

After perhaps two hours, the herders' dogs became very agitated. In their inventory, they also had the scent of the three Dostoyevskian wolves -and there was something else. Volkov noticed an unusual number of birds circling one particular spot, to which the dogs were now hurtling, unstoppable. The reindeer riders duly followed.

They heard fierce yowling and yelping long before they saw anything. The guttural snarls, which chilled the blood and made human hackles rise, grew louder and louder. The reindeer bucked in terror under their riders.

As they drew nearer to a clearing in the trees Volkov witnessed a gladiatorial stand-off of Roman proportions. A black mass of carrion birds flew up cawing bitterly. On the snow-covered ground lay five bodies. On one side of the natural arena three wolves paced and growled, ears down, teeth bared. On the other side, six dogs displayed in exactly the same way. On the far side, Volkov could see the figure of a man, bearded, crouching behind a large conifer. That was their man. He could see that he was about to run and he took his rifle from his shoulder –the new-issue Kalshnikov- and aimed it at the figure and fired off one round. He fell to the ground as he crawled for cover.

All at once there was a terrible silence as the two groups of animals launched themselves at each other. A signal had been given and the combat begun. Volkov was stunned. Were these wild animals actually protecting the killer? There was not an ounce of altruism in their canine souls. Surely it was their food source they were defending? He was wrong. Two of the herders were running toward the fallen man and as they did, one of the wolves –Mitya- intercepted them, fighting off the two dogs who were determined to bring him down. He barred the herders' way to the wounded figure, repeatedly throwing the dogs almost bodily out of the way with his powerful jaws. But he was growing tired. The herders took their opportunity and put a bullet into the wolf and he fell dead immediately.

At the sound of the shot, the animals dispersed but such was their frenzy they quickly regrouped and returned to the fight. Along with the other herders, Volkov dismounted his kicking, plunging reindeer and let it run into the forest. He ran closer and was witness to the sheer brutal power of these animals as they clamped teeth to back and throat and tore gobbets of flesh one from another. The snow was red with blood. The odds were now three to one and the wolves were growing tired as they leapt at their attackers. But as they launched from the front, a dog would come in from the side and another from behind. The dogs were neither as big nor as desperate as the wolves but their number was deciding the outcome of the contest. The biggest hunting dog finally got his teeth into the throat of the second wolf –Alyosha- and held on, tearing deeper and deeper till the jugular was pierced and it was all over for him. Finally Vanya was the only wolf barely standing. He made a heroic leap at the lead hunting dog and left him yelping, his muzzle torn and bleeding, in a flurry of snow. But the rest of the pack were on him in an instant and all Volkov could see then was a shattered kaleidoscope of teeth, blood, claws, flank, fur and vulpine eyes widened in terror and aggression. Vanya was down and he gave a miserable yelp -one of the few sounds in a contest that was for the most part eerily silent- as the dogs finished their work and he lay still.

As the herders kept their dogs away from the dead bodies of the soldiers with whips and curses, Volkov steeled himself to examine them. He had seen many dead soldiers and dead civilians. They had just fought the bloodiest war in history and he had been a starved and desperate combatant and budding revolutionary in the one before that, but his sense of the sheer waste of lives never left him. He wondered why he had been spared when so many others had perished alongside him. He walked past the fallen boys. For that's what they were as far as he was concerned. Little more than children. Their heads were thrown back as if in some grotesque choral exultation. Their throats slashed, a knife brutally plunged into their entrails, their bowels coiled on the snow. He saw where the choughs and the jays and the buzzards and the crows had torn at the flesh, pulling the guts further from the boys' bellies, in one case pecking out the eyes. The cheated birds raised a collective cry of protest and a couple of the Evenki let off a few shots to disperse them. They flew up as one, only to resettle again and scream angrily at the herders.

Volkov then turned and strode toward the monster who had perpetrated this evil. He was sitting on the ground holding his foot. Apparently Volkov's shot had grazed his instep, not enough to cause him any serious harm but enough to prevent him running away. This was to Volkov's satisfaction as the bastard could now be taken to Moscow and brutally interrogated before being put on trial.

Volkov watched as the Georgian pulled off his boot then his bloodstained sock. The bullet had gouged the flesh and exposed bone. Semyon, grunting with pain, used the sock as a bandage to tie around his foot. He put the partially-destroyed boot back on and stood slowly. The herdsmen pulled back as he did so. He glowered at them as they pointed their rifles at him. Volkov noticed his torn and swollen hands.

'So, here is your wolf-spirit,' he said. 'He's just a man, like you or me. A common murderer.' However, he couldn't help feeling that the sight of this bearded, bloodied giant, staring arrogantly at his captors, in a field strewn with corpses, his three guardian wolves dead in the snow, carolled by massed choirs of cawing carrion birds and surrounded by the dark mystery of the taiga had something of legend about it. Out here, in the middle of nowhere, it was easy to believe in spirits.

Volkov watched as the herdsmen bound Semyon roughly with reindeer hide rope and made him walk -for a second time- behind one of the grunting beasts. He limped but never made one sound of protest or pain. Volkov rode next to him.

'So what have you got against my men, these boys you've slaughtered? What did they do to you?' Receiving no answer, he continued. 'Yes they were chasing you, hunting you and you had every right as prey to evade capture, even to retaliate. But this…' He gestured as they passed the rapidly freezing corpses. 'I can't even bury them. They will be food for the animals and the birds. They have mothers at home waiting for them. Girlfriends, wives maybe. Why? And why so sadistic, why so … ritualistic?' That was the word he was searching for. They had been butchered like sacrificial animals by a self-styled priest of some barbaric religion. But didn't the militiawoman say he was Orthodox?

That he sang hymns, attended banned religious services? And his demeanour. Almost Christlike in his endurance of suffering. He was the crucified not the crucifier. It would seem. But then, he thought, I'm just a simple soldier. What do I know about such things?

Semyon looked up at the thickset military man on his reindeer mount. 'I didn't kill those boys. I found them. I have killed no one. I am innocent.'

He said this simply and with magnificent dignity, Volkov thought.

'Then how do you explain the death of one of my other men at the scientific station? Who killed the herder and kidnapped the boy? You left an officer of the Soviet people to die in the freezing cold….'

'She was going to take me to Moscow for trial. I hadn't done anything but no one would have believed me. It was either me or her. What would you do?'

He asked this question with a childlike innocence. It wasn't rhetorical. It was almost pleading.

'Well, you will be facing trial now that's for sure, that's if these guys don't get you first!' He laughed and gestured to their herders riding behind them. They were grim-faced and deep in thought. Volkov knew what they were thinking. They have their killer and don't want to be cheated of revenge by some Russian arsehole in uniform. Maybe I should let them string him up from the nearest pine tree. After all, I am a military man not a law-officer or a politician. Things happen on the field and they need to be settled on the field.

These were his thoughts as he rode alongside his captive. He took in the passing landscape. How did people live here? A man could go mad with the endlessness of it. These herders, they were another race. They survive because of their relationship with the noisome, stertorous creature carrying me. Without that, there was no reason to be here in this desolation. And yet evil could flourish, even here. Men were beasts. They murder to survive. They murder because they can. This 'wolfman' was no wolf. He was one hundred per cent man. He killed for the pleasure of it. It's what men do. Not wolves.

It took them several hours to reach the herders' encampment and when they arrived they were met by a rider who tore up to Innaksa's father and delivered an urgent message. The rider was visibly disturbed. Innaksa's father looked at Semyon, who stared back without comprehension. Volkov demanded to know what was happening.

'Shaman is dead,' was all the reply he got.

Volkov was stunned. What could this mean? He wanted more information but was ignored as the herders spurred their reindeer towards the smoking tents. Semyon was forced into a painful, limping trot, almost being dragged along through the wet snow.

As they came nearer, they could see a fire burning. Again the vertical hollowed-out pine log was sending up twisting orange flames next to a birch-tree frame. Across the frame was spread-eagled the naked body of the shaman, his skin torn in sheets from his body, his intestines hanging in a bloody coil from his abdomen. The flayed visage stared at them and seemed to be mocking them as they passed. From the camp they could hear wailing and screaming, sounds of abject fear and distress distilling in the winter air. The wolfman was still out there and they had arrested an innocent man.

8

Lord help me to eliminate the savages and the Bolsheviks.
Come to me when I sleep and when I wake and speak to me.
I am chosen. I am a Believer. Guide me. Your Annointed.
Your Angel of Death.

Stepan Stepanovich Fedorovski was thinking. He ran his
fingers along the chain round his neck where the cross his
mother had given had been. He was thinking. That is to say
thoughts ran through his head, but it was not what could be
called thought in the sense that it was reflective. Reflective
thoughts double back on themselves, circle a little, go ahead
and come back, pause, and change direction. But these had
no place in Stepan Stepanovich's mind. He did not reflect.
He couldn't. His mind was ironclad and moved in one
direction. His thoughts had the single-mindedness of prayer.
The purity of instruction. Reflection only served to confuse.
From birth he had had no sense of what others felt. He had
observed pain in the animals he had caught in traps. As a
young boy-soldier fighting for the Whites in the Civil War,
he had watched men writhe in pain when shot in the stomach
on the battlefield. He had looked at them, head cocked to
one side, as they begged him to end their lives, begged him
to help them, begged him to tell their loved ones. Sometimes
he put a bullet in their skulls, other times he did not. It was a
practical decision. It depended on whether he could spare

the ammunition. Stepan Stepanovich was steeped in violence, bloodshed, death. When the Reds had invaded Ukraine, he had fought to keep them from over-running his homeland. A decade later, he had sat by the roadside and sold the limbs of the dead to anyone who could afford them. The only food they had were the corpses of those who had starved to death. There was little meat on their bones but people who had money or something to trade bought the arms, the legs, even the heads of the dead. This is what the Reds had done to Ukraine. His Ukraine, bread-basket of Russia. They had watched the corn ripen and then loaded it on trains to Moscow. His own mother had been shot by the zealous Young Communists who patrolled the edges of the cornfields. She had a handful of stolen corn in her hand. She was Ukranian. She was not entitled to corn. Stepan Stepanovich cradled her in his arms as she bled to death, vomiting blood over his clothes. He had dragged her body to the hut they lived in and after making the sign of the cross over her as she took her last breath, he dismembered her, cooked and ate her body. As he did so, he said the words of the Agnus Dei and crossed himself again, asking God's forgiveness. He sang a hymn and swore revenge. But he wouldn't weep. He never had nor ever would, for he didn't know what weeping was. But his God had told him that the Reds had done this and for that they must suffer and die.

Stepan Stepanovich murdered the two Young Communists patrolling the cornfields. He cut their throats with the same knife he had dismembered his mother. He took the arm of one of them and wrapped it in sacking and fled north into Siberia. The arm sustained him long enough until he had become adept at trapping and hunting small animals. He had been caught trying to steal a reindeer calf from a herding pen and had been chased for days into the taiga by herders whom he knew would show no mercy if they caught him. He had eluded them at one point by digging a hole and almost burying himself alive and staying still for two whole days while the dogs searched in vain for a scent of this feral human imbued in every pore with the *chernozem*, the black earth, that extended from his home even into this wilderness. But eventually they caught him and hung him naked from a skinning frame, flogged him savagely with reindeer-hide cord, then let him go. Now they too were on his death-list. He wandered deeper and deeper into the taiga, for survival befriending a pack of Siberian Grey wolves who tolerated him but kept him at the bottom of their pecking order. He murdered a lone, drunken fur trapper and stole his rifle and sled, his reindeer and his dogs, and made a livelihood trading with the local kolkhoz, but living alone, staying away from all human contact. As another war raged beyond the Urals, he had stayed hidden in the forest and bided his time.

Now he was a thing unleashed. The herders were beginning to pay. He had despatched two, almost three. And the Bolsheviks. Those boys he had tracked and slaughtered like deer. He had their rifles and their ammunition. The stupid jug-eared fool playing with himself instead of staying alert to his up-wind, silent approach. The big wounded man-bear, almost as strong as he was, manacled in the wolf compound, the vicious little she-wolverine who had succeeded in wounding him, those Bolshevik scientists who kept the wolves, his peers, in cages. They were next. He couldn't help but howl his anticipation into the bitter, icy air. A pack not too far away took up the call and howled in response. He grinned to himself, showing brown, tobacco-stained teeth long as any wolf's, eyes grey-green and merciless. The godless Reds, the heathenish herders. They were all going to die tonight. He knew the herders called him *Aboraten*. Wolfman. *Let them hear me and fear for their lives.* He lifted his face into the air and howled. *Almighty God I come to do your bidding!*

9

Volkov ordered that Semyon be released and his wounds dealt with. He ignored the disorder and grief in the camp. Always deal with the practical aspects of any situation, his thoughts ran, no matter how terrible the emotional circumstances. An older woman came out with some sort of poultice made from mosses and her husband brought a hammer and chisel and, laying Semyon's arms across a birch stump, severed the handcuff chain. The bullet wound on his foot was cleaned with vodka and bandaged. Through it all, Semyon remained impassive, too weary even to feel anger for the brutal injustice he had been forced to endure. He stared at the three herders who were taking down the body of their priest with as much care and respect as they could. Volkov was watching them too. After a few moments he turned to Semyon.

'We owe you an apology, comrade. That poor bastard wasn't butchered by you. That's obvious. Unless you can fly. We will go back to the field centre and make another plan. You can rest and recover.'

Semyon was aware of the older man's gruff attempt at kindness but was in no mood to respond. He had been degraded to the role of a hunted wild beast, his only friends instinctive, uncomprehending wolves who had shown him more humanity than any of his pursuers. He stared blankly as the herders laid out the remains of the shaman on a sheet of reindeer hide. He was exhausted, weak, desperate, seemingly incapable of feeling anything but the pain in his hands and in his foot, the biting easterly wind on his face and the aching in every part of his body. Then the old colonel touched his shoulder and squeezed. At that single demonstration of human contact, Semyon broke down and wept.

Volkov watched the big man convulse and snort back tears, then release a high-pitched whine before breaking out again into hacking laugh-like sobs as he curled into a foetal ball and covered his face with his huge swollen paws. His own eyes pricked with tears as he felt something of the Georgian's pain. He felt the sense of desertion, the uncomprehending fury, the justifiable self-pity as if these feelings were his own. He glanced again at the weeping man, checked the sky for more signs of snow and went to organise an escort back to the field station.

Ludmila checked the cage fom which Semyon and the Brothers Karamazov had escaped. There was no point returning her prisoner here unless he was chained to something more solid. Picking her way though the wolf shit, she established that the central heartwood pillar would be strong enough. There were already cleats driven into it through which she could thread a chain. Irina came out to see what she was doing. The wind was gathering strength and the snow was starting to whirl in spirals across an increasingly white terrain.

'I wouldn't be sure they will be back tonight,' she said to the militiawoman's back.

'Marshal Stalin gave him 72 hours. I am confident they will find the murderer and bring him here.'

'What are we going to do with the commissar?'

'He has temporarily lost his mind. He must be cared for until he regains his senses.'

'Everything is so simple in your world, isn't it?' Irina could barely keep a sneer out of her voice. In reality she felt as low as she had ever felt in her life. Hatred of this other woman gave her some semblance of strength.

Ludmila turned on her suddenly, so suddenly that Irina jumped backwards and a shot of adrenaline surged through her. She regained her balance and stood her ground defiantly as Ludmila approached her and spoke to within inches of her face.

'Where were you when the fascists were trying to invade our Motherland? Where were you when the bullets were flying and the tanks were crushing women and children, when the buildings were being blown to pieces? Here? In this nowhere place? Cooking up treachery with your father, the *scientist?* I defended our country while *you* were trying to destroy it. Yes, everything is simple in my world. It is either right or wrong. I am right and you are completely wrong.'

Her forehead now was against Irina's. Irina smelt her breath on her face. It was sweet, familiar. Her skin too had a familiar scent. Like raspberries blended with cream. And yet as far as she knew, this woman used no perfume. Ludmila gave one vicious little butt with her forehead to the bridge of Irina's nose – the discrepancy in height put the forehead of one and the bridge of the other at the same level. Irina fell back with the disabling pain. She put her hands to her nose. Blood was gushing from her nostrils. She wiped it away with the back of her hand and faced her attacker.

'I wish I'd never called you here! I wish you'd died in the forest! I wish Semyon had cut your throat and … left you torn apart by wolves, like … you've torn our lives apart, you evil fucking bitch!'

Ludmila looked at her coldly. 'Everything you said will be duly noted and recorded.' With that she walked away.

Tears of anger welled up in Irina's eyes. Tears or frustration and impotence. Never had she felt so feeble in the face of someone like this woman. Staring miserably after her, she wondered what it must be like to be such a creature. There was no way of escape. Snow was crystallising in the air and soon the already boggy terrain would be impassable. Ludmila had taken all the weapons and put them under lock and key.

Just then she felt a warm wet muzzle and a rough tongue on her hand. Kolya came and stood next to her, gave a whining yawn, then sat on his haunches. *Kolya!* Irina looked down at him in shock. If Ludmila saw him, he would be dead. She called him quietly to her and motioned towards Semyon's tiny cabin a dozen or so yards away. Kolya needed no second bidding. There were always scraps of deer meat and offal in and around the hut and she knew he would be ravenous.

She very rarely went inside Semyon's cabin. As a little girl she had gone there daily but as she grew up and realised he needed his privacy, she went less and less. There were several game birds hanging head-down in the narrow porch. Irina reached up and and gave one to Kolya. He tore it to shreds and gulped it down in seconds and Irina gave him another, which he despatched in the same way. She pushed open the heavy pine door and peered inside. It was dark and gloomy and the stove had long gone out. Kolya followed her in, his nostrils alive to the rich array of scents: blood, fat, animal hide, tobacco and all the fetid human odours of a tightly-sealed room. She opened the wooden shutters and the windows and let in air and light. The first thing she noticed was a tiny icon of the Virgin and Child on the wall, its colours dulled with age and smoke, the gold leaf all but worn away. Various knives lay on the rough-hewn table by the stove. Semyon had sharpened all of them on the foot-operated grindstone outside his cabin. Without thinking, Irina picked up the biggest, wrapped it safely in a piece of greasy cloth and tucked it into the back of her skirt. She looked around the cabin she had played in as a girl. She would sit on the bed eating an apple, as Semyon skinned a rabbit or gutted a game-bird for his pot, bombarding him with questions, begging him to take her hunting, to show her how to shoot and skin animals like he was doing, to play hide and seek. He would answer gruffly in monosyllables until finally he would pick her up by the ankles and carry her screaming and laughing outside, depositing her none too gently on the ground. Tears streamed again down Irina's face and then other inexplicable memories flashed through her mind. She had been here with someone else, someone her own age, another little girl. They had played together on Semyon's hard straw-filled mattress. Laughed and fought. She recollected pain. Bruising. Being pushed from the bed. Hurt. Semyon shouting.

The light from the doorway was suddenly extinguished and the hairs on her neck prickled. She knew it was Ludmila who was standing there.

The militiawoman was about to order Irina back to the cabin when she was pushed to the ground by the powerful body of Kolya, whom she had failed to see until too late, as he made his escape through the open doorway. He fled into the forest as the wolves in the compound set up yet another baying chorus. Ludmila scrambled to her feet and aimed her rifle at the departing wolf. She let off a couple of rounds but the terrified animal had disappeared.

Irina's reaction was to burst out laughing. It came flooding up through her, volcanic and joyous. She laughed so hard she thought she was going to suffocate. She couldn't stop. Even when Ludmila shouted at her to be quiet and threatened to hit her with the butt-end of her gun, she laughed loud and long. Nothing had ever felt so wonderful as this. She was disintegrating with joy. In the end, Ludmila found an enamel jug of water Semyon used for washing and threw it over her. Irina stopped briefly and coughed and spluttered then started laughing again. It was the most subversive thing she had ever done. Ludmila, short of putting a bullet into her, was powerless in the face of it. Irina, in between convulsions, was sure she saw Ludmila stamp her foot like a child. In the face of laughter, her authority was meaningless.

As she watched the helpless Irina laugh herself into hysterical oblivion, Ludmila was also overcome with unwelcome, alien thoughts. Memories she didn't recognise. *I know this place!* Ludmila shook her head like a dog would, to shake off water and let the thought, the memory, the dream, whatever it was, disperse. She stepped over the now supine Irina and tore the icon off the wall. *More evidence.* Seeing the knives on the table, she gathered them up and ordered Irina to return to the cabin. Helpless now with laughter –a phrase Irina had often heard but never experienced- she staggered to her feet and still laughing openly at Ludmila, stumbled to the cabin.

Before they got to the door, they heard Petrenko screaming about a wolf. He had seen Kolya run by the cabin and was as hysterical now with terror as Irina was with laughter. They found him standing completely naked on the table, only the bloody bandage round his throat, holding a ladle and daring any wolf to come near him. Grigori was trying to encourage him to come down from the table but Ludmila unceremoniously swiped his legs from under him with her rifle and told him to be quiet the wolf was gone. Slowly, he calmed down and, clutching his hands to his private parts, slunk away into Ludmila's room and closed the door. If this was a signal for Irina to stop laughing, it had completely the opposite effect. She broke into more paroxysms and lay back on the couch holding her sides. Her father went and sat beside her and looked at Ludmila questioningly. Ludmila shrugged and said she was hysterical but that if she didn't stop soon, she would gag her.

Gradually, Irina calmed down and began to sob quietly into her father's neck. He stroked her hair and whispered to her tenderly. She murmured over and over again, 'Why is this happening, why is this happening?'

Ludmila returned to the doorway and looked across the open area in front of the cabin toward the dark line of the taiga. The evening was drawing in and there was no sign of the search party. She was about to turn back into the cabin when she detected movement out of the corner of her eye. Automatically, she pulled the bolt on her rifle and peered into the gathering gloom. She scanned her field of vision methodically and her nostrils widened and her ears twitched. No doubt it was their damn pet wolf prowling around the perimeter. She lowered her rifle and went into the cabin and closed the door.

Darkness fell quickly. Irina made a thick soup and served it with black bread and a hard reindeer-milk cheese. Petrenko, now in shirt and trousers, joined them at the table and offered his apologies to Ludmila. She nodded and told him to eat. Grusha and Masha sniffed around the diners, making most of the time for Petrenko's ankles. He kicked out at them. Masha yelped and kept her distance whereas Grusha set up a vicious high- pitched growl and her hackles rose visibly. Ludmila told Irina to move them to another room or she'd shoot them. Irina locked them in her father's study where they howled and whined and pawed at the door.

By nine o'clock a wind had picked up outside. Somewhere a shutter banged against the cabin wall. Grigori offered to go out and see to it, but Ludmila told him curtly to stay where he was. She went outside and found the offending shutter and secured it. The clouds had blanketed out moon and stars, and the snow was heavy and deep underfoot. The desolate keening of the wind obscured every other sound but something made Ludmila stop and her ears prick up. The darkness was almost complete apart from the yellowy spill from the cabin windows. She listened intently, desperate to hear the sound of Russian and Evenk voices returning successfully from their expedition to bring back the Georgian murderer. A sudden crash made her heart race. She cocked her rifle and tried to gauge where the sound came from. Seconds past. She heard nothing but the low moaning of the polar wind. She moved around the side of the cabin and discovered the door of the privy wide open. She went and shut it and began to walk back to the cabin when she caught the scent she had smelt once before. The acrid, stale smell of an unwashed human male. It brushed her olfactory nerve-endings briefly, but it was enough to alert her that someone was –once again- stalking her.

As soon as Ludmila left the cabin, Irina had eyes only for the miserable Petrenko and not in any way he would have liked. She cleared away his bowl and cutlery and put them in the sink. He watched her, head down, face averted, eyes peering under brows. Irina thought she also detected an arrogant sneer. She put her hands behind her back and into the waistband of her skirt. As she spoke, she pulled the wrapped bundle up slowly and let the cloth fall to the floor until she could feel the handle of Semyon's razor-sharp boning knife in her right hand.

'Have you had enough to eat, comrade Petrenko?' she asked sweetly.

Petrenko nodded.

'Good. It's simple but I hope it filled you up before ...' She paused.

Petrenko blinked, suddenly very alert.

'Before what?' he asked.

Irina went over to the cabin door and turned the old key that always sat in the lock but was very rarely used. Grigori, deep in his depression, started up.

'Irushka, what are you doing?'

'Nothing. Just locking the door.'

'Irushka ...'

'Comrade Sirotovska is outside. I demand you unlock the door!' Petrenko sounded panicked as he made his way to where Irina was standing.

Irina pulled the blade from behind her back and in a single movement lunged at Petrenko. In the same instant Grigori was on his feet not knowing whether he should stop his daughter or help her carry out her plan.

Irina's aim was calculated and cold-blooded. As Petrenko came toward her, she stepped slightly to one side and lunged at him with the knife, aiming at his heart. He put out his hand and deflected the blow, receiving a gaping wound to the side of his palm. Blood gushed out all over Irina. At the same time Grigori used all his body weight to thrust his daughter aside and prevent her using the knife a second time. Petrenko looked at his hand in horror but had the presence of mind somehow to turn the key, wrest open the heavy door and flee into the howling wind.

Irina couldn't believe what her father had done. 'Why did you do that?' she screamed at him. 'Why?'

Grigori couldn't answer. As he lay over his daughter whose eyes were wild and terribly focussed, she squirmed and tried to push him off her, but he wouldn't let her up.

'We have no choice, dad. They're going to take us to our deaths! It's either us or them. Now he's out there with her! You … fucking idiot!'

Grigori relented and knew she was right. He let her get up.

'What are you going to do now, Irushka?'

'What am I going to do? I'm going to kill them both and then we'll be free!'

She felt a blow to her wrist and the knife flew across the room. She looked up and Ludmila was standing above her, her eyes blazing. The muzzle of her cocked rifle was inches from Irina's face. Irina squealed in pain but looked up at the other woman defiantly.

'Get up,' was all Ludmila said.

Irina got to her feet without taking her eyes off the militiawoman. Ludmila ushered them over to the table and made them both sit. She backed to the door and looked out into the blizzard for the whereabouts of the Narkom commissar. She could see nothing.

Petrenko stumbled blindly holding his bleeding hand. The blood pumped furiously. He felt faint and nauseous. He had no idea which way he was going, but he could smell the wolf compound and he could hear them pacing their cages and making low menacing growls as he passed. They could smell the blood. If he followed the cages round he would come back to the cabin, he felt sure. He was beginning to feel light-headed and virtually blinded by the swirling snow. Ahead of him he made out a human form. Was it the militiawoman, his own Ludmila? The woman he had been so gloriously intimate with, the beautiful creature who was so violent, so unpredictable, so utterly attractive? *Was she coming to save him?* As he drew nearer he could see that the figure was not that of a woman, but a large male. He had a branch or a pole in his hand. The wolves were growling louder now in anticipation. He could smell their disgusting breath, their shit, their stinking wolfish bodies. *What was he doing?* The figure raised the pole and smashed it into the cage. He cried out involuntarily and the figure turned toward him. Petrenko stopped in fear and ran in the opposite direction, by now completely disoriented. He was sure he heard the man laugh as he rained blow after blow on the cage door. Petrenko fell in the snow and quickly scrambled to his feet, then fell again. He ran as fast as he was able. Behind him he could hear the freed and panting wolves gaining on him. The stuff of nightmares. The stuff of *his* nightmares. In seconds they were upon him.

The three in the cabin heard his screams and looked at one another. Ludmila still had the door open but could see nothing. The high-pitched screaming grew louder, more pleading, more despondent but was eventually drowned out by the darker, more guttural notes of wild beasts tearing their prey to pieces with ruthless efficiency. Soon, there was nothing but the lowing of the wind.

'Someone has released my wolves,' was all Grigori could say in a dead voice.

Ludmila immediately went from window to window and closed the internal shutters, then she ordered Grigori to lock and bar the cabin door, while she secured the back door. All she knew was that someone was out there and he meant to kill them all.

10

Two of the older women in the camp were singing. To Volkov's ears it wasn't exactly music. More like a nasal moan. They were singing over the remains of their priest. As the wind picked up outside the tent where he had been offered hospitality, it had a haunting, disconcerting quality.

Volkov had been brought up as a peasant. He knew what harsh lives so many in Russia had to live. He knew and was used to the barbaric lack of care human beings showed each other in his homeland. He had never really had anything to compare it with and he knew through newsreels and films and radio broadcasts and newspapers that outside Russia, human beings were even more barbaric. Capitalism was where dog ate dog and ultimately devoured itself.

Russia was under siege. She had to act ruthlessly toward anyone inside or outside her borders that threatened her very existence. And those threats were very real. He was a soldier and he knew from experience that this was true. First the Whites, then the West and always those parasites, saboteurs and vermin within, who would bring down a system that had freed him and millions of others from feudal slavery.

He had always believed this and would continue to believe it. As he sat with these thoughts, smoking one of his own cigarettes and listening to the women sing their funeral song, he realised however that he knew very little about *this* Russia. This Siberia, which was still truly wild, inhabited by people whose lives had changed little in ten thousand years. He knew they were reluctant to embrace the opportunities that Communism offered them. They were as stubborn as kulaks and were being treated in the same way his mother's family –some of whom had made money and gained their freedom from the tsar- had been treated after the revolution. Punished, fined, imprisoned, executed. He recalled with unease how he had had to disown his mother's relatives formally before he was allowed to ascend through the ranks.

Yet these people weren't kulaks in the strict sense. They just needed their vast empty spaces in which to follow their herds. Volkov knew agriculture. He had farmed land, grown crops, herded livestock. It was absurd to follow the creatures you relied upon for sustenance instead of constructing fences and keeping them close. And yet this is how they lived, how they had always lived and how they would continue to live. His thoughts turned like tumblers in a lock. He knew these musings were taking a direction that was not constructive, perhaps even subversive, but here in this smoky tent smelling of pine resin, infrequently-washed bodies, tobacco-smoke and tea, his mind wandered and he felt able to make observations he would never have been able to make from a position of Soviet authority.

He discerned a pattern in the womens' singing. It wasn't as random as he'd assumed. He hadn't been listening properly. He now recognised repetitions and was starting to be infected by the sad snatches of melody he could make out. It was a true song for the dead.

Volkov despised religion and yet he had been steeped in its traditions and beliefs as a child. He was never as religious as his mother was. He could not feel the faith she showed and held deeply, despite the thrall in which the priests and their doctrines held all poor, uneducated people. The herders' own priest, their shaman, had been dismembered and mutilated by a creature they believed was some sort of devil. He had seen what this creature could do, but Volkov knew he was only a man. A man who had butchered his soldiers and who the Georgian giant, now sleeping in a corner of his tent, had been the only –innocent- suspect.

He looked over at the snoring bulk of the man he had captured, and felt a deep remorse.

Volkov took a last mouthful of his glass of tea, dragged hard on his dwindling cigarette, stroked his moustache and got to his feet and went out into the building snowstorm.

Somewhere out there, not that far away, was their wolfman. Volkov walked around the camp. He discovered Innaksa's father and two of his companions securing the makeshift birch fences. He impressed upon them that the killer was still at large and that they must be extra vigilant. The herders looked at him without replying. Volkov was suddenly aware of how ridiculous he sounded, how pompous. Any military authority he had was meaningless here in this bleak wilderness where Nature made, and unmade, the rules.

It wasn't a comfortable feeling for a man who was used to giving orders and having them obeyed without question. His son was a high-ranking officer in the Red Army, twice decorated with the Order of Lenin. His daughter had married a naval officer. Both grandsons were going to enter the military. He missed his wife Sonya, who had died from tuberculosis during the War. She would have understood what he was thinking and feeling and would have been able to give it context. She had been his beating heart and thinking head. She had been able to rein in his boyish impulses and channel his childish outbursts. She had cautioned him to curb his tongue when all those around him were seeking favour and waiting for him to make his first -and last- wrong move. He felt very alone and vulnerable.

He sighed audibly and the three herders looked at him with curiosity, then turned away and laughed. The wind stung his face and penetrated his thick woollen great coat as if it were paper. By contrast, the darkness was impenetrable, almost palpably dense. All he could hear was the wind moaning in the conifer branches, the occasional grunts of the corralled reindeer and the endless, endless threnody sung by two elderly women in a wild Siberian night.

In the cabin, Ludmila, Grigori and Irina sat silent as the wind blew around the house and down the stove chimney. Ludmila had secured all the internal shutters and they had nothing else to do but listen for the slightest sound. All the wolves had gone now. Irina was the first to break silence. She had placed a cushion on her father's lap and lay with her head on it. He stroked her hair absently.

'Wolves rarely kill humans,' she said almost inaudibly.

Grigori murmured something in assent and Irina continued.

'They do in the fairy stories. Wolves always eat people in fairy stories. But then sometimes they help people. Like Prince Ivan. The Idiot.' She laughed. 'Other times it's people who eat people. Like Baba Yaga. She tried to eat princess Vasilissa. Didn't she?'

Her eyes rolled up towards her father. 'Didn't she?'

'Yes. She did.' His daughter was nine again and he was telling her fairy stories. 'She tried and failed because her little doll …'

'Because her little doll saved her.' She laughed softly. 'Her doll always looked after her. Like my doll Kuklushka when I was small. Like Innaksa's Uluki.' She smiled a distant smile. Grigori looked down concerned and shushed her gently and continued to stroke her hair.

Ludmila looked at the pair stony-faced. She despised their intimacy, their collusion. It was something she had never known. Her mother had told her fairy stories. She knew about Vasilissa the Beautiful and her little doll and how Baba Yaga had tried to eat her and how the doll had foiled her plans. But it had brought her no comfort. Her mother intoned the stories to her as if they were a spell to ward off evil. Her mother's stories were always dark. Vasilissa had gone to fetch light for her wicked sisters and her stepmother, but she returned with a skull whose eye sockets blazed fire and burned them all to ashes.

'Did you ever have a doll, Ludmila?' Irina asked. A nine-year old's question. In its lightness and innocence all the more disconcerting.

'I am an orphan. We weren't allowed toys. I had no childhood.' Ludmila spoke without bitterness.

'That's sad. It explains a lot.' She felt the warning pressure of her father's hand.

'What does it explain? My mother died when I was seven. She hanged herself as I told you. They took me and put me in an orphanage. There is nothing to explain.'

'Where was your father?'

'Irina ...' Grigori's voice was firm.

'I don't know. My mother said he died. In a country far away. She had to bring me up by herself. But her mind was weak. Things were hard. She tried her best. She hadn't the strength to survive.'

'I never knew my mother. Well, I feel as if I did know her. My dad has told me so much about her and I have a photograph. Have you a photograph of your father?'

'No.'

'Irushka, this is hardly the time …' Grigori tailed off.

Ludmila spoke without looking up.

'My mother told me a story once which I've never heard before. It was about a cruel man who had two children. To one he gave presents. To the other, beatings. In the end the mother could take no more of his cruelty and one night she took the child from her bed in darkness and fled many miles, but when she got to where she felt safe, she realised she had brought the wrong child. She had left the other child whom the father hated. It was too late to go back.'

'That's a horrible story.' Irina looked at Ludmila appalled. She turned to her father and could see that he felt the same. He looked as if he might be sick. His face was grey and his eyes stared unblinkingly at the floor. She placed a hand on his arm.

'Yes. But it's just a story. It means nothing.'

Irina looked at Ludmila for a moment. 'Who *are* you?' she said finally. 'Why are you here?'

'I'm a police officer and I'm here because you called me.'

'And who is out there?'

'I don't know, but my guess it is your Georgian kulak.' Ludmila spoke evenly without any fear in her voice.

'For the last time, whoever is out there it isn't Semyon,' Irina spoke through gritted teeth.

'You don't know that. He has obviously eluded Colonel Volkov and has come back to kill us all.'

'If it is Semyon, he won't have come to kill us all. Only you.' Irina couldn't keep the grim amusement out of her voice.

At that moment the lights went out. Their attacker had found the generator and turned it off. The cabin was lit only by the dull glow of two hurricane lamps. A loud crash against one of the shutters at the rear of the cabin caused Irina to shriek and Grigori to shout, 'My God! What's that?'

Ludmila ran automatically to where the sound was coming from, which she guessed was the window of her room. Without hesitation, she let off two shots. The deafening reports were followed by the sound of shattered glass and splintering wood. Then nothing.

Ludmila, every sense alert now, tried to track the movements of their stalker.

'You'll have to let us have some weapons to defend ourselves,' Irina said.

Ludmila waved her to be quiet. Another crash, this time at the front caused her to spin round and fire off a single round through the shuttered window at the side of the door. Again, silence.

Ludmila's heart was beating fast. She tried to second-guess the attacker. He would be looking for a weak spot obviously. She was sure she had secured all shutters. *He might get on to the roof. He might …* suddenly she heard the metallic click of a rifle being armed. She screamed at the other two in the room to move out of the way of the door then in the same moment threw herself to the side as a burst of automatic machine gun fire blasted through the thick front door of heartwood pine. *A machine gun? Where would he have got a machine gun?* Then she realised that the only people carrying an automatic weapon were the soldiers sent out to capture the killer. A glacial trickle of fear slid down her spine. The heavy door held but it wouldn't survive another salvo like that.

'For God's sake give us something to defend ourselves with!' shouted Grigori. 'That's not Semyon!'

'Stay down and don't move!' was all the militiawoman said. She felt helpless imprisoned in the cabin. She needed to be out there, the hunter not the hunted. The fifteen-year old who had pinned down German soldiers from her ruined aerial hideout in Leningrad was not used to being a target herself.

Outside, Stepan Stepanovich cursed the new machine gun he had taken from the soldiers. The recoil had sent him sprawling, the gun had been flung from his hands and now the mechanism was jammed. He tried to release it a few more times, then threw it aside. Whoever was inside was armed so he would need to be more careful. The snow was swirling around and the wind tore through him, but he didn't feel the chill, only a predatory urge to kill everyone in the cabin and burn it to the ground.

He crept into the outbuildings and wrenched the padlock from one of the doors with a machete. He quickly found what he was looking for.

Ludmila smelt the kerosene first. They had remained still, listening for the next assault. Grigori gripped Irina's hand as they crouched helplessly behind the big leather couch. He whispered over and over again, 'I'm sorry, I'm so sorry, Irushka, so sorry.' Irina didn't know why he was sorry nor did she care, but she squeezed her father's hand in return and shook her head, dismissing his apologies. She caught the smell next.

'He's going to set fire to the cabin!'

'Please officer Sirotovska, Ludmila, for pity's sake give us some thing to defend ourselves with! We promise we will help you. If you don't we're *all* going to be killed!' Her father's voice was hoarse with pleading.

'Ludmila, we know it's not Semyon. We will help you, we promise!'

Ludmila looked at the pair of them briefly and decided the risk was too much. She could sense the hatred in the other woman and shook her head.

'We will leave the cabin by different doors. You' –she indicated Irina – 'will come with me and you can go out by the back. He can't cover both of them.' She took hold of Irina and held her in front of her, locking one forearm across her throat. Irina struggled but Ludmila hissed at her to keep still. 'Make for the truck and whoever gets there first will start it. Is it fuelled up?'

Grigori nodded then crept to the study door, unlocked it and went inside. He heard someone singing a hymn. It was their attacker, singing a deep-throated 'Kyrie'. Was it Semyon? Could they both be wrong? He looked across at his daughter. It was obvious Irina had the same thought but something in the timbre of the voice told her that it wasn't Semyon. She shook her head. All of them smelt the burning kerosene.

'Are you ready, go!' Ludmila shouted, dragging Irina to the door. 'When I say open it, open it! Understand?' Irina nodded, her windpipe crushed by the other woman's arm. 'Now, open the door!'

Irina pulled open the bullet-peppered door. The blizzard swept into the cabin and Ludmila dragged Irina outside, scanning the windswept darkness for any sign of the intruder. At the same time she kept an ear on Grigori as he opened the back door. The through-draught sent books and crockery and ornaments crashing to the floor. The back door slammed twice, three times in the wind. Ludmila pushed Irina ahead of her towards where she knew the truck was parked. The darkness was all-consuming. Ludmila hoped that together with the shrieking wind this would work to their advantage. *Where was he?* She blundered on guessing her way, pushing the other woman towards the truck. Irina ran and stumbled in the snow. As she neared where she knew the truck would be, a face loomed at her out of the darkness and she felt herself thrown to the ground. She screamed in terror and felt a huge stinking weight bear down on her. Whoever it was roared in her face. She smelt the foulness of his breath. Ludmila lashed out with the butt of her rifle and the figure sprang away groaning in pain. Ludmila reached down and pulled Irina up and made the last ten steps to the ZIS.

Grigori was already there. He pulled the distraught Irina to him.

'Never mind her! Start the truck!' Ludmila shouted above the wind.

Grigori dived for the handle which was searingly cold to the touch. He could feel the skin of his hands adhering to the metal. He yanked the handle. Nothing. Again. Nothing. And then again and again. Finally the frozen machine roared into life. Ludmila shoved Irina into the cab, then climbed on to the tailboard. Grigori clambered in and slammed it into reverse, the cogs in their sluggish lubricant crashing and grinding, refusing to mesh. Eventually the truck moved backwards easily on its tracks over the thick snow. Grigori slammed the accelerator to the floor. The engine whined to an impossible pitch. He had to guess when they were free of the fenced bay in which the truck was normally parked. He guessed badly as a birch fence was demolished. He spun the wheel and rammed the gear into first, then second. He turned on the lights. As he did so, a huge figure leapt out of the way of the accelerating lorry. The blade of a machete smashed through the side window, showering Irina with glass. Their maximum speed was barely twenty miles an hour but it was enough for them to make their escape.

The sudden lurch of the truck as Grigori gunned the engine threw Ludmila backwards and she lost her footing and fell. As she recovered and ran to jump on to the tailboard, she realised she needed both hands. A moment's calculation and she threw the rifle to Irina and grabbed door handle and sill to pull herself aboard. Irina kicked savagely at one hand and then the other and the militiawoman fell backwards once again and disappeared.

Irina said nothing to her father hunched at the steering wheel. They were heading toward the herders' encampment steering only by memory and the compass mounted on the dashboard. Visibility was almost zero outside the cab. Then Grigori noticed that Ludmila wasn't with them. He slammed on the brakes. Irina lurched forward and stared hard at her father.

'What are you stopping for?'

'We have to go back for her,' Grigori said.

'Why?'

'Because she will be killed.'

'But if we go back, we'll be killed. Besides, she's probably already dead.'

'Irushka, how can you be so callous?'

'But, Dad, we don't stand a chance!'

'I know, but think of what that monster will do to her. You've seen what he's done already. He's not human.'

Irina said nothing. She didn't care. Besides, rescuing Ludmila would only sign their death warrants.

'We have to go back for her.' Grigori's face was set as he looked out through the rattling glass of the windscreen at the swirling blackness.

11

Volkov watched as two boys were being taught by an old man how to braid reindeer hide into a lariat. His gnarled arthritic brown fingers with the long yellow tobacco-stained nails flew over the thin strips of leather, twisting and threading and tightening. The two boys had their own material and were clumsily trying to follow the old man's movements. Their mothers in the corner of the tent by the low stove were cooking and chatting and laughing at their sons' incompetence. Volkov looked on, intrigued and impressed. He felt like a child watching adult skills he could only dream of and yet what were they doing? Braiding strips of leather. Despite the raging storm outside, which seemed to threaten to demolish the tent, and despite the grim outcome of his mission so far, he felt elevated, light as air, without a drop of vodka having passed his lips.

Semyon stirred and grunted then shot up into a sitting position, momentarily unsure of where he was. Volkov put out a calming hand and made reassuring noises.

'It's all right, comrade, no need to worry. No one means you any harm.'

Semyon listened to the wind howling round the tent and causing the reindeer hide to flap angrily. He looked at Volkov, then winced as the pain surged through his hands and foot.

The two younger women looked up briefly, eyed the big man suspiciously, then went back to their cooking pots. The smell of stew cooking with herbs filled the tent.

The older women had paused in their singing and were now muttering what Volkov guessed was some sort of prayer for the dead to themselves.

Volkov felt for his pistol just in case the Georgian decided he was cornered like a desperate animal, but once he saw him relax, he pulled his hand away from the gun.

'When the storm dies down, we'll carry on our search for the killer at first light,' Volkov said to Semyon. 'You need to stay here and rest.'

Semyon couldn't believe the kindness in the Colonel's tone. Not more than a few hours ago he had been hunted like a mad dog. He remembered breaking down and weeping and felt ashamed of himself.

'I'll come with you. If that monster is out there, Irushka and the professor will be in danger.'

Irushka. Volka noted the diminutive. As if she were his daughter. That one word made him ache with a loneliness he couldn't quite place. Sonya was his wife's diminutive. Her full name was Sophia. He had never called her that. She had called him Mitya or sometimes Colonel Volkov depending on her mood. He smiled to himself. His own children and grandchildren were in Moscow and he had never felt so far away from home as he did now.

'You were very close to the professor and his daughter?' the colonel asked.

'I still am,' the Georgian growled.

'You know they have been arrested for sedition and betrayal of the Motherland?'

'Yes. Like I was arrested for being a murderer. It is all lies. The professor is a good Russian. A good communist.

That bitch and her lapdog are the ones who should be in jail.'

'Talk like that could get you thrown in a labour camp, comrade. Be careful.'

'Breathing could get me thrown in a labour camp. I'm coming with you in the morning,' was all the Georgian said and he rolled over and went back to sleep.

Volkov doubted it. Not with his injuries. He shrugged, admiring Semyon's guts and resilience, and resumed watching the boys' fumbling attempts to make a lasso.

Grigori drove the roaring truck into the compound. Without a word, he slammed on the brakes. Mystified, Irina got down from the truck as if she were hung with lead weights. Why was he doing this? Let her die. She won't be grateful and she will destroy us both.

Her father jumped down into the flailing snowstorm. Irina could barely see him, but she followed as best she could. A loud scream came from the wolf compound. It was female and could only be Ludmila. The creature had obviously overpowered her. Irina could feel nothing but pleasure at the thought.

Good.

Grigori ran faster toward the sound. Both of them knew the layout of the compound and were there in seconds. There was light from one of the cages. A hurricane lamp was hanging from a central pole and swinging in the wind sending huge magnified shadows careening over the illuminated snow.

They could just make out the figure of a man dragging something toward the cage. It was the creature and he was pulling a bound and twisting Ludmila- just as Semyon used to drag the carcasses of reindeer for the wolves. They saw him pull her into the cage and then punch her hard in the head. Ludmila was momentarily stunned and he was able to lift her to her feet, first slinging the rope he was dragging her with over a low cross-beam. Then he began to haul her up.

Irina took aim. From this distance and conveniently illuminated, she would have no trouble in killing their stalker. She had had a rifle in her hand since she was little girl. She had brought down small animals and game birds for food and challenged Semyon to see how many cones they could blow off a pine tree. She had even shot a reindeer stag that had charged her. She lined up her shot. The creature was now securing the rope to a far post in the cage. Grigori could see that his daughter had a clear shot at the killer. He was confident in Irina's marksmanship. In the gloom, he could just make out where she was taking aim and realised she was moving the weapon from left to right and to left again.

'Irushka! What are you doing?'

Irina had him in her sights. He was the size of a brown bear and made an easy target in the swinging light. She took in the limp form of the woman hanging fom the rope. She remembered what the creature had done to the herdsman and the soldier and what he had tried to do to little Innaksa. He was a ferocious cannibal who was endangering their lives and he deserved to be eliminated, like any other threat. Her rifle moved to the right and in her one open eye she saw the slight figure of a half-conscious young woman who had ruthlessly pursued the man who had looked out for her all her life. *They both deserve to die.*

Grigori could read everything in his daughter's mind.

'Don't kill her, Irushka! You mustn't!'

Irina turned to him coldly. Then she turned back to her rifle.

'Give me one reason.' She slid the bolt of the rifle back and squeezed the trigger. She had her sights lined up on the woman.

Irina fired at the same time as her father pulled the rifle from her. It blasted harmlessly into the air. Grigori pushed Irina to one side with all his strength and aimed at the killer, whose face was momentarily turned toward them. He pressed the trigger and the creature fell. Grigori ran toward the two of them, followed by a wildly protesting Irina. The wolfman lay still on the cage floor. Not trusting his daughter with the rifle, he ordered her to release Ludmila. Irina did as she was told, letting the rope go and having the petty satisfaction of seeing Ludmila collapse heavily to the ground.

'Help her to her feet, Irushka and get her inside!'

Irina felt physically revolted as she hauled the other woman to her feet and dragged her toward their now-smouldering home.

The fire was beginning to threaten the whole rear of the cabin. Grigori slung the rifle across his back by its strap and ran to the water butt. Seizing a wooden pail, he smashed the surface ice, filled the bucket then threw the water on the flames. Again and again he did this until he had the fire almost out. It had eaten away at the lintel of the door and was creeping up the outer wall. In a few moments it would have engulfed the whole place.

Irina let Ludmila drop on to the couch. The militiawoman was groaning and her hands were swollen and purple from the tight rope around her wrists. Irina had no urge to loosen them. In the weak flickering glow of the hurricane lamps, she watched as Ludmila slowly came round and her father finished putting out the fire. Never had she felt so much revulsion for another human being. Never had she wanted another human being to die as much as she wanted this woman to die now. She was furious with her father.

She heard the chug and throb of the generator, as her father gunned it back into life and the electric light came back on.

Grigori entered the room, wheezing and gasping for breath, his hands and face scorched and blackened with soot. He went over to Ludmila and immediately untied her. Ludmila yelped as the blood flowed back into her hands. She sat up, rubbing her wrists.

'Give me the gun,' she said. 'You're both under arrest.'

Irina burst out laughing. 'Just be thankful we didn't kill you. If I'd had my way, you'd have been dead before that beast outside.'

'Give me the gun or it will be worse for you.'

'Worse than what? Being executed or worked to death in a labour camp?' Irina laughed again.

'This isn't a joke. Give me the gun.'

'Kill her dad. Now. Put her out of her misery.'

'Irushka …'

'Irushka *what*? You had the chance to be free of her, of all this and you let her live. What's the matter with you?'

'Darling, make us some tea. There's things I need to talk to you -to both of you- about.'

Both women looked at him curiously as he opened a bottle of vodka, poured out three glasses and handed them round. They took them without a word. Grigori threw his back and poured another. He spoke softly to his daughter.

'How's the stove? It's nearly out. Put another log in.'

Irina did as she was told, shooing the two wolf cubs, who had lain curled up together and terrified, away from the stove. She filled the samovar and lit it, then swallowed some of her vodka. It was poor quality stuff but its fire revived her and she finished what was in her glass. Ludmila held the glass in both hands but didn't drink.

'What do you want to talk about?' Ludmila asked. She stared straight at the scientist.

'I want to talk about … us,' Grigori said. He swallowed his second glass and poured another one. He offered the bottle to Irina. She shook her head.

'Dad, what do you mean, us? Who?'

'You, Irushka and … this young woman. It's important.'

'What's so important about her?'

Grigori finished his third glass, paused and looked from one woman to the other. Then he stared down at the two wolf cubs, took out his pipe, dismantled it and blew it and put it back together. The two women were silent. They watched the older man as he unfolded his oilskin tobacco pouch and began to pack the bowl of his pipe with tobacco, using his forefinger. He found matches and lit the pipe, shook the match and tossed it into the ashtray on the table. He took one, then two puffs and blew the smoke into the air.

Finally, Grigori spoke. 'You've both seen the films I made of the wolves and the little girls. What did you make of them?'

'Dad, you know what we thought of them …'

'No really. You Irushka, what did you think I was doing?'

'You were observing human behaviour … animal behaviour, but …'

Grigori cut across her. 'Lieutenant Sirotovska?'

'You were abusing your role as a scientist. You were treating human beings like rats in a laboratory. Just as the Nazis did.'

Grigori seemed to ponder this for a moment. Irina knew it was an act, so did Ludmila. The faux-academic style was to cover something else.

'Get to the point.' Ludmilas's voice was harsh but Irina thought she could detect a tremor in her voice. Was she frightened? If so, of what?

'The darker girl in the film. I lied about her. She wasn't the daughter of a colleague.'

'So ... who was she? Dad?'

Grigori turned to his daughter. 'Irushka, you have to understand that what I did was to prove a hypothesis. It was a scientific study. I didn't mean to hurt you. Either of you.'

A chill went through Irina.

'What are you trying to say?' Ludmila snapped.

'The two little girls in the films are related. They had to be. For the experiment to work.'

'In what way related?' Irina asked.

Grigori assumed the professorial tone. 'The two subjects were sororial twins. They were born from the same womb at the same time but from different ova. Just like these two here.' He pointed his pipe stem at the two curled-up wolf cubs.

Irina felt sick. 'But dad, the other girl is ... me ...'

'Yes, she was your twin sister.'

The news came as a physical blow. Irina gasped.

'Where is she now? Is she dead?'

'No. She isn't dead.'

'Then where is she?'

Grigori turned to Ludmila. She stared back at him, a mixture of loathing and distrust in her features.

'Comrade Sirotovska,' he said, 'when your mother told you the story about the wrong child, how did the story end?'

'Like I told it to you. She found she had taken the child the father loved and left the one he hated.'

'Didn't she have a happier ending?'

'I don't follow.'

'Didn't she look at your sad, angry eyes and wide-open mouth and chuck you under the chin and say, 'Don't look so sad, little one, that's not how the story ends. No. For the mother finds a magic horse called Gavrila who takes them both back to the father's house on the wings of the wind and while he sleeps they take the other child and flee to a land where the wicked father can never reach them.'

Ludmila looked as if she had been struck.

'How did you know that?'

Grigori said nothing but continued to look at the cubs who stared back at him warily, still traumatised by the night's events.

'Dad, what is this about? You're telling fairy stories?'

'Your mother told that story to you when you were small. You won't remember it because you were too young, but she no doubt repeated it to you' –he looked up at Ludmila- 'when you were older and you did remember it.'

Ludmila looked at the scientist with hard, searching eyes, Irina with only wild panic in hers. She could not make sense of what she was hearing.

'Are you saying … dad, are you saying, my mother is … *her* mother?'

Grigori nodded. The wind slammed one of the window shutters several times.

'This is nonsense!' exclaimed Ludmila. 'You are saying she is my sister? That is …impossible!' She stood up and paced the cabin. The cubs whined in fear.

'Dad, my mother is dead. You told me she was dead. She had no other children. She died. Of diphtheria. You told me. She's buried. Out there. Every year we remember her. I've got her photograph.'

Grigori turned and looked at her and gently shook his head.

'The woman in the photograph isn't my mother?'

'Yes she is your mother, but she isn't buried out there. She left a long time ago … with your sister.' He spoke slowly, almost in pain as each word was torn from him.

Ludmila turned on him. 'What you are saying is that we are sisters, that my mother took me away from you and … her … and moved to Moscow. In that case, the other girl in the films you made, that girl is … me?'

Grigori nodded.

Irina was aghast. 'You're not saying you think it's true, are you? Dad? Tell her it isn't true! Tell her!'

She sounded like a frightened child and Grigori instinctively put out his hand to stroke her hair but she pulled away angrily.

'Your mother didn't like the work I was doing. She was a scientist herself. She knew what I was trying to prove but she was also a mother and we had a daughter who was … unruly, who bullied her twin. She was cruel where her sister was kind. She was selfish where her sister was generous. Dark where the other was light. Their personalities couldn't be more different. But your mother only saw two little girls who needed love and attention and who would change as they grew older, whereas I … I was not so optimistic.'

Ludmila stood up.

'Where are you going, officer Sirotovska? You need to hear this. It's not something I want to say.' He said that so matter of factly it could only be true. 'What happened in Moscow, Nadya? That's your name. Natasha Grigorievna Medvedenka. What happened to your mother? To my wife? To the woman I loved?'

Ludmila whirled on him. 'Is this how you torture people in your *experiments*?'

Irina screamed. 'This is insane! Dad, what are you doing? Why are you saying these awful things?'

'Because ... I have reached the end of telling lies and ...' Words deserted him. 'This woman is your sister and ... she is my daughter.' The words when they came were halting but precise. The scientist did not want to be misunderstood. Now that all the evidence pointed in only one direction.

'You have no proof!' Ludmila was trembling.

'How else did I know how your story ended?' Grigori's tone was unnervingly calm, reasoning. 'And the scar on your forehead. Shaped like a bird's claw. I remember when that happened. One of the wolves snapped because you'd been tormenting him with a stick and he bit you. I had to prize his jaws away from your skull. He would have crushed it like an egg.'

Ludmila involuntarily stroked the small keloid scar on her forehead. She remembered no such incident. But the dreams ...

'You always fought, the two of you,' the scientist continued. 'It caused your mother so much pain. She couldn't understand why Nadya could be so cruel so young. She wanted my help, my support, but I was just fascinated how two creatures born from the same womb at the same time could be so different. It meshed seamlessly with the work I was doing. I was studying wolves but ultimately I was studying human beings.' He looked up at Irina and Ludmila, almost with wonder. 'You two were to be my life's work.' He smiled, a distant, wistful smile.

Irina was crying from sheer incomprehension. What was her father telling them? All the cherished memories of her dead mother, all the stories her father had told her. Were they all lies? Was this other woman she loathed really her sister? Her *twin*?

Ludmila's mind was working furiously also. She was powerless at the moment. She had no weapon and she was in the middle of a vast empty land where no one would know if she lived or died. She was shaking with the force of powerful subterranean emotions. How did he know the story her mother had told her? How did he know about the dog she dreamed of so often, the dog that attacked her and locked her head in its iron jaws? The name of the magic horse, Gavrila. He called her Nadya. Her mother called her Nadya. The orphanage gave her the name Ludmila- so she could forget her past and be reborn. As a loyal daughter of the Soviet Union.

Grigori broke through both women's thoughts. 'Your mother was slim and dark. Very beautiful to my eyes. She could sing and fill the house with flowers and laughter one day, then the next she could become still and silent as her life-spirit abandoned her. She often became depressed and she blamed me. She said I was distant and cold and that I was not a proper father to our children. We fought and argued. She would throw things. She even picked up the rifle and threatened to kill me once. She said she'd take our daughters away with her. One day, she did.'

Grigori seemed to be talking to himself now. Releasing thoughts he'd held captive for two decades.

Irina felt herself standing back from the three of them in that dimly lit cabin with the wind slowly subsiding and the only sound the dull roar and occasional crack of new birch logs burning in the stove. She saw three miserable figures, not one of them able to connect with the other. The revelation was too much for any of them to bear.

That this ...creature, as much an animal as the killer who lay dead outside, that *she* could possibly be her sister was unthinkable. It made her feel physically sick. And yet it seemed all so familiar. The flashes of memory ignited by scent or dream or angle of the light. She had to admit to herself that somehow she *knew* this woman and that her father's words were true. She looked at him and out of the depths of her own misery she could see how utterly broken he seemed. The whole pantomime with his pipe and professorial manner, the way he delivered his findings as if concluding a scientific paper, all that was so false. What she could see and what she could feel, over and above her own emotions, was his profound collapse. She turned her head and looked at Ludmila with what felt like a huge physical effort. This was her sister. Her twin. So beautiful but so brutal. A woman she had come to revile, to loathe, to want to kill. She had never had such feelings in her life except … except when she was small, at the watershed age of just under three when memories have not formed in any solid, coherent way. She could remember feeling frightened but of what or whom she couldn't say. But now the evidence of the films and her father's testimony gave those fears a shape and a solidity. Ludmila. Nadya. Whatever her name was. She had always been afraid of this beautiful cruel monster, now in the uniform of the militia, but then just a tiny, ferocious child.

Ludmila could feel the other woman's eyes on her. She didn't return her gaze. She was doing her best to control a volcanic rage within herself. She looked down at her freshly bleeding hand where the stitches had burst. She looked at the blood as it seeped and pooled and dripped. This man she had arrested as a traitor and an abuser of children was her own father. She didn't want to believe it but she couldn't deny the evidence. She was a police officer. She dealt in evidence, just as he did. He had revealed things about her he could not possibly know had he not been her father. All the self-sufficiency that had helped her to survive a siege by a foreign army, the predatory sexual attention of men, the craven ruthlessness of Party officials, the violence of city drunks and thugs, her friendlessness and lack of anyone to cherish, the barriers that her dead German lover of one night had almost broken through, they were breaching in a thousand places. She felt dizzy and sick. This man was her father. This woman her sister. She wanted to kill them both. She watched the blood drip from her hand because to look anywhere else was to acknowledge the absolute bleakness of her situation.

'Let me take those stitches out and clean up that wound.' Grigori's voice startled her out of her reverie. Almost against her will she extended her hand to be examined by this man, her father.

Grigori looked at the pink healing flesh, the swollen tender flesh that was starting to infect, the black sutures and the new blood, then he got up and found his surgical kit. He asked Irina to fetch him a bowl of hot water from the samovar.

She moved sluggishly and brought the bowl of water to her father. He used fresh cotton wool to clean the blood and paused apologetically at Ludmila's sudden intake of breath. He applied surgical spirit in the same tentative manner, then snipped the sutures one by one and applied a new clean bandage. Ludmila looked down at his thinning scalp. The smell of fresh tobacco smoke was clinging to him and his hands were soft and gentle. When he finished tying the bandage, she snatched away her hand and experienced a surge of emotion that threatened to engulf her. The last thing she would do in front of this man was cry. She stood up suddenly and went to the window and looked out. All she could see was her own reflection and tears were pouring down her face.

Irina suddenly burst out. 'I don't believe you! It's lies! I don't believe you!' It was a cry of pain. 'If it's true, why did she only take *her*? Why not both of us? Why did she leave *me*?' Irina was hoarse with weeping, her eyes swollen and bruised. She lost all feeling for the man in front of her. It was her pain, her naked suffering, and hers alone. He must explain himself. He was the one who held the knife.

Grigori looked up. *As you reap so shall you sow*. The biblical text ran through his head in a repetitive loop. *As you reap …*

'Your mother wanted to take both of you away from me. I couldn't let her do that. I loved you. I loved … both of you. I was your father … I couldn't let her take both of you.'

'So what did you do, draw lots?' Irina broke into a spasm of hysterical laughter.

Ludmila looked hard at Grigori, her father. 'How did you choose which daughter went and which one stayed?'

'I asked her to choose,' answered Grigori, 'but she refused. She said … she said a mother must never be asked to choose between her children. I said, what about their father? She said ... I don't remember what she said … she was angry with me. She was … not fully in control …'

'What happened?' asked Irina. It was a simple question but hideously pregnant with an answer she didn't want to hear.

'I begged her to stay, Irushka. You must believe me. I said I would discontinue the … observations. For the sake of our family. She said it was too late. She said she didn't believe me. She had your clothes packed, I …' Grigori finally broke down into tears.

Ludmila pounced. 'What? *What* did you do?'

'You have to understand the situation, you have to understand the circumstances …'

'What. Did. You. Do?' Ludmila said each word slowly, like a hammer blow.

Grigori looked up. 'Nothing. I just stood my ground. And she left.'

Ludmila continued the interrogation with a sense of dread. 'With one child?' Then, 'With … *me*?'

Grigori nodded.

'It can't have happened like that! She wouldn't just leave, with just one of us!' Irina looked pleadingly at her father.

Grigori looked from one woman to the other, miserably. 'She made a decision. She knew it was the right thing to do. She was a strong woman. A rational woman. She made a decision.'

'To take her and not me? Is that the *rational* decision she made? To leave me with a father she regarded as cold and cruel while she took my …' -she couldn't bring herself to say 'sister'- 'While she took the other one to safety? I don't believe you!'

'Irushka, it's the truth. She knew she couldn't take you both. She felt –wrongly, wrongly!- that Nadya was in danger, that I was not treating her properly …I told her I would stop, that the observations would stop, that I would burn my papers and forget all about it if that would make her stay, but …' He tailed off.

'But what?' Ludmila's tone was harsh, professional.

'She didn't believe me.'

Grigori sank into the armchair and covered his face with his hands.

The three became still and silent. Words had lost their meanings. Thoughts had become unhitched from their moorings. Emotions seemed to have no logical connection to events. What was there to say, to think, to feel? Any action which followed would be absurd. It would have no sense. It would neither heal nor hurt, make nor destroy. It would just happen, like so many other things had happened.

Grigori had self-immolated. Ludmila was smashed senseless against the wall of her own inquisitiveness. Irina was haemorrhaging twenty-three years' innocence.

Grigori was the first to stir. 'I have a letter. From your mother.'

He got up and went to the study. He returned with a creased and grimy envelope. Irina was the first to grab it, though Ludmila reached for it too. She tore open the envelope and unfolded the cheap white notepaper on which was a scrawl of closely-packed text. Irina read it, gasped and threw it aside and bit hard on her fist. Ludmila seized it then read aloud, without expression, monotone.

'Dear Irushka,' she said, 'my beautiful baby girl when you are old enough to read this if you ever do read this I have hidden it where no one can find it which sounds silly doesn't it but I know that if I gave it to your father he might never let you see it you have to know Irushka that I love you very much and it breaks my heart to have left you like this but I do love you with all my soul you are the sweetest girl a mother could wish for but I cannot let you and your sister be together any longer you are twins and I know this will seem strange if you read this and you never even knew you had a sister just a dim memory of someone else never mind a twin sister born at the same time from your mother's womb but anyway I'm losing track of my thoughts it's something that happens to me now and again things go dark like night time and I get very sad and I can't talk or laugh or sing your father doesn't know I am leaving this for you I will put it in the back of your picture frame the one with you and Semyon and the little wolf cub you are my little wolf cub and one day

I will come back for you darling but for now I leave you all my love your mother …'

Ludmila looked up from the letter. 'What did she mean she couldn't let her two daughters be together?'

Grigori shrugged. 'You were always fighting. There was no love between you or at least there didn't seem to be. You were very young but …' He shrugged again as if to say that in his opinion things would never change.

Irina erupted. She flew at her father, fists flailing. 'You bastard! You fucking bastard!' she screamed. Grigori held up his forearms to defend himself as Ludmila roughly pulled her sister off him. She held Irina's arms pinned behind her back and dodged the latter's murderous backward head-butts until she had calmed down.

'Irushka, I am so sorry. I never wanted you to know … never wanted you to suffer … it was all so long ago.'

'Don't you realise, I have no idea who I am anymore!' Irina fell backwards and sobbed and wailed. 'You killed my mother! You killed my mother!' she said over and over again.

Ludmila confronted Grigori. 'And me? What about me? If all this is true then you let me go with a mentally unstable mother to a city where she knew no one, you let us both live in poverty, my mother barely making a living in a … a boot factory, then commiting suicide and leaving me to be brought up in an stinking orphanage without anyone to care for me! Why did you let that happen?'

'Your mother said she would stay with family. She cut all contact with me. I tried to find her -several times!- but it was impossible. No one knew where she was. Believe me, Nadya, I tried to make her stay. I begged her, but she …'

Ludmila finished his sentence. 'But she didn't trust you. She didn't trust you because you are a liar and a traitor and a coward and a cold-blooded Nazi!'

'No! No, that's not true. I was –I am- a loyal Russian. A scientist. I only wanted the best … for humanity.'

'But not for your own children!' Irina screamed at him.

'Please, Irushka, believe me … you're my child, my daughter. I love you. I wouldn't want to hurt you in any way!'

'And what about her? My alleged sister? I should throw my arms around her. Rejoice that we found each other. Instead, I loathe her, loathe her from the depths of my heart!'

'Even though I saved your life. Twice.' Ludmila sneered but inwardly she was trembling. This was becoming too much for her. It was outside anything she had experienced. Until now, she had managed to keep a distance from anything that would threaten her, anything that would cause her emotional pain. She was militia. She hunted, tracked, captured and, if necessary, killed. She was predator not prey. But now she was vulnerable and her whole being revolted at the thought.

'You saved my life because you arrested me and you wanted to take me to face trial, not because you cared about me!' Irina replied. 'When Semyon left you for dead, it was me who said we should go and find you, rescue you, bring you back.'

'That was your duty. I don't have to thank you for that.'

'I should have left you to the wolves. How could you be my sister? We're so different. I don't believe it! I *won't* believe it!'

'There is too much evidence whatever you want to believe.' Ludmila tried to find the tone she used as a police officer –objective, firm, assured- but it faltered badly. Irina could sense this.

'You're not so sure of yourself now, are you, *sister*?' She spat out the sibilants. 'You're lost. You've no one to arrest, no one to take into custody. You don't know what to do next, do you?'

Ludmila went to strike Irina again, but regained control of herself.

Suddenly a long howl of despair came from Grigori. He clutched hands to the side of his head and emitted a single cracked note of anguish that caused his body to curl up. In response Irina screamed repeatedly at her father, her teeth bared and saliva spraying from her lips. Ludmila roared helplessly for them to stop. She punched and kicked whatever was nearby. The wolf cubs scampered into a far corner of the room and quaked with terror.

Finally, they stopped and sank into mortal silence. There was only blank despair, nothing else. No joy in reunion, no solace in reconciliation, just the bleak revelation of a truth long dormant.

Irina, spent and breathless, was the first to speak. Despite her agony and her fury, she had questions she wanted answered.

'My mother. Our mother. You said she … committed suicide. How did you find her?' She wiped her mouth and looked at Ludmila.

'She was hanging from a rope in the kitchen. I was seven.'

'That must have been horrible.'

'It wasn't good.'

'Did she leave you a note … anything?'

Ludmila paused. 'No. Yes. She left a note. It said, 'To my little Vassilissa. I'm sorry.' I tore it up.'

'That's a terrible thing.'

'Yes. But I survived.'

'She must have been so unhappy.'

'She was a woman on her own with a child and no money. Yes, she was unhappy.'

Grigori uncurled from the couch into which he'd sunk. His grip was still round the rifle.

'Did she … did she ever mention … me?' he asked tentatively.

'No.' Ludmila's reply was brutal and dismissive.

'What are we going to do?' Irina spoke softly, desperately.

'When the colonel returns with the prisoner, you will hand over the weapon and you will all accompany me to Krasnoyarsk and then on to Moscow.' Ludmila was regaining some of her official tone. 'You will be tried for anti-Soviet activities and the Georgian for my attempted murder.' There was comfort in the official. It steadied her.

'Don't you ever stop?' asked Irina incredulously. 'You have no power now, you have no authority. More to the point, you have no weapon. There are two dead men outside. One of them is the murderer you should have been after in the first place, the other is a Party official. How do you think that's going to look to your colonel?' She turned to her father. 'Dad, give me the rifle.'

Grigori passed it to her in silence.

'What are you going to do?' Ludmila looked at her sister with an animal curiosity but no fear.

'Nothing. Yet.' Irina checked the magazine. It held five cartridges. It was full. She snapped it back into place.

The emotional fog in Irina's brain suddenly cleared. The other woman had said that she survived. Well, she too was going to survive. That was all she knew for the moment. All that was left to her was an animal instinct to live. Her thoughts rolled smoothly as if on oiled wheels, one after the other. They had the advantage of remoteness. The woman was on her own. The other man was dead. There was the colonel. They would tell him the killer got her. It would be simple to stage. Her father was weak. She would look after him. She didn't care if the woman was her sister or her father's daughter. There was only one way that this situation could be resolved and that was with the death of the sister she had never known, who had treated her badly as a child and who had now destroyed their lives here in the wilderness of Siberia. But … she couldn't do it. She couldn't kill this woman in cold blood.

'What are you thinking, Irushka?' her father asked, though he knew exactly what was running through her mind.

'Take off your uniform,' was all Irina said.

'No.'

'Take it off and put it in the stove. Everything. Boots, hat. Everything. Now!'

She pointed the rifle at Ludmila and cocked it.

'Irushka …' her father began.

'Dad, be quiet. Uniform. Stove. Do it!'

Ludmila paused a moment, then began to take off her boots, then her coat, followed by her tunic and trousers. She took off her hat, looking briefly at the gold badge. She stood in her underwear looking directly at Irina.

'You can leave your underwear on. Dad, put her uniform in the stove, then go and find her some of my clothes.'

Grigori did as he was told, first feeding the boots into the flames, then going and fetching whatever came to hand in Irina's room. He poked at the burning boots, then fed in the trousers. The coat was too big to go in, so Irina made him cut it along the seams into smaller pieces with kitchen scissors. Meanwhile, Ludmila silently put on the skirt and blouse and thick woollen cardigan Grigori had brought in. She remained bare-legged and bare-footed. To Irina, she looked suddenly vulnerable. Without her uniform she was no longer a threat.

Ludmila watched her uniform slowly consumed by the flames. In truth, it was so much a part of her that she now felt suddenly drained of all her strength. She had not so much worn that uniform as inhabited it. It was a part of her, an extension of her power. In this other woman's clothes, she was no longer herself.

As her father fed the stove and her sister sat motionless on the old leather couch, Irina looked out at the falling snow, feeling lost and alone. The wind had died down now and the snow was falling softly, blanketing everything. The ravaged corpse of the Narkom commissar Petrenko would be buried, as would the body of the cannibal Stepan Stepanovich. The snow covered the blood and the muddy tracks, the footprints and the charred wood, the suffering and the pain.

It fell interminably, millions of crystal fragments, each one unique, like the spirits of the dead coming to rest on the vastness of the Siberian plain.

12

Dawn. The sky was blue and snow covered everything. At first light, Volkov stood impatiently as the herders saddled their animals and argued among themselves. Innaksa walked up to the old soldier and looked at him. Volkov looked down and smiled. He ruffled his hair but the boy continued to stare.

'Are you going to catch the Wolfman?' he asked eventually.

'Yes and we'll take him away and you won't see him ever again.'

Volkov's certainty of tone, inculcated by years in the military, belied the fact that he wasn't at all confident of completing his mission.

'What's that you're holding, a doll?' he asked, changing the subject.

Innaksa looked offended. 'No it's not a doll. It's Uluki. A squirrel'

'I see,' said Volkov. 'Can I have a look at it?' He held out his hand.

Innaksa wasn't sure he could trust this white-haired Russian in uniform. He pondered for a moment and decided to give him the benefit of the doubt. Volkov looked at it and turned the figure in his hand. It was indeed a squirrel and quite finely carved. He handed it back.

'Does he bring you luck?'

'If I don't have him something bad happens. The lady took him away from me but then she gave him back. Look, here comes the big man now.'

Volkov turned to see Semyon emerge limping from the tent behind him. He was clearly in pain from the tense look around his eyes, but he was determined to go with the group.

'I advise you not to come. I don't want any one holding us back.' Volkov's tone was harsh but not unkind.

'You can't stop me. There are no rules out here in the wilderness. I can do what I want.'

Volkov looked at him a moment, then said. 'It's your decision. Be ready to move when we are.' He turned back to Innaksa and chucked him under the chin. 'See you later on, when we've caught your wolf man.'

The boy was thoughtful for a moment, then he thrust the carved figure at the old colonel. 'Uluki will help you. But I want him back when you've caught him.'

Volkov took the figure, kissed it theatrically like a relic and put it into his greatcoat pocket. 'Thank you,' he said and smiled. 'Now I know I'll catch him.'

Volkov looked at the herdsman preparing to leave. Semyon was being offered a place in the sledge. He was too big for a reindeer. He took it gratefully and sat cradling a loaded rifle. What a ragtag band, Volkov thought, but as the Georgian said, out here he had no one else to rely on. Instead of feeling afraid, however, the notion thrilled him. This was life stripped to its essentials. It was about survival and the true comradeship of the pack. It was what a soldier was, he thought. A human being trained to live like a well-adapted animal. It was pure existence. It wasn't about currying favour or manoevring for position or watching your back or wearing a unifom. This moment for the 71-year old war veteran was what life should always be. A life lived in the present with only two options: to live or to die. He knew even as these thoughts flashed through his mind that this was bourgeois romantic nonsense, worse it was jejune, but nevertheless it was how he felt. He knew there were more important things like family and friendship and of course the historical dialectic of Marx and Lenin. But still ...

When he saw that the herdsmen were mounted, he gave the order to move out. Whether the Evenki heeded his order or just moved because they were ready, was hard to tell.

13

Eventually, they slept. It was all that was left to them. The psychological shocks had left them exhausted and completely drained of emotion. Their bodies demanded sleep. Masha and Grusha, glad of the silence after all the shouting and movement, curled up together. Grigori fell asleep, mouth open, a corpse. Ludmila head forward on her arms at the table. Irina sunk into the battered leather couch curled around the rifle.

Grigori got up and answered a knock at the cabin door. His wife, still 24 years old, stood there smiling. He went to kiss her but she shook her head. She held a bundle in her arms and offered it to him, still smiling. Grigori expected to see a small child. Instead there was a dead animal, a wolf cub, with blood at the corners of its mouth. In Irina's dream, she was dancing with Ludmila. She didn't want to dance but for some reason the other woman gave her no choice. As Ludmila slept, she dreamed she was naked running from something or someone, but her legs sank into the snow and she was making no progress at all. Whatever it was, it was getting closer.

They awoke more or less at the same time. Ludmila went to the window and looked out on to endless white. A few crows broke the silence with inane laughter.

Mechanically, each of them rose. Irina fried eggs because she needed to do something. Grigori observed her nervously, knowing she had something in mind but not certain what it was.

When Ludmila was out of the cabin using the privy, Grigori asked her what she was going to do, but Irina refused to answer.

'Irushka …'

'Don't call me that! It's my pet name, my little girl's name. I don't want to be your little girl anymore!'

'Irina. Please. Forgive me. What I did … I did it because I was looking for something, trying to understand … I thought it would help our people. The revolution was the greatest thing to happen to any country in the world, ever. It was a massive shift in the evolution of our species. We were showing the world justice, equality, humanity, progress. We were climbing out of the swamp of war and starvation and … and oppression that had dragged us down for millennia. We were leading the way. Finally the people were in control. When I saw a way to expand this power even further, I … I grabbed it with both hands ... do you understand? Irina? Irina. Talk to me.'

'What is there to say? You lied. You drove my mother away. You hid the truth from me. You used me in an experiment. What father would do that to his child? Or rather what *loving* father would do that?'

She flung a plate of two eggs in front of him and went back to the stove. She saw everything now with a fatal clarity. She no longer felt like a child. The love that she had always felt for her father had curdled into disllusion and was setting into hatred. Even as she acknowledged this, she was appalled. How could she hate this man who had always shown her nothing but affection, who had always been kind, put her first –or so she thought? But no human being, she repeated to herself, no human being would destroy the lives of others for the sake of knowledge. It was grotesque. And what was worse, she began to feel a creeping complicity in all of it. She had been her father's loyal and loving assistant. She had looked after his domestic needs, she had worked with the wolves, typed up his research -or some of it. *His work*. The dividing of siblings, the clinical observation of innocent children, making them no more than laboratory animals. *His life's work*.

She looked over at the two cubs curled up together. Masha was licking Grusha and whimpering. For the first time, Irina noticed that Grusha was injured. She went over to the little wolf cub. Grusha growled at her but on closer inspection, Irina could see that she was bleeding. Flesh had been torn from her back, probably from the door splinters or shards of glass. She glowered up at Irina, her eyes betraying no obvious sign of pain but a deep snarling suspicion of anyone who came near her - apart from her sister. Masha was uninjured but was caring for her sister as best she knew how, by licking the wound. How could this be? She was just an animal. But here it was. The pup was doing everything she could to make her sister's injury bearable. Irina made sure the wound was only superficial and then stroked Masha behind the ears and the little wolf licked her hand.

Ludmila came back into the cabin. Irina stood up from the cubs alert again. She checked the rifle and moved back to her seat at the table. She observed her own sister. Her loathing was so intense she could never imagine bathing the wounds of this woman, supposing her injuries were ever more than skin-deep.

Grigori asked meekly if he could visit the privy. Irina nodded, unable to look this man in the eye. She loathed her sister, she had despised the commissar, she loved Semyon, she loved Kolya, but she hated her father. And hate she came to realise was not an uncomplicated emotion. Its shadow was a deep feeling of love. She watched the man she had loved for so long walk slowly with head bowed toward the door. She wanted to cry out in pain and anger. She wanted to hold him. She wanted him to hold her with the gentleness and ease and reassurance that he had always held her. She let him walk out of the door.

Ludmila was looking in turn at her.

'What?' Irina snapped.

The militiawoman's voice was hoarse, subdued, but full of menace in reply. 'What will you do when the search party comes back?'

Irina ignored the question. In her mind she rammed the butt of her rifle into the other woman's face.

Ludmila continued in monotone. 'Because they will come back and you will have to face consequences.'

Irina reflected that last night she had nearly killed this woman. It would not be a huge step to complete the act. She slid the bolt on the rifle and pointed it at her sister. Ludmila stared back without expression. She looked her twin straight in the eye.

'You couldn't kill me however much you wanted to.'

Irina was furious that this woman knew exactly how she was thinking, how she was feeling. She lowered the rifle. She thought she saw Ludmila smile.

Grigori sat in misery, his bowels turned to stone. He wept. Wave after wave of convulsive sobs escaped from his core as he sat half-naked in the bitter cold. Self-pity, remorse, self-loathing, sheer visceral anguish. There were no words, only inarticulate sounds erupting from an inconsolable animal quivering on its haunches in despair.

He pulled up and belted his trousers and pushed open the privy door. The sky was grey and low, the cold damp and raw. Instead of going back into the cabin, he walked past the door. He wanted to see the results of last night's carnage. A hump of blood-stained snow drew him to where the wolves had finished off commissar Petrenko. The remains had been pulled this way and that as the animals had gorged themselves. The liver, lights and gut had been devoured and the carcass was now being picked clean by buzzard and chough and jay. A bloody skull grinned at the sky. Grigori couldn't help crossing himself as he had done as a child at funerals an age ago. He looked around for evidence of the other victim of the night's events. He walked toward the compound where Irina had brought down their stalker. He imagined a similar desecration. But he could see nothing. There was blood on snow but no rendered corpse, no scattered bones, no raucous scavengers. A sudden fear gripped him. Where was the second body? Wasn't this where Irina had shot him dead? *Surely he couldn't still be alive?*

He looked up. The hackles rose on his neck, his bowels loosened. Silhouetted against the grey-whiteness of the dawn was the creature who had tried to kill them all the previous night. Bear-like, blood-stained, limping. Grigori couldn't move. He watched as the creature lumbered painfully away and vanished behind the cages. Grigori followed, drawn on against better judgement by fascination and curiosity. This was the creature –the *man*- who had tried to murder them. This was the thing –the *human being*- that had flayed and mutilated and eaten other human beings. Grigori knew that he should get back into the cabin as fast as he could and make plans to rid them of this menace forever. How could it –*he*- still be moving? He was a good shot.

The light had been poor but they both saw him fall. Fall and lie still. Grigori crept forward, the visceral thrill of fear spreading through his whole body. The creature was wounded, possibly dying, what harm could he be? They must capture him somehow, tie him up, interrogate him. Yes, talk with him! Converse with the devil. With the wolf. With the primal genetic stock of which *we* were the mutation. First came the wolf…

A powerful stench- half human, half animal- assaulted his nostrils, followed by a blow to the back of his head that threw him forward. He lost consciousness for a second but recovered enough to turn and see the giant –ragged, filthy, blood-matted beard and hair, blackened teeth, jaundice eyes, a mask of wrinkled leather and disfiguring scars- reach out with a hand like iron, grab him by the throat and pull him into the nearest cage. With one thrust of his arm, Stepan sent the scientist sprawling across a floor strewn with straw, offal and wolf shit.

Stepan looked at his victim with contempt. The wound in his ribs caused him to cough blood and gave him intense pain. The spindly Russian Bolshevik was holding his hand up in supplication. Stepan grinned a canine grin. The sense of power was a momentary relief.

Grigori summoned up the presence of mind to speak to his attacker.

'Please, don't hurt me. I … I want to know more about you. What is your name? Where are you from? Please. Tell me.'

Stepan looked at him and a puzzled frown crossed his features. No one had ever asked his name before. No one cared where he was from. He had been hunted like an animal for nearly twenty years. The man clearly playing for time.

'Talk to me. I want to know more about you. I know what you did was wrong, but … can I ask you … can I ask you … first, tell me your name. My name is Grigori. I am a scientist. I work here with animals … wolves … I have a daughter … two daughters …'

A guttural sound came from Stepan's lips. He hadn't spoken to a human being in a long time. He had almost forgotten speech. He wanted to say something to this babbling Bolshevik before he killed him. He didn't know why, but he felt a need to reply to the man's stumbling questions. With a final effort, he drew buried words back into the light.

'Step … an Step … ano …vich Fed … Fed … orovski. From Ukraine. You killed. My mother. You let me starve.'

The words came as he remembered them, haltingly, in Russian. Grigori looked at the creature he now knew as Stepan Stepanovich. There was contact. Curiosity overwhelmed him. He wanted to know more. His own speech grew in confidence.

'Why did you kill the deer herders? And the young soldier? What had they done to you?'

Stepan felt again the lashes from the herders that had brought him close to death. He saw his mother dying in his arms. He felt the gnawing pain of hunger that had made him eat the flesh of his own kind. No words came. He roared into the morning air and pulled the machete from his belt. Pain seared through him. He clutched his side and felt the blood ooze between his fingers. Rage consumed him.

'Listen! Please, Stepan, don't! I can look after that wound. You need it treated. Let me help you. I want to talk to you, please!'

The Ukrainian found one word – 'Why?'- before a shot rang out and he was thrown backwards.

Grigori let out an involuntary 'No!' before looking round and seeing Irina about to fire again as Stepan staggered to his feet.

'Irushka, no! His name is Stepan Stepanovich. I need to talk to him. Don't kill him!'

Irina looked at her father with blank astonishment. She paused for a moment as the mortally wounded killer lurched toward them. Ludmila appeared behind her.

'Shoot! What are you waiting for?' The militiawoman's tone was commanding.

'He's injured,' Grigori shouted. 'He can't harm us. Let me talk to him. I need to talk to him!'

Irina looked at her father as if he'd lost his mind. Ludmila ordered her to shoot again as Stepan advanced.

Grigori rushed forward to the Ukrainian and stood in front of him.

'Stepan Stepanovich! Listen to me. We won't hurt you if you put down your weapon. You hold so much knowledge---!'

'Dad, get out of the way! He's still dangerous!'

'Irushka, he's critically injured. He can't do us any harm! Don't you see *he's* the wolf in our midst, we're just farmyard dogs … lapdogs compared to him! If you shoot him you'll have to shoot me too!'

'Very well!' Ludmila said. 'Shoot them both!'

'Dad, get out of the way, now!'

The world was closing down on Stepan Stepanovich. He was seeing through a long tunnel and a single deep note drummed loudly in his ears. A gauze fell across his vision as the blood pumped from his chest. The Bolshevik was in front of him, calling his name. Stepan saw only the murderer of his mother. He lifted his machete with the last ounce of his strength and brought it down on the man in front of him. The man fell.

Irina screamed then fired again and Stepan crashed into the snow. Irina ran forward to her father. There was a gash across his head and left shoulder. The blade had glanced off his skull and through his collar bone.

'Help me get him inside!' Irina demanded of her sister.

Ludmila was looking at the felled giant, her hand on his neck, checking he was dead.

'Now!'

Ludmila moved from the body and helped her sister carry their father into the cabin.

The three of them were soaked with blood. Irina pressed her hand hard to the base of her father's neck. The blood seeped between her fingers and her father's face was a grey-white. Blood poured from his scalp. They laid him on the couch. Irina removed her hand and checked the wound. She screamed at Ludmila to fetch anything that would serve as a bandage. Ludmila ran and pulled sheets from her bed and, first slashing it with a knife, tore it into ragged strips. Irina made a pad and bound it tightly in place. She used remaining strips to clean the blood from Grigori's head. She looked in utter dismay as the makeshift bandage was suffused with a deep red in seconds. She felt helpless and resumed pressing her hand to the wound. She wanted him to tell her what to do but her father was already drifting somewhere else. He was whispering something. They both bent closer to hear. His hands gripped each of them by the arm. His strength astonished them.

'I didn't mean … any of this …any of this to happen. I begged her to stay. You … you must believe me…' His breathing was becoming laboured but the grip remained tight. 'I loved you both … both of you … your mother was angry … so angry… Nadya … Irushka … my lovely girls. I watched you being born. I helped you into the world, even though the babushka tried to send me from the room …' He attempted a laugh which turned into a cough and the breath came in gasps. 'You were two precious bundles …purple, naked, wrapped in blankets … I held you both in my arms and looked at your mother … she was weak … but we smiled … at each other. There was love, please believe me … I came to find you Nadya … but the city is so big … so big … I couldn't find you … I'm so sorry …' He half raised himself but the effort was too much. Irina pushed him back gently and shushed him. His chest was heaving. 'Wolf sisters … that's what we called you … we laughed about it …your mother and me … but when the…the *tiny insect* in my brain kept … gnawing ... arrogant … telling me that in my own two little girls was the key to all human behaviour … the buzzing in my … brain … was too much … I didn't look at you as a father should but as a … a …Victor Frankenstein …' The huge gulps he was taking in seemed to provide him with little or no air to breathe. His grip however tightened. The two women bent closer to catch the hoarse, broken whispers. 'My monster was not something I created. It was something I *was*. The creature Stepan … he was not a monster… my little Nadya is no wolf … I am that monster … forgive me …'

Irina looked at Ludmila and saw that she was weeping. Tears filled her eyes and ran down her cheeks. She made no effort to wipe them away. Irina realised that she herself hadn't shed a single tear.

She looked down at her father. The breath came at longer and longer intervals. He wanted to say more but it was impossible. As the air passed over the build-up of fluid in his throat and produced a moist rattling sound -the death rattle- the scientist's eyes widened in terror and he clung to his daughters to save him.

His depleted heart stopped and he was dead.

Ludmila cried unashamedly while Irina watched. She looked at her sister in wonder. She couldn't believe the tears. Was she crying for herself or her father or her mother? Why don't I feel anything? She was stone. Tears would simply run off, like rain over granite.

Irina closed her father's eyes. Ludmila had completely broken down and her wailing was uncontrolled. She started to hit at the body of her father. Blow after blow on his rib cage. Irina was tempted to put out her hand and hold her sister, restrain her from her violent grief, console her, kiss the top of her head, rock her slowly until the tempest blew over. But even as the impulse began, she cut it short. She took back her hand.

Eventually, Ludmila became calm and silent. She was kneeling on the floor at the side of the couch. She let her head fall on to her father's chest and was still.

Irina rose and found the vodka. She poured two glasses and handed one to Ludmila. Outside the clouds had returned and the light was poor. More snow was in the air. Winter had arrived. Irina put another birch log into the stove. Ludmila drank the vodka in one and held out her glass. Irina filled it. Ludmila drank this more slowly.

'So what happens now?' Irina paused. '…Sister?'

Ludmila looked at Irina sharply. Then, 'We must bury our father before the ground gets too hard.'

Her eyes were red and swollen. She sniffed loudly and wiped the clear mucus and tears from her face with her sleeve. She stood up.

Irina looked at the other woman. Dressed in her clothes, bare-footed, hair falling over her face, weeping, grieving, now trying to appear strong and capable again. She held out her arms to her. Ludmila responded with the momentary wariness of a wild animal. She flinched. She walked toward Irina and fell into her arms.

14

The herders arrived at midday. For two hours before then, Ludmila and Irina talked. They shared stories of their childhood. Of school. Of their teenage years, spent so differently. Of the war. Of wolves. Irina asked about her mother. Ludmila-Nadya about her father. There were no tears just a rhythmic exchange of memory. A narrative ballet choreographed by their own senses, their need to talk, their need to listen, above all their need to listen. And to understand.

Ludmila-Nadya spoke without obvious emotion about her mother's depression and their life of hardship in Moscow. Irina spoke of her loneliness in the vast wilderness of Siberia, but also of her growing up and the love she had for her father, for Semyon, for the animals in her care. Comparing herself to her sister, she felt like a child, and said so. Ludmila-Nadya shook her head and said she would have given her own teeth to have had her sister's life. Irina asked how she could be so cruel and so certain of everything. Ludmila-Nadya told her that Stalin had been her father and everything that he said gave her strength and certainty. She had been in awe when the Leader arrived. She couldn't believe he was there in the same room and she would have given her life to save him if anything had happened. 'He was… he *is* my father,' she repeated. Irina said she wished she had known her mother and had been able to take care of her, soothe her sadness, help her cope. Her sister said that if Irina had been there then maybe she wouldn't have been so sad. Irina nodded and said perhaps. They sat either side of their dead father on the big leather couch, now sticky with blood, and talked. And talked. Speaking, listening, then speaking again. A dance whose movements were courteous, tentative, seamless, clear of all misunderstanding.

A commotion outside the cabin announced the arrival of Volkov and the deer herders.

Innaksa's father cocked his rifle. He fired it into the air, once. The herder surveyed the scene around the cabin. He dismounted and walked forward. The old Russian soldier shouted something to him but he pretended not to hear. His fellow herders –brother, brother-in-law, nephew, uncle-followed him in a wide arc, their rifles cocked. Innaksa's father smelt blood before he saw it. They came across the remains of Petrenko and prodded them with their boots. They moved further towards the empty wolf compound. Innaksa's father stopped and shouted to Volkov. He came over quickly, moving like a much younger man, the herder thought. On the ground was the body of what could only be the wolf man, a bullet hole in his forehead, blood congealing on the snow behind his head. The Evenk took in the huge frame, the matted hair and beard, the mouth fixed in a snarl. This was their *aboroten* for sure. The herder pulled out his knife, slit open the dead man's clothing and plunged the weapon under the ribs. Face reddened with effort, the veins snaking at his temple, he cut out the killer's heart within a minute. He held it up steaming and bloody in his hand. His fellow herders cheered as Innaksa's father threw it away from the body and the dogs ran straight for it yelping and growling to secure the meat. The lead dog took the heart in his jaws and challenged the others. They backed away and slunk angrily back and forth as the lead dog gorged on the still-warm hunk of muscle and fat, its chambers brimming with blood. Innaksa's father and the other herders laughed.

Ludmila-Nadya by now had emerged with her sister from the cabin. The sound of the shot tore them away from their storytelling. Volkov approached them and asked them whose the body was.

'The killer,' Ludmila-Nadya said.

'His name is Stepan,' added Irina. Volkov stared at her.

'You know his name?'

'He told my father.'

'He told-? Where is your father?'

'In the cabin,' said Irina. 'He's dead.'

'How-?'

'Stepan the wolfman killed him,' said Irina sounding as open and honest as a young child.

The reindeer and sled, slower than the rest of the party, drew up in the compound. Irina caught sight of Semyon, before he saw her.

'Semyon! Semyon!'

At the same time the Georgian saw her, he also saw Ludmila-Nadya. He cocked his rifle. Irina froze.

'No, Semyon! She ... she's changed ... different now!'

Semyon aimed the weapon at Ludmila-Nadya's heart. Volkov intervened.

'Don't shoot her, big man. Or I will shoot you.'

He pointed his automatic pistol at Semyon.

'She destroyed our family. I was innocent and she arrested me. She was going to take me to be executed in Moscow! Why shouldn't I kill her? What is to stop me?'

'I said I will shoot you and I will,' said Volkov firmly.

Semyon slowly lowered his weapon. Irina could see that he was visibly trying to control his rage. His mouth was tight shut, and he breathed rapidly through dilating nostrils. When Volkov saw that he wasn't going to use the rifle, he holstered his own weapon. He looked at the scene in front of him. A light wind sighed as it travelled round the buildings, across the snow. The corvids circled, hungry and protesting. The dogs fought over the last portion of gristle from Stepan's heart and the herders beat them away from the corpse. Volkov guessed they would probably burn the remains of the killer. So, let them. He looked at the gaping hole in his chest, the snarling features, the huge bulk of the man the girl had called Stepan. How did she find out his name? His eyes returned warily to the other giant, the one he knew as Semyon. He was gaining control of himself. He felt a surge of pity, for the Georgian, for the herders, for the two young women, for their dead father, even –the strangest of feelings– for the killer. There was no justice out here in the *pustinya*, the wilderness. What was the Marxist-Leninist analysis for this carnage, this human devastation, this piteous loss? Tragedy was not a word in the communist lexicon. Everything was determined by the economic conditions, governed only by the materialist dialectic, the class struggle. He knew this. How did it account for the raw brutality exhibited here, the bloodshed, the compassion, the grief? He watched the two women, standing close to each other and for the first time noticed a resemblance between them. Not an obvious one. Just something across the bridge of the nose, the spacing of the eyes, the width of the mouth. Something had happened in that cabin that he would never understand. As a soldier, he didn't want to understand. He needed to assert control, ensure order, contain it in a report. As a man? Well, that was something that would have to wait. He longed to go home.

Irina moved to Semyon. She flung her arms around him and sobbed loudly. He hugged her in return and she felt his powerful arms around her body, crushing her to him as if he would never let go. Ludmila-Nadya stood and watched. For the first time she felt conflicting emotions. In her young life there had never been any room for complexity. She knew how to survive and all her energies had been harnessed to that one instinct. But now, something had burst within her, all the seeds of doubt and vulnerability and anguish and anger and pain, spilled at once and she could not control their violent flowering. She trembled with the sheer physical impact this made on her. She didn't know who she was anymore or what she was or even *why* she was here under the looming snow-bellied clouds on the Central Siberian Plain. She had gained a sister and had lost a father in the space of a single month. What massive movement in the cosmos had brought her three thousand miles to this desolation to find her sibling, her twin, to witness the death of her father and learn the awful truth of her own origins?

She knew there was no cosmos, of course, other than the physical reality of stardust and planet, there was no divine plan, no significant congruence of events. Like Volkov, she knew there was only dialectical materialism. Human beings were the authors of their own destiny, animal brutality was the product of a corrupt and vicious economic system and the mass of human beings would one day take control of the planet for the good of all. She knew this. We were not animals. We were human beings.

She walked over to Irina and Semyon and stood and waited until their embrace came to its natural conclusion. The big Georgian looked at her and she returned his gaze. She held out her arms, vulnerable, courageous, unconditional. And waited.

Epilogue

Kolya watched everything from a safe distance.

The violence of these bipeds was truly frightening. His bloodstream was laced with adrenaline and cortisol. His vulpine brain ran calculation after neural calculation. What to do next? Where to go? Who to trust? His olfactory sense absorbed the scent of blood and picked up pheromones exuded by the humans. He watched the dogs fight and scrabble for remnants of flesh. His stomach growled with hunger. There was fresh meat slowly freezing in minus temperatures. There were bones to be picked. He observed his dominant female and the other aggressive female -who had tried to kill him- and the big biped -who fed him- close together. It confused him. He whined with jealousy, but fear prevented him from approaching them. Something had happened that he didn't fully understand and his instincts demanded caution.

Another scent penetrated his sensory nervous system, accompanied by two distinct high-pitched squeals. His nostrils flared and his ears twitched. He turned to see the female wolf cubs scampering toward him, unsure of everything after the violence of the preceding night. Perhaps they imagined one of their own kind might offer protection. Kolya felt the urge to kill them on the spot, but the urge passed. They padded toward him and sniffed at his lowered muzzle. They cowered - as they should. They rolled on their backs - as they should. They knew instinctively that submission meant survival. Kolya licked each of them briefly. One snapped at him, the other begged to be licked again. He nipped both of them in the belly and with a last look at the scene below him, set off into the taiga. The cubs followed at an ambling trot and soon all three were gone.

Acknowledgements

My thanks to Jan Anderton for giving me the original idea; to Maison des Scènaristes in Cannes for having faith in the story in its early -but substantially different- incarnation as a film script; to Caroline Goetzee, Mark Roberts and Jim Morris who read and commented on various stages of the manuscript; to my wife Gillian who is eternally encouraging; and to Jack, Katharine and George for their support and for not taking me too seriously, ever.

About the Author

Paul Goetzee was born in South Korea in 1956. He was educated at Liverpool and Leeds Universities and was at one time Arts Council resident playwright at Essex University. He has worked as an arborist in a Welsh woodland and continues to work as a writer and director in the theatre. He is married with three children and lives in Liverpool. This is his first novel.

Lightning Source UK Ltd.
Milton Keynes UK
UKHW010003010921
389797UK00004B/1190

9 781839 754487